Mrs. Pratt's War

Sarah Richmond

There is no remedy for love but to love more.

Henry David Thoreau (1817-1862)

Journal, July 25, 1839

Dedication

This book is dedicated, with thanks, to the men and women who serve in our armed forces and to those who love them.

Chapter One

❯❯❯❮❮❮

England, 1915

Livinia Pratt put on the blue dress with the old-fashioned Belgian lace collar that had belonged to her great-aunt after whom she'd been named. Yes, they still dressed for dinner at Fairview Farms, even as the world swirled in disarray around them. It was the one thing Livy insisted upon.

Thankfully the dress still fit, although the buttons did strain a bit against the buttonholes, and the waistline could use a letting out—a task she would see to when she had a spare minute. She'd like a new dress, but there was no extra money. They were a country at war.

The Great War, some called this horror.

As expected, the Army had taken away most of their livestock, leaving them with Jenny, well into her third decade and no longer fit to pull a plow, and a few chickens to provide eggs for the children. The rest would go to the soldiers.

Their fighting men, boys by most accounts, needed to be fed. She'd given the army a good quantity of beef, milk and grain gladly.

One must persevere in the face of hardship. She couldn't despair in front of her children. They needed a mother who could be strong.

With her mind unsettled and weary and the day's work having taken its toll, she arrived at the dining room where the children waited in their chairs around the dining room table. Wyatt—almost nineteen, a man and yet still boyish in his features—held her chair as his father had done. He looked very handsome in his starched shirt and tie. Elizabeth, a year younger, nine-year-old Grace, and eleven-year-old Winifred looked pretty and feminine in chiffon and lace.

As she sat down, her children looked at her with eager faces. Their innocence made her heart ache. She wanted to hold them close and not let anything outside these four walls touch them. Thank goodness Wyatt would soon return to in his studies at the agricultural college in Wye. By the time he was finished, the war would be over.

Livy kept the glaring headlines about the atrocities in Belgium and France from the girls. She tried her best to keep the war as far away as possible.

Livy sniffed. "Grace, take the dog to his kennel."

Grace's angelic smile turned into a frown. She didn't protest but pushed back from the table. The spaniel jumped from her lap and followed her out of the room.

"I told her you'd be cross about the dog," Winnie said. Only two years older, she seemed infinitely wiser.

"I'm not cross," Livy ladled out the soup from her

mother-in-law's chinaware tureen and handed her a bowl, "but as you well know, your father disapproved of animals in the house." In truth, she would've done the same at that age and with the equivalent result.

"Did you know there's a new resident at the Ashers' gamekeeper's lodge?" Elizabeth took her bowl.

"Really?" Wyatt's brows came together. "The place is barely inhabitable."

Elizabeth turned to her brother. "He's Gwendolyn Asher's uncle, just returned from the front. They say he's a major."

"By Jove, a real major? I'd very much like to meet him."

"He's recovering from a battlefield wound, and not inclined to want company, I'm told," Elizabeth answered. "In fact, people say the old boy is rather a curmudgeon."

Livy wondered why the major chose to recuperate in the lowly cottage rather than the Ashers' lovely home. She would ask Gwendolyn at the first opportunity. It seemed unworthy of her friend that she'd let her uncle stay secluded in such primitive conditions.

"No doubt he has been through a great deal and needs his privacy," Livy replied. "We should not criticize. Indeed, we owe him our thanks."

"No other family, I presume?" Wyatt said.

Elizabeth scoffed. "Apparently none that will have him."

"That's quite enough," Livy said. She didn't mind their curiosity about the new arrival, but she wouldn't tolerate unkindness.

Wyatt opened his mouth to reply when Grace returned, skipping as she came into the room. Noticing how all eyes were upon her, she slowed to a walk. When she reached her chair, she pulled a long face directed at her sister. Winifred, for her part, didn't respond, and Livy hoped this would be the end of hostilities this evening.

After everyone had been served, Livy bowed her head. Wyatt rushed through the prayer. Livy said amen and spread her serviette across her lap. Thankfully nothing more was said about the major and his wounds. Livy didn't wish to talk about the war.

"Leek soup again?" Elizabeth grimaced.

"Indeed." Livy reached for her spoon. "We are grateful to have plenty of them to eat."

"I love leek soup." Winifred picked up her spoon and slurped the first spoonful.

Grace giggled.

"Must you be so indelicate?" Elizabeth frowned. "It's not lady-like to make such noises at the table."

Winifred glared at her sister. Livy continued to eat her soup. The battle with Winnie to act like a lady wouldn't be won in one day.

Elizabeth modeled herself after her grandmother, a Londoner, who possessed exquisite manners and expected everyone to follow her example. The girl's patience with others was always razor thin, and she locked horns with her sisters more often than Livy would like.

Winnie put down her spoon. "Mother would be very

displeased to know you entertained Mr. Morehouse while she was helping old Tom in the orchard."

Elizabeth's dark eyes shot daggers at her sister.

Livy hadn't thought Mr. Morehouse so bold to attempt a rendezvous with Elizabeth here at Fairview.

"I hope you told him to come back at a more appropriate time," Livy said.

Elizabeth turned sharply to face her mother. "I invited him in to tea—I only wanted to be hospitable. Redding had come down from London, and I couldn't very well turn him away."

"Who joined you for tea? Wyatt, did you?"

"'Fraid not, Mother. I spent the better part of the afternoon in the barns."

Livy returned her gaze of her oldest daughter. "You two were alone?"

"How alone could anyone be in this household?" Elizabeth emphasized her remark by turning an accusing frown upon Winnie and Grace.

Livy was angry but she wouldn't argue at dinner.

"Winnie, no one likes to hear tittle-tattle," Livy said.

The little girl shrank from the rebuke but didn't protest.

"As for you," she addressed Elizabeth with as much calm as she could muster. "We'll talk about this later."

Elizabeth squared her shoulders. She'd disobeyed Livy on the subject of Mr. Morehouse again. A girl of seventeen had no business in the company of a man who hailed from London and was twice Elizabeth's age.

They knew nothing of his family or his reputation. What kind of man accepted an invitation to be entertained at a home with the parents absent? Not a gentleman, obviously.

Elizabeth could be shockingly naïve.

Satisfied she'd quelled all dissent for the moment, Livy took the soup away and delivered the beef left over from Sunday's dinner to their plates, along with some boiled potatoes and swedes.

"Isn't this lovely." It wasn't a question but a statement of gratitude.

Wyatt's face was creased into a frightful frown. He'd been quiet most of the meal. His plate remained untouched.

"Is the roast all right?" Livy asked him.

"Yes, Mother." He smiled weakly. "I'm not very hungry."

Wyatt didn't look sick, Livy decided. What could be the problem? His appetite was always so keen.

"Should I be worried?"

Wyatt cleared his throat.

Oh dear, Livy thought. There is something wrong.

"Mother, I wish to speak to you about a matter of importance."

"Very well." She put down her fork. "You have my complete attention."

Her son regarded her with woeful eyes. "I'm not going back to school for the Michaelmas term."

"I beg your pardon?" Livy found his unexpected announcement alarming.

Wyatt lowered his gaze.

Livy glanced at Elizabeth, believing her son might have confided in his sister. Elizabeth shrugged, looking bewildered. Whatever troubled Wyatt was a complete mystery. What could have brought on this sudden decision to leave school?

Livy turned back to Wyatt. Every now and again she would see glimpses of his father—the set of his mouth, the strong jaw, the ears that were one size too large for his head. She could imagine Charles now as her son prepared to make an important announcement.

"I've joined the King's Army." He spoke with pride, and to Livy's dismay, finality.

The declaration brought a gasp from Elizabeth. Livy shuddered as if she'd been hit by a sudden blast of cold air.

"Just this afternoon." Wyatt's words came out in a rush. "I went into town and signed up."

"Don't be a silly goose," Elizabeth said in strident tones. "You can't be a soldier. You promised Father you'd take a degree in agricultural economics."

Wyatt rounded on his sister. "I know what I promised."

"Who will run the farm? We are short on laborers, as you well know," Elizabeth said.

"Mother has Fairview well in hand. The harvest is almost done and in the barns. As for the winter chores, there is old Tom Martin and his grandson to help. They can manage what's left of the livestock and do the repairs that need to be done." His tone was defensive, but he'd obviously known what their arguments would be.

Elizabeth narrowed her eyes. She was very good at putting her brother in his place. "What will we do when spring comes?"

Wyatt straightened. "The war should be over by then."

"How can you be so sure?" Elizabeth scoffed.

Wyatt ignored her and turned to address Livy. Her nerves were so brittle they were ready to snap.

"Mother, it is my duty to serve, and I want to go. You and the girls will get along splendidly I shouldn't wonder. Aren't women all over England pitching in and doing a man's work?"

Livy folded her serviette into small squares. "That is not the point. It's all been decided what you should run the farm when you've finished your studies."

Wyatt snorted. "Am I not to have a say in the matter?"

The air seemed to have gone out of the room, making breathing difficult. How could her only son have gone against her wishes and done this grievous thing? This was not the boy she had borne and raised. He was somebody else, a stranger living in her son's body.

"What has caused you to be so impetuous?" Livy asked.

"The Miller sisters came up to me in town and gave me a white feather," Wyatt said. "They called me a coward and told me I was shirking my duty."

"How very stupid of them," Elizabeth countered.

The little girls were thankfully silent.

Livy's heart broke to hear him speak so solemnly. The locals believed he lacked the courage to be a soldier. She could see how miserable that made him feel.

"I do understand," Livy said, trying to be supportive. She unfolded her serviette and spread it across her lap. "The Miller girls were wrong to criticize."

"I fail to see how you could object to me going. The country needs fighting men."

"You're a farmer, not a soldier," Elizabeth said. Her tone contained an element of Livy's own panic.

Livy fought to keep the tremor out of her voice. "Wyatt, you won't be eligible for a few more days. Do give what you are proposing careful consideration."

"I have, Mother." He stared at her with defiance. "Don't you see? If we all don't get in the fight, then no one is safe."

Much as Livy appreciated the sentiment—defending the homeland and all he loved was noble and fine—she would not let him take this course of action. The Army had taken away her livelihood. She would not sacrifice a son.

"I understand you don't feel you're helping the war effort by staying in school," Livy said with a calm she didn't feel. "As you know, farming is very important to feeding the troops. You can take a leave of absence from school and serve your country here at Fairview."

Wyatt's shoulders fell. He made no attempt to hide his unhappiness. "I cannot stay here while a war wages on in Belgium and France."

Livy grasped her shaking hands together and put them in her lap. "I agree with you, Wyatt, we all need to serve. Your duty is here."

Wyatt exhaled noisily.

Elizabeth wore a smug expression.

The little girls squirmed in their chairs.

Livy could weep from frustration. He'd gone and enlisted without discussing it with her first. Why the subterfuge? The answer was obvious. He'd known she would have tried to dissuade him. He'd known she would have worn him down, made him promise to reconsider.

"I have made my decision," Wyatt shoved back his chair and stood. "The deed is done. I signed a contract. I cannot take back a promise."

Livy looked up and saw he'd turned beet red. Wyatt was not asking for permission but telling her his decision. He was growing into a man and hoping to take his place among other men.

"Where are you going? You haven't finished your meal."

"I'm not hungry." He tossed his serviette on the table and bolted from the room.

Livy blinked back tears, fighting to regain her composure. She couldn't let the children see how frightened she was. The world was intruding and she'd no way to stop it.

She smiled to reassure the girls. "Doesn't this beef smell delicious?"

The clatter of silverware on china was the only response.

Chapter Two

➤➤➤❬❬❬

"**B**last!" Major James Gunnison hated when things weren't in their proper place. A good soldier relied on discipline and order and couldn't carry out his duties when what he was looking for couldn't be found.

He continued his search in a foul mood, the pain in his knee a constant reminder of what happens when discipline goes lax and order becomes chaos.

To his surprise, the tea canister was where he'd left last night, on top of the Welch cupboard next to a single cup and saucer.

He ladled a modest amount of tea leaves—one must economize in wartime—into a chinaware pot and added steaming water from the kettle. The aroma of freshly brewed tea was bracing.

After replacing the lid, he returned the kettle to the stove. The sound of drops of water sizzling on the hob's surface irritated him and he growled. This was what he'd been reduced to, drinking tea and idleness.

James carried the tray into the Spartan sitting room, a fire popping and crackling in the grate. He used to find the crisp October air invigorating, but now these cold mornings only served as a reminder of the long, dark days of winter ahead.

The cottage was built of stone, with sturdy English oak beams in the ceiling and a fireplace that drew well. The previous resident had left an upholstered chair and ottoman, moth-eaten and soiled, to be sure, but serviceable, and a small oak table—badly stained and scarred.

They were all James needed.

His leg throbbed, stopping him in his tracks. He set the tray on the table and leaned against the chair, gripping the backrest like a vise.

"Blast and blast!" He yanked his handkerchief out of his pocket and wiped the beads of perspiration from his forehead. When the pain finally subsided, he collapsed into the lumpy cushions.

Pull yourself together, soldier. It's only a bit of shrapnel.

He'd thought a rest in the country would put him right, but the stubborn wound hadn't improved. The pain tablets provided a respite, but made him sleepy in the middle of the day. He couldn't very well spend his days napping like some old moggy in front of the fire, could he?

Not with a war on. He ground his teeth, hating how he'd been forced to leave his command in the middle of a campaign. He should be in the trenches taking care of his lads, not here, nursing a blighty wound. A good soldier was, above all, devoted to his men.

James poured himself a cup of tea. The hot brew reminded him of his officer's club, of cozy London parlors, of civilization. These were the things worth fighting for.

Unhappily, he might not be in the fight much longer. If his wound didn't heal, the Army would offer him a desk job or even more concerning, a discharge.

A desk job. Bah!

What would he do with a discharge? The military life was all he knew, had known since he was out of knee breeches. He wasn't ready to pack it in, to retire. He had plenty of good years ahead of him.

If only his leg would heal.

The chatty postman was coming up the path whistling and continued his tune as he opened the stubborn gate and walked up the path. A missive of some kind dropped through the postal slot but thankfully the postman didn't knock.

"What is this?" James pushed himself out of his chair and winced as he bent down to pick up a cream-colored envelope.

He read the return address: *Mrs. Livinia Pratt, Fairview Farm.*

Looked like an invitation: Dinner or a garden party so he may be introduced to the locals.

Bah! He was in no mood for a party.

He tossed the envelope on the table and slumped back into his chair. The effort cost him a streak of searing pain from his knee to his thigh. Eventually the pain passed and he propped his leg on the ottoman.

Convalescence was overrated, in his opinion. These minor flesh wounds were only a matter of the mind overcoming the demands of the body.

James glared at the missive on his side table. Other neighbors had stopped by with words of encouragement. Some indulged him with pies and cakes. Didn't they know a war was on?

He hadn't let them in. Hadn't he told Gwendolyn in no uncertain terms that he didn't want company? Hadn't he made his preferences perfectly clear? And yet they all continued to seek him out.

Why did their persistence exasperate him so?

He picked up the envelope and tore it open. The writing was all swirls and curlicues. He inhaled the scent of lavender.

Just as he'd suspected, Mrs. Pratt had sent him an invitation. The woman explained the occasion was her eldest son's birthday.

In other circumstances, James would've begrudgingly accepted. Not that he wanted to attend. He hated parties, but his attendance would be required as a regimental officer and gentleman.

This time there were practical matters to consider. He'd no means to get there and wouldn't impose any more on his niece and her husband. Even if he could find transportation, he hadn't brought any formal attire.

He rose clumsily from the chair to search for ink and pen. He found neither.

"What the blazes!"

James had no choice but to walk up to Gwendolyn's house for supplies. He could perfectly well manage the half-mile walk to the Hall. In fact, fresh air and exercise were exactly what he needed. He picked up his hat and squashed it on his head, ready to do just that.

As James slogged up the hill to Asher Hall, the pain in his knee cut like a serrated knife against the bone. He planted his stick in the soft dirt, every step a challenge, determined not to yield to this wound's tyranny.

A rock under the shade of a poplar provided a place to rest. He sat. A wren flitted to a branch overhead, looking concerned.

"You needn't worry," the major told her. "I'm perfectly all right."

It was a lie. He'd thought he was getting better but, in his foolishness, this walk had made matters worse. The half-mile should've been child's play. The constant throbbing in his leg convinced him he'd taken on too much.

Bloody nonsense. He wasn't an invalid and shouldn't act like one.

The chug of a motor claimed his attention. The noise carried from the direction of the estate.

As he struggled to his feet, a motorcar came over the hill. Puffs of dust followed it.

The klaxon blared. The driver had seen him. The motor slowed and then stopped.

Gwendolyn was behind the wheel. She shifted the gear into neutral and poked her head out the window. Every time he saw her, he marveled at what a splendid young lady she'd become.

"Uncle, how delightful. Are you paying us a visit?" The feather in her hat bobbed as she spoke.

Her sunny disposition reminded him of her mother. Judith had always radiated warmth and caring in her expression and her manner. People were drawn to her laughter. She'd been the perfect debutante, and suitors had lined up at her father's door.

Gwendolyn was waiting for his answer with brows arched.

"Actually, I am in need of some paper and a pen," he said.

"So, you wish to correspond with someone?"

He'd no doubt she was teasing him. "I wish to respond to a birthday invitation."

"Do you mean Wyatt Pratt's birthday? I'm so pleased Livinia has invited you."

"Unfortunately, I cannot attend."

"Why ever not?" She eyed him as he leaned on his stick. "Ronald and I would be happy to pick you up in the motor if that is your concern."

"I thank you for the offer, but circumstances…"

"Circumstances?" She'd interrupted because she needed particulars. What excuse could he give that she wouldn't pester him with additional questions about his injury?

"Suffice to say I'm not prepared for a formal evening."

"Fiddlesticks. You could borrow one of Ronald's evening suits. I'm sure my housekeeper could alter the coat and trousers to your satisfaction."

She'd set her mouth. Her gaze bore into him, daring him to say no. This was the Gunnison side showing through. They all were a stubborn lot.

James shouldn't have hesitated.

She smiled triumphantly. "I'm so glad you changed your mind. Don't trouble yourself with a response. I will telephone Livinia and let her know you accept and send the tailor around for your measurements."

"Hold on. I didn't say I would go."

She wasn't listening. She ground the gear into first, slipped the clutch, and was off, driving down the middle of the road.

Remarkable how these young people were always in a rush, James decided. He headed back to the cottage, cross with himself for having been so easily persuaded.

He'd not been able to say no to her mother, either.

By the time he reached the front garden, he was hot and thirsty. He loped up the path to the door, trying to ignore the pins and needles digging into his knee with each footfall.

The cottage was thankfully cooler. He tossed his hat on a wooden peg and made his way into the kitchen. The hob had gone cold. The stone pitcher for water was empty. The well in the back garden seemed miles away.

Blast!

Tinned beans were all that was on offer in the larder.

Beans it would be for his noon day meal. He opened a tin and stared at the thin, pinkish sauce. The sight made him grimace.

He was a soldier. He'd eaten worse.

He set the tin on the table and slumped into a rickety wicker chair, exhausted.

A neighbor has asked him to a birthday party, a local affair for her son. She wished to include him, a stranger, in an evening of frivolity.

Bah, humbug.

He'd plenty of excuses for refusing, but Gwendolyn wouldn't hear any of them.

Make no mistake. It would be the first of many invitations, some out of kindness and others out of curiosity.

The locals would seek reassurances. He'd none to give. They would ask about any progress on the front. How could he tell them progress was measured in inches and the blood of soldiers? That the dead were too many to count?

That the war meant to last only a few months showed no sign of ending?

He couldn't. Nor would be try.

James pushed the tin away, his appetite gone.

Chapter Three

>>>×<<<

Livy had tossed and turned all night trying to think of a way to appeal to her son to give up the notion of joining the army. It wasn't too late. There must be a way to undo what Wyatt had done. In a fatherless family, a farm boy his age could be exempted from service.

Wyatt was so very young and impressionable. Well-intentioned villagers had influenced him. They'd called him a coward, but they were mistaken.

Didn't she depend on Wyatt more and more to fill his father's shoes? Hadn't he shown an abundance of courage since Charles had died?

The farm needed a man's firm hand. Wyatt must take charge. How could he if he was away in France or Belgium or some other foreign land?

Yawning, she finished making up her bed and went straight to the kitchen.

Wyatt came in the back door and sat down at the breakfast table. He didn't look at her. He didn't wish her good morning with his usual cheerfulness.

Livy was bereft that there should be this chasm of hurt

and ill-will between them.

"Would you like a fried egg?" It was the only thing she could think to say.

"Porridge will do." He poured his own coffee, added a splash of milk, and studied his cup.

Livy returned to the sink and looked out the window. She loved this land and couldn't imagine living anywhere else. Was she being selfish asking Wyatt to stay here? Or was she being protective as any mother would be?

"I'm sorry to have been so abrupt with you last night at dinner," she said, turning around, facing Wyatt adult to adult. "Only you took me by surprise."

Wyatt set his coffee on the table and crossed his arms. "There never seemed to be a good time to discuss the matter with you."

She affected a smile. "Have I been so neglectful?"

Her son met her gaze and shook his head. The strain in his expression was palpable.

Livy changed the subject. It seemed the prudent thing to do. Obviously he wasn't ready to listen to what she'd prepared to say.

"I've sent an invitation for your birthday party in the morning post to Major Gunnison," she said.

"Thank you, Mother—for all you've done." Wyatt managed to smile.

She was grateful they'd managed to find common ground.

"Now you eat a good breakfast. There are a hundred things to do today." Livy filled a bowl from the pot of porridge on top of the cooker and brought it to the table.

Wyatt sat down and picked up his spoon. Livy set the bowl in front of him but resisted the urge to brush a lock of hair out of his eyes.

Livy checked the clock on the mantelshelf. She'd immersed herself for the last three-quarters of an hour in paying the bills. It was a task she put off until the last minute and she hurried now to get them done.

Mrs. Heath would want to see her about the menu for the birthday banquet. A few other details had yet to be decided on before tomorrow's fete.

A soft knock at the door interrupted her.

"Come in," she answered, turning from the desk.

Mrs. Heath stood in the doorway, her notebook in her hand. "I'm at my wit's end about what to serve for the dinner."

"We still have a few chickens left." Livy put down her pen.

"We need the eggs." Mrs. Heath sighed. "We must be mindful about having enough. How ever am I to make a cake without eggs?"

"This is a very special occasion indeed. We will have to be creative." Livy thought a minute. "Perhaps mushrooms, barley and leeks?"

"I may have a recipe," Mrs. Heath said, and she wrote in her notebook.

They'd known each other for nearly twenty years. Livy had been a bride when the housekeeper came to Fairview. Charles had insisted. Hiring a housekeeper was one of the many improvements he'd made to the farm.

Mrs. Heath had been patient and wise. In the intervening years, they'd shared the good times and the bad. They'd become friends and even confidants.

"I can't believe Wyatt will be nineteen," Mrs. Heath said.

"Nor can I. He was such a good baby." She remembered those early days well and wished sometimes that she could return to the past.

"He's grown into a fine young man."

"I've raised them to be independent, and now when they are ready to spread their wings, I am shattered."

"To be expected."

"Yes, well…" Livy fought back tears, appalled at how she could fall apart so easily.

Mrs. Heath looked at her hands. Livy had made her uncomfortable with her show of emotion.

"I'm sorry." Livy cleared her throat and straightened. They all needed to be strong for each other in these most trying of times.

"It is not an easy task to let them go, but we must. They are not ours to keep."

Livy exhaled, the full weight of Mrs. Heath's pronouncement was a heavy burden to bear.

"Mrs. Pratt, are you all right?"

"Yes," she answered. "I was thinking about what I

will do without Wyatt here on the farm."

"He'll be finished with his studies by June," Mrs. Heath replied. She'd not been told about Wyatt's plans and Livy couldn't bring herself to tell her now.

"We will carry on until then, won't we, you and I?" Livy said.

"Indeed, we will," Mrs. Heath replied without a trace of doubt.

Livy drew strength from her dear friend's confidence.

"I've written Major Gunnison asking him to attend Wyatt's birthday party."

"Major Gunnison?" Mrs. Heath's forehead creased.

"I'm told he's staying at the gamekeeper's cottage over at Asher Hall. He's Mrs. Asher's uncle."

"So I've heard." Mrs. Health made no additions to her sparse comment.

"Wyatt wants him to come."

"Very well." Mrs. Health opened her notebook. "I will add his name to the guest list."

Livy heard the tone of caution, even disapproval. "Is there something about Major Gunnison that I should know about?"

Mrs. Heath shifted slightly in her chair. "Only he was rather abrupt with Iris Bellwether when she and her daughter paid a call to welcome him. They even brought him a fresh batch of Iris's cream tarts. A most unpleasant man, she told me. Didn't ask them in or even thank her."

"Oh dear," Livy said. Had she made a mistake inviting the major? Would her family and friends be on tenterhooks all evening with the major there?

Livy remembered what Elizabeth had said at dinner last night. The man had the reputation as a curmudgeon.

"He's made it plain as day he doesn't want company." Mrs. Heath went on.

"We must make allowances," Livy said. "After all he's been through on the battlefield."

Mrs. Heath nodded. "Of course. What he must have seen…" She could not finish.

She'd been widowed by an Afrikaner's bullet in the Transvaal. Mrs. Heath carried her own pain, had endured more than her share of sacrifice.

"I cannot imagine. How could anyone?" Livy shivered. Now Wyatt wished to join the major and the rest. At times, it seemed the entire world was unraveling before her eyes.

How would they ever get through it?

A commotion outside diverted Livy's thoughts. She rose to peer out the window. A black Daimler, the boot piled high with cases, had stopped at the front steps.

"My mother-in-law has arrived," she said.

"Would you like to continue this discussion at a later date?" Mrs. Heath asked.

"Yes, I must go and greet Mother Pratt. It won't do to leave her unattended."

Mrs. Heath rose from her chair. "I'll send up a menu for your approval."

Livy's relief was immediate. "That would be lovely."

"Will there be anything else?"

"Not for the moment." Livy smiled. She didn't want Mrs. Heath to worry. "I am grateful to have you to depend on."

Mrs. Heath acknowledged the compliment with a nod, and then exited, a model of enviable efficiency.

Chapter Four

➤➤➤◄◄◄

L ivy whisked down the hall, wringing her hands in anticipation of the reunion about to take place. Her mother-in-law could try a saint's nerves.

Wyatt had agreed that he must not discuss his wishes with his grandmother until after his party. Livy had sworn the girls to secrecy. It'd seemed the sensible thing to ask for the sake of family peace and harmony.

As heir and only son, Wyatt had never done any wrong in his grandmother's eyes. Still, Livy dreaded what would be most certainly a blistering confrontation if Mother Pratt found out what Wyatt intended to do.

Wyatt's birthday party must be, by all means, a celebration.

There'd be no long faces if Livy had her way.

The double doors opened and Mother Pratt breezed in with Winnie and Grace at each elbow, peppering her with questions about what gifts she'd brought for them.

Their grandmamma lifted her veil, not in the least perturbed by the children or set off course by their poor manners. When she saw Livy, her gaze intensified.

"There you are," she said as if she'd been kept waiting for hours instead of minutes.

"Mother Pratt, how good to see you." Livy bridged the gap and gave her mother-in-law a quick peck on the cheek. The scent of lemon verbena was overwhelming. "I trust your journey wasn't too tiresome?"

"Only a little," she answered as she surveyed Livy from head to toe. Thankfully, no comment was made about Livy not wearing mourning clothes.

"Did you bring any chocolates?" Gracie's small voice interrupted them.

"We shall soon find out, won't we?" Mother Pratt drew off her gloves and handed them to Livy, followed by her duster and traveling hat. She wore black, of course, relieved only by a swirl of gray hair and a pale complexion worthy of a city dweller.

The chauffeur came inside laden with several cases. A lady's maid followed.

"Please put them in the east bedroom," Mother Pratt said.

Livy hid her consternation as she handed over the traveling garments to the maid. This was her house, a fact of which she'd like to remind Mother Pratt. Instead of a confrontation, she guided her mother-in-law into the parlor. "I imagine you are ready for your tea."

Mother Pratt didn't reply. No doubt she found a response unnecessary. She glanced around and frowned before she sat down on the horsehair sofa.

Grace perched on the sofa's arm. "We are having a

wonderful birthday party for Wyatt."

"Yes, I know." Mother Pratt tilted her head, her movements very sharp and bird-like. "Your brother is turning nineteen."

Winnie nodded. "All our friends are coming. There will be dancing and so many kinds of good things to eat."

Mother Pratt smiled indulgently. "I suspect the evening will be a pleasant affair."

Livy averted her gaze. The woman didn't know how close the evening had become to being a disaster.

"Are you cold?" Mother Pratt asked. "Grace, be a good girl and find my maid. Time these windows were closed."

Grace looked at Livy.

"Never mind, Grace," Livy said, and she shut the window. Mother Pratt's maid had enough to do.

Mother Pratt cleared her throat. They all waited for her to speak, but she suppressed whatever had been on the tip of her tongue when Elizabeth made her entrance wearing the dress that she had been working on for days.

Oh, my, Livy thought. She'd not believed the finished product to be so daring.

"How good to see you," Elizabeth said to her grand-mamma as she kissed her.

"My dear, what on earth are you wearing?" Mother Pratt's tone was not complimentary as she glared at the girl.

Elizabeth twirled around to show her an exotic con-coction of colorful strips of cloth. "It's the latest fashion from France. I copied the design from an illustration in the *Daily Mail* using some old dresses."

The combination of colors complimented her daughter's fair skin, Livy reflected, and the pleated skirt was flattering as well, but the hemline was scandalously high, and a lot more than her pretty ankles were exposed.

"Go take that awful costume off at once," Mother Pratt asserted quite forcefully.

Elizabeth froze. "This is what all the girls are wearing."

"Maybe country girls, but not a Pratt." Her speech was clipped. There was no room for discussion, let alone compromise. Livy blamed herself. If she'd known her daughter's intentions, she would've supervised her more closely and could've spared her from her grandmother's wrath.

"Perhaps your grey wool skirt would be better," Livy said, unhappy Mother Pratt's visit had so quickly hit a sour note.

Elizabeth straightened, cast Livy a hostile look, and exited the room.

"The very idea," Mother Pratt said. "What were you thinking?"

Livy lowered her gaze. "You know how young people are. Always challenging the status quo."

Mother Pratt harrumphed. "A hemline must be modest. To wear it above the ankle would invite the wrong kind of attention."

"Yes, Grandmamma. Elizabeth will not leave the

house dressed thus." Livy prayed that would be the end of the woman's objections.

Her mother-in-law appeared to be mollified for the moment.

"I suppose you've invited the regulars to the party?" Mother Pratt asked.

"I have indeed." Livy sat down wearily. "With one addition. This year I included Major James Gunnison."

"Is he local? I don't remember meeting him." Mother Pratt's voice was like cut glass.

"Oh no, he's only just arrived from the battlefield. He's Gwendolyn Asher's uncle and recovering from a wound to his knee."

"Not serious, I hope?"

"I don't think so," Livy replied. "He seems to be getting along without the benefit of servants in that old cottage on the Asher estate."

"How very odd."

"I thought so myself, but the major insists on solitude as he recovers."

Her mother-in-law relaxed her shoulders, but did not change the tautness in her expression. "Don't you worry the activities of your party will be too much for him? You know how curious everyone will be about any progress in France. They will be sure to bombard him with questions."

"Hopefully the major will understand."

"I've read about a soldier in last week's *Sunday Telegraph* who took his life while on leave," Mother Pratt said.

"How terrible."

"To be sure," her mother-in-law continued. "Men returning from war need time to recover their bearings. Sometimes their nerves are quite brittle."

"Hopefully the condition is temporary." Livy wondered if the major suffered from a case of nerves. Was that why he stayed at the cottage rather than in the big house with Gwendolyn and Ronald?

Mother Pratt sniffed. "I hope you won't regret your decision to include this man."

If Mother Pratt wanted her to rescind the invitation, Livy would disabuse her of the notion.

"Whatever the major's physical and mental state, all of us will welcome him," Livy said so there wouldn't be any misunderstanding.

Livy saw by the woman's pinched expression she understood perfectly.

"Whatever you decide, Livinia. I didn't come to interfere."

Livy turned her head so Mother Pratt wouldn't see her grimace. For no falser words had ever been spoken.

The conversation had sowed seeds of doubt. Would a party be too much for a man recovery from the war?

Livy didn't even know if the major would come, she hadn't yet received a reply, but she hoped he would because what could be better for the mind and spirit than a celebration with friends and family?

Chapter Five

"Was that the telephone?" Elizabeth presented herself in the parlor in a dark blue serge skirt with the hemline only slightly above the ankle, appropriate for a girl her age.

"Yes," Livy answered. "Gwendolyn Asher rang up to say her uncle will be attending Wyatt's birthday party."

Elizabeth frowned. "I don't understand why you invited the major."

"Because he's a neighbor, and Wyatt was keen on meeting him."

Elizabeth sat primly on the sofa.

"Thank you for not opposing your grandmother's wishes," Livy said. She could speak freely. Mercifully, Mother Pratt had gone to her room for a lie down after her tea.

"I don't know why you take her side." Elizabeth's eyes narrowed with indignation.

"I took no sides." Livy wouldn't quarrel. She understood Elizabeth's need to be fashionable, envied her at times the freedom she embraced to try new things. "I don't want there to be any arguments with your grand-mamma here."

Livy looked over the menu Mrs. Heath had presented to her but had difficulty concentrating. Her daughter's behavior had become more and more troublesome, and even the locals looked askance at the girl's erratic temperament. Of course, the loss of a father at such a tender age had made her this way. Livy was willing to give her some latitude to avoid a mutiny. A mother must make allowances for a child who was hurting.

Mother Pratt was another kettle of fish. She did not tolerate defiance. Her wishes were always obeyed. It was the way things were done in families, had been done for generations.

Elizabeth chafed against the old ways, much as Livy had done, but tradition served a purpose, in Livy's opinion. Following the rules set in place so long ago assured the world was predictable and safe. Her daughter would learn this in due course.

"I didn't mind the dress, you looked lovely in it, but it's your attitude that concerns me," Livy said.

Elizabeth pulled a face. Her disposition couldn't have been less agreeable, but there was no argument.

"Good. I'm glad we can discuss these things with some degree of maturity."

The girl responded with a shrug.

Livy sensed Elizabeth had something else on her mind besides the dress and Mother Pratt's quick reprimand.

She would rather continue with her preparations for

the party, the list of things still to be done was quite long, but she had learned her daughter's sulkiness must be addressed before it affected the rest of the household.

"Tell me what else is bothering you."

Elizabeth lifted her gaze. There was an honesty there Livy found refreshing. The girl didn't know how to mask her feelings—yet.

"Why do you resist inviting my friend, Mr. Morehouse, to the farm?" She took a deep breath. "I asked Mrs. Heath to add his name to the guest list for Wyatt's birthday party, but she refused. You told her he wasn't welcome. Frankly, Mother, I believe all of you conspire against me."

"Don't be ridiculous."

"Why, may I ask, do you find him so unworthy?" Elizabeth pouted most disagreeably. "You know I'm terribly fond of him."

"So you have told me many times."

"And yet, you exclude him."

What Livy had to say would take a great deal of diplomacy. Her daughter was young and shockingly naïve and would take offense at any suggestion of impropriety.

"He's not suitable for you," Livy replied. Her darling girl had become infatuated with a man Livy knew little about and what she did know, she didn't like.

"In what way, may I ask?"

"What kind of man would call on a girl your age without her parents in attendance?"

Elizabeth scoffed. "Your generation is so old-fashioned. Nobody uses an escort these days."

Livy wasn't offended. "Is that so? I'll have you know I'm not exactly a fossil."

Elizabeth's face bunched into a terrible scowl.

Livy had thought a bit of humor would ease the tension between them, but she could see she was wrong.

"I want you to marry a considerate man," Livy said, "one who would be your equal in the adventures to come."

Elizabeth sighed. "You are being most unfair. You haven't even given him a chance."

"I'm your mother. I'm doing what I think best."

Livy would not be swayed by her daughter's flare of temper. She had a duty to protect her and would do her best to keep any contact with Mr. Morehouse to a minimum and spare Elizabeth the heartache of a relationship that would prove to be false.

Still, Livy's heart swelled with tenderness for the girl struggling with her feelings.

Her beautiful child was so very young. Elizabeth's confidence in her abilities to make her own choices should not be discouraged, but she had no experience with men.

If Elizabeth would only let her, Livy would hold her close and assure her there would be other men, fine, worthy men for her consideration. She feared, with so few suitors available, Elizabeth might think she needed to settle for the first man who paid her any notice.

"Don't think I'm going to stop seeing him." Elizabeth thrust out her lower lip. There was fire in her eyes. She glared at Livy in a way she wouldn't have dared if her father was alive.

And yet their personalities were closely aligned when it came to defending those they loved.

Elizabeth stood, ready to bolt. "There will come a time when you won't be able to treat me like a child."

"Until that time arrives, you will do as I say." To explain further, Livy decided, would only invite more contempt.

"If Mr. Morehouse isn't invited, then what is the point of my attending Wyatt's party?"

"Your absence will be noted and commented upon. Why would you want to spoil the party by drawing attention to yourself?"

Elizabeth's eyes widened. "It's not me who will spoil the party."

"Isn't it?" Livy was having difficulty reining in her patience with the girl. "A party is a celebration and your only consideration is to ruin the occasion with your petulance."

"Mother, you are being so unfair."

"I will not hear any more of Mr. Morehouse. Am I clear?"

Elizabeth glared for several seconds and then marched out, leaving Livy with a heavy lump in the pit of her stomach. A storm was brewing, and she'd no idea how to protect her daughter from her own willfulness and imprudence. Aware this was only a skirmish, Livy was at a loss about what she must do.

The girl would not miss Wyatt's party. Of that, Livy was certain.

Chapter Six

➤➤➤◄◄◄

L ivy wore her lime green crepe dress with a very pretty square neckline for the birthday party. As she checked herself in the mirror, she decided the dress was not the most fashionable design, but not a dress for a fossil, either.

Mother Pratt had strongly suggested she wear black, but Livy had put away her widow's weeds in the back of her wardrobe and that's where they would stay. She was determined to present herself as cheerful this evening.

She added a pair of elbow-length kid gloves. They'd belonged to her grandmother, who'd not had much in the way of luxuries but wouldn't be seen at a gathering without her gloves.

Thankfully, Wyatt had mentioned any thing more about his future plans. Hopefully, after some reflection, he'd realize the implications of enlisting and changed his mind. As far as anyone knew, he intended to return to college.

She was nervous about Major Gunnison's attendance. Would he be difficult? She would try and be the perfect hostess, of course, but some men could be belligerent and demanding.

Livy descended the stairs and went into the parlor. She straightened the family photographs on the mantelshelf and took a quick look around the room.

Mrs. Heath had done wonders with the decor, and Livy was delighted at the result. Garlands of wisteria were draped in the entryway. A vase of late roses, deep reds and vibrant yellows, had been placed on the side table. Their scent was a reminder of summer gone. Extra chairs had been brought in for the older ladies who would retire by the fire and gossip—away from the noise of the dancers in the back garden.

To Livy's gratification, the other rooms were equally adorned.

If only Charles could be here to celebrate with them. He would be bursting with pride at the man their son had become.

Livy did not dwell on what could not be but hurried to the dining room. Tonight, she would do her best to keep the black clouds at a distance for Wyatt's sake. He would not gaze upon one frown or tear if Livy had her way.

The best flowers had been reserved for the dining room. Gleaming silver urns were filled with orange chrysanthemums and wild grasses. The collection of family crystal sparkled in the waning light.

Satisfied all was ready, she returned to the parlor. In the quiet moments before the first guests arrived, Livy reflected on what she must do tonight. Above all, the celebration must be happy. The evening must be filled with gaiety and laughter. The gathering of family and friends would talk of happier days so their fear of the future might be forgotten for a while.

Livy must hurry. Her guests would be arriving. Young Tom—who did the work of two grown men most days—met her in the hall. He'd been recruited as a footman and looked very distinguished in his Sunday suit of clothes. He wore white gloves, as was the custom.

"Good evening, Mrs. Pratt." He bowed from the waist.

"Evening," Livy replied. "You look very handsome tonight."

Tom straightened and rocked on his feet. "Thank you, Mrs. Pratt."

He'd assumed a heavy burden for his tender years, and it was a credit to his character that he tried to make the best of a difficult situation.

"Have you heard from your brother?" she asked, fearing the answer.

Tom stood straighter. "Mum had a letter from him only yesterday and he sends his regards."

"Will you tell him I am remembering him in my prayers?" She smiled.

"I will indeed."

"I'm sure he will be home soon." It was a wish they all shared and spoke frequently. Their brave men must return to their homes and to their families in all possible haste.

Tom pressed his lips into a thin line, his gaze stretched far away. To a foreign land, no doubt. To grassy fields and rutted pathways soaked in English blood.

Hopefully, the war would be over before this boy would be eligible to enlist. So many had already been lost. Livy couldn't bear to lose another fine English lad to this war's greedy clutches.

As Livy adjusted her gloves, she heard reins jingling and wheels crunching over gravel in the driveway. Tom opened the front door.

The air was warm for October and the light was just beginning to fade. Her guests would be able to stroll in her back garden and admire the last of her flowers before the local musicians took their places and the music started.

Tom had lit the lamps and they bathed the steps in light.

A trap pulled up and stopped. Livy positioned herself just inside the door by a display of deep purple delphiniums flanked by an oil painting of the rural countryside. It'd been their custom when Charles was alive to greet their guests together. Her husband hadn't liked parties as much as she had, but he'd indulged her fancy. He'd always been an affable host. Many at his funeral had commented on it.

The guests began arriving in twos and threes. Each looked at her tentatively, no doubt to gauge her mood. The time since Charles's death had been filled with sadness for all of them. They'd lost a good neighbor and friend and done their best to comfort a grieving widow.

She welcomed them all with the heartiest of hellos and the most genuine of smiles. How thrilled she was that they had put on their best finery and come.

"Just like old times," George Bellwether said with a wink before his wife elbowed him in the ribs.

"Almost," Livy replied, swallowing hard.

Much to Livy's consternation, right behind Iris and George Bellwether stood Mr. Redding Morehouse. He wore a white silk scarf flung carelessly around his neck and an evening suit with a high stiff color and narrow bow tie.

No doubt he thought he looked very debonair dressed thus, or perhaps he didn't care a fig how he looked. Even so, the man was as pompous as a peacock in full feathers.

She'd read London's Bohemian society was at odds with tradition. Some even took pleasure in shocking their family with their strange manner of dress and off-putting behavior.

If it was only his appearance, she might not have minded so very much. However, there was a challenge in his eyes, a hostility that made Livy shiver.

What did he want with her daughter? If Charles had been here, Mr. Morehouse wouldn't have been so bold to crash their house party. Her husband would've known how to deal with this interloper.

"There you are," Elizabeth said behind her, making Livy jump. Elizabeth reached for Mr. Morehouse's hand

and tucked it in the crook of her arm.

"Mother, you remember Redding?"

"Indeed, I do." Livy was furious at her daughter for inviting him—Redding, is it now? How dare Elizabeth go against her wishes.

She was quick to remember her own admonition. There would be no controversy tonight. No arguments. Only good will and cheerfulness. She put on her most engaging smile. Elizabeth seemed to breathe easier.

"Mrs. Pratt." Mr. Morehouse bowed, a little too exaggerated, a little too theatrical for Livy's taste. "How good of you to include me in your little soiree."

"We are celebrating Wyatt's birthday," she said, welcoming him, if not with open arms, at least with a modicum of good will. She couldn't ask him to leave now—as much as she'd like to.

"I dare say a happy occasion." He bowed again, acknowledging her with a second glance, then turning his attention to Elizabeth.

Tom helped the man with his coat and took his hat. Mr. Morehouse's hair was heavily oiled and gleamed in the electric light.

"Let me introduce you to the others," Elizabeth said, pulling him away.

"Don't forget your grandmother," Livy said.

Elizabeth cast an uncharitable look over her shoulder.

She was such a lovely girl with high cheekbones and delicate mouth—at this moment clamped tight.

Livy suppressed a sigh. Elizabeth was of the age where

a mother's opinion could be annoying. Livy believed Mr. Morehouse not to be the genuine article.

The world was changing so rapidly. In Livy's day, a girl's life was planned for her down to the kind of crockery she should own. She married the man her father chose for her.

Charles had sought land, and Father had needed money to make improvements to the farm, so their marriage had been arraigned. Even though theirs had not been a love match, look how well everything had turned out.

Elizabeth wanted to explore another path. She wanted to make her own choices, even make her own mistakes. Livy envied her for that freedom, but she feared where such headstrong ideas might lead.

A motorcar approached, headlamps lit. The arrival of a motorcar could only mean Gwendolyn and Ronald Asher had arrived. The chauffeur jumped out of his seat and opened the back door. Gwendolyn stepped down, looking so pretty in a taupe satin gown and her mother's pearls. Ronald followed, dressed to perfection in a tailcoat with a black tie. The two of them ascended the stairs arm in arm and with such grace you'd think they'd arrived at a royal palace.

The pair would cause a stir in such finery, especially since the locals couldn't afford new clothes with a war raging. Livinia was grateful they had come. The Ashers had always been good neighbors, and she didn't want such strong ties to be broken.

Regrettably, Major Gunnison didn't seem to be with

them. Excuses would be made for his absence. No doubt Gwendolyn would apologize profusely.

"How good to see you both." Livy was rewarded with a kiss on the cheek from Gwendolyn.

"We wouldn't miss a birthday party." Gwendolyn spoke with a lilt in her voice. She appeared content no matter the situation. Livy wished she could be so carefree.

"Ronald, I'm so happy you came," Livy said.

"Awfully good of you to invite us." He took Livy's hand and brushed a kiss across her knuckles.

Livy patted his clean-shaven cheek. He smelled heavily of South Sea spices.

"I'm sorry your uncle couldn't attend," Livy said.

"Oh, but he is here," Gwendolyn said as Tom helped her with her satin cape.

Livy checked again and saw another passenger emerging from the other side of the motor.

"I wouldn't let him stay at home." Gwendolyn leaned closer as if sharing a confidence. "You were so good to include him."

"I was glad he accepted the invitation."

"Not that Gwendolyn gave him a choice." Ronald smirked.

"Don't be rude," Gwendolyn said. "Of course he wanted to come."

"His knee still bothers him," Ronald stated neatly. "The old boy won't be dancing the waltz tonight, I dare say."

"Ronald, please," Gwendolyn admonished her husband.

"No matter," Livy replied. "I didn't expect the major's attendance to reach the dance floor. To have him here at all is an achievement."

"You're very kind to say so." Gwendolyn glared at her husband, who thankfully remained silent.

Her uncle must be a source of strain between the couple, Livy thought, although for what reason she couldn't fathom.

"Livinia, when are you going to sell me the farm?"

"Ronald, do be considerate," Gwendolyn scolded, "we aren't here to discuss business."

Her husband ignored her. "Farming's not a job for a woman. You can't last much longer, you know. Especially now, with Wyatt off to the continent."

His comments put Livy's back up. "You've got it wrong," she said, vexed the gossip had reached his ears. "Wyatt has no such intentions."

"I beg your pardon," he replied without a grain of sincerity. "I'd heard he'd enlisted in the army."

"Wyatt will be going off to college for his final term," she corrected them. "After his graduation in the spring, we'll discuss his future."

"Of course you will," Gwendolyn said. "With any luck, this dreadful war will be over by then." She turned to her husband for confirmation.

"We'll see, won't we?" Ronald Asher replied.

Livy forced a smile. His family had wanted to buy Fairview for ages. Well, he wasn't going to have it, not if she had any say in the matter.

"You'll find the others in the parlor," Livy said, putting an end to the conversation.

Gwendolyn nodded, and guided by Ronald, the pair made their way in that direction.

Livy turned back to see a gentleman grimacing as he labored up the steps. He leaned on a stick and struggled to keep his balance with each step.

This must be the contentious Major Gunnison, she mused. She met him at the top step. He stood a head taller. His jaw and long nose were in good proportion, a symmetry that was pleasing to her eye.

His gaze met hers. Livy's heart fluttered, unbidden. And unwelcome.

"How wonderful to meet you at last, Major Gunnison," she said, a little breathless. "I'm Livinia Pratt."

"Mrs. Pratt, thank you for the invitation."

"Thank you for coming, even though I understand you are recovering from an injury."

"A slight wound to the knee," he said. "The pace of healing isn't at all what I'd like, but I'll be right as rain in a couple of day."

He spoke as if he'd given his knee a direct order and had been disobeyed.

"These things take time," she replied encouragingly.

"Indeed, they do. It takes discipline to overcome obstacles. My father believed in discipline. It's what made me the man I am today."

Livy would never contradict a guest, and yet she had

her doubts. Healing took a great deal more than discipline.

"I'm very glad you came," Livy said. "Everyone will be delighted you are here."

Tom took his coat and top hat. To her relief, the major hadn't worn his uniform, but looked very dapper in an evening suit. Old school, to be sure, and showing off a fit physique.

"Thank you, young man."

Tom bowed. "Sir."

Livy had not thought Major Gunnison would acknowledge the boy. It was a small thing, but she was impressed nevertheless. She caught a glimpse into what kind of officer he must be.

The result was clearly evident. Tom's eyes beamed with obvious adulation.

To her surprise, he handed over his stick.

There could only be one explanation. He didn't want her guests to see his condition. Was it vanity or the need to be strong for their sake?

A little of both, she guessed. In her experience, a man doesn't like to admit to any weakness.

Young Tom carried the major's things away to the cloakroom, leaving the two of the facing each other.

"How becoming you look this evening, Mrs. Pratt."

The compliment was of the generic variety, she'd heard it a dozen times already this evening, but she was ridiculously pleased anyway. "You're very kind to say so. Would you call me Livinia? All my friends do."

His smile was a little off-center. "I would indeed."

"What shall I call you? Major Gunnison seems so very formal."

"My Christian name is James. Call me that."

She would be happy to do so.

"Then you will be returning to France as soon as you are able?"

"Yes, and I am most anxious to do so."

Livy admired his dedication. James was a professional soldier and wouldn't shirk his duty. He would be an inspiration to her other guests.

What would he think of her and her opposition to Wyatt's enlistment?

"Would you be so kind to accompany me into the parlor?" She couldn't ignore her other guests a moment longer.

He offered her his elbow. There was a time when she would've been tentative, even timid to take the arm of a stranger.

She intertwined her arm in his, closing the gap between them. She was comfortable in her role as hostess and he could be at ease with her.

"Come, meet my family and friends, Major." They will do you a world of good, she wanted to add.

His arm flexed to accommodate her. When they reached the doorway, the conversation stopped. He tensed as the room of unfamiliar faces looked to see who'd arrived.

Livy had no doubt the other guests were asking each

other questions about her charge. So, this was the major everyone was talking about, they would be saying. This is the man who could be rude and even hostile come to join our ranks.

They strode arm in arm into the parlor. How very good it felt to be ushered into the room filled with family and friends on the arm of a handsome gentleman.

Livy was almost giddy—the thought made her laugh.

"Is there something amusing?" James was looking at her.

Livy realized what she had done, and a rush of heat threatened to expose her. "The occasion requires a degree of gaiety from us, don't you agree?"

He smiled. It was only a brief smile, but endeared him to her in the most fundamental way. It was what she'd wanted from him and required of herself. To make him smile, relax, and forget about the horrid war for the evening.

Livy introduced him to the crowd that gathered around them, hanging on to the major's arm as she did so. It was a coquettish thing to do, but having him here seemed a triumph over all he'd been through on the battlefield. To her satisfaction, they all greeted him with their thanks and appreciation.

Livy was grateful, but she could no longer delay the inevitable.

"Major, come meet my mother-in-law. She's come down from London for Wyatt's birthday." Livy led him away.

"She doesn't live with you?" He quirked a brow.

"Heavens, no." Lest she sounded too pleased, Livy hastened to explain. "Grandmamma never liked country life."

How would her mother-in-law react to the major? They all had questions to ask, of course. Livy hoped Mother Pratt's inquisition wouldn't take long.

Mother Pratt sat in a high-backed chair, presiding over old neighbors and friends. When she'd returned to the city to live, she'd taken on airs of *noblesse oblige*. Why these people tolerated her was nothing short of miraculous, in Livy's opinion.

Livy didn't care for London. She didn't like city smells or the constant rush of having to be somewhere. A country girl, she would never move from Fairview.

She hoped Mother Pratt could carry on a conversation without mentioning London society overly much or worse, dragging them into a discussion about things they couldn't afford and would never have. With the Ashers present, so would be the temptation to impress them.

"Of course, one must own a motor in this day and age," Mother Pratt was saying, "but I will never get used to them. Their noise is intrusive and the engine petrol fouls the air."

She was met with a chorus of agreement.

"My dear cousin Rosamund insisted I take the motor car when I came to Fairview. She didn't want me suffering from chilblains. Trains can be so drafty."

Just as Livy had suspected. Such comments only

served to be aggrandizing. Petrol was strictly rationed. Where had Mother Pratt managed to find enough to travel to Kent?

"Mark my words, motor cars will never replace a horse and a good trap," Iris Bellwether said. A farmer's wife, she was known for getting in the last word and seemed to have succeeded this time.

The women looked up at Livy and her guest as they approached. Her mother-in-law's pursed lips, for some reason, irritated Livy.

"Grandmamma, allow me to introduced my neighbor, Major Gunnison."

He bowed slightly. "Ma'am."

Livy introduced the other ladies.

Mother Pratt surveyed him closely. "Isn't an officer expected to wear his uniform?"

The major affected a smile. "Good lady, I was hoping to be a civilian tonight."

Mother Pratt sniffed.

"I gather you are from London. I'm a city man myself," he said. To Livy's great delight, James could be charming.

"Livinia, you should've told me." Mother Pratt turned to James. "What part of London may I ask?"

"I grew up in Mayfair. My family resides there still," he said.

Mother Pratt acknowledged his reply with a nod. "I understand you are related to the Ashers?"

"My brother is Mrs. Asher's father." He did not volunteer anything more.

"How trying these times are, you must be glad to be away from the conflict." Mother Pratt's interrogation continued.

"To be frank, I would prefer to be at the front with my men."

"Such a terrible war," Iris Bellwether said, shuddering.

"Tell us, are they making any progress?" Gertrude Finley asked.

"As best as can be expected," he replied.

Regretfully, the conversation was becoming grim. Livy must shift the topic to one that was more pleasant.

"How lucky we are that the weather cooperated," she said.

"Yes, October can be so unpredictable," Gertrude agreed.

"Too hot for me." Iris fanned herself with her hand. "I prefer a crispness in the air. So much better for one's constitution."

There were murmurs of agreement and the rustle of bombazine as the women shifted in their seats.

"There you are, Uncle." Gwendolyn swept up to her uncle's side.

Livy was happy to see the affection in his gaze.

"Would you be a dear and rescue Ronald?" Gwendolyn pulled a face as she gestured in the direction of a group of animated men. "He's over in the corner discussing politics."

"I will join him." James bowed slightly.

"Splendid."

"Ladies," he bowed again, "if you will excuse me."

"Such an attractive man," Iris whispered.

Gertrude giggled and then clapped her gloved hand over her mouth.

Livy agreed as she watched him retreat.

"He seems to be getting around rather well," Mother Pratt said. "I was told he had been injured."

"That's right," Iris answered.

"I confess to being surprised," Gwendolyn said. "When I found him walking up the road to Asher Hall the other day, he looked rather spent."

Livy drew the only conclusion possible. "He must be getting better."

"It's his knee," Gwendolyn explained to the other women.

"A bullet wound, they say," Iris said.

Gwendolyn shook her head. "Shards of metal from a bomb."

"Oh, dear," Iris replied.

"I think it's a bit odd he has shut himself up in your gamekeeper's cottage." Mother Pratt spoke so all could hear.

"I assure you he is perfectly tame." Gwendolyn laughed. "He insisted on the cottage. I couldn't persuade him to stay with us. Uncle prefers his seclusion, I'm afraid."

"How very inconsiderate of my daughter-in-law to invite him tonight," Mother Pratt replied.

Mother Pratt's barb stung, but Livy would not let her mother-in-law undermine good intentions.

"We all welcome him into our small community as he recovers," Livy said. "It's the very least we can do."

Mother Pratt ignored her. "Still, he must suffer walking about with a sore leg."

"Apparently not, as you have just said." Livy stifled her irritation. It took everything she possessed to control the tone of her voice.

"I should think a bit of exercise is just what the doctor ordered," Gwendolyn added.

"One must not overtax one's self." Mother Pratt shot Livy a look of hostility.

"I will do my best to see that doesn't happen," Livy replied, her temper severely compromised.

Mother Pratt blinked back her surprise at Livy's bold reply.

"If you'll excuse me, I see Mrs. Clark. I must ask her where she bought such an exquisite broach." Gwendolyn took the opportunity to flee, leaving Livy and Mother Pratt shooting sparks at each other.

Livy dared the old woman to say one more word about the major. One more word! Mother Pratt shifted her gaze to the others, who averted their eyes. No one seemed willing to take sides, which was just as well.

"Where is the cider?" Mother Pratt sniffed. "You can't expect us to sit here in this heat with nothing to drink."

Thankfully, the woman's interest in the major's affairs

seemed to be satisfied. For now.

"As you know, we are short-staffed," Livy replied. "I will go see what's keeping them."

She excused herself, her nerves frayed. The woman could be so tactless. Her criticism bordered on spitefulness.

Livy glanced over her shoulder at James Gunnison, who was conversing with the men. He shook hands as he was introduced and exchanged pleasantries as any gentleman would. Something he said made them laugh, which pleased her. There was pride in his bearing, even a touch of arrogance. If the men noticed, they wouldn't take offense. All appreciated his service and made allowances.

Livy was delighted how everyone accepted him so easily and how he responded favorably to their good wishes. She'd worried needlessly.

The evening had not started out as planned with Mr. Morehouse's arrival, Elizabeth neglecting her duties as hostess, and now the refreshments overdue. James Gunnison's presence at the party made up for these unfortunate ripples in the pond. Despite her mother-in-law's misgivings, Livy had no doubt inviting him was one of her successes this evening.

Where was Wyatt? Had he come down from his room? She hadn't seen him.

Why hadn't he presented himself in the parlor to greet his guests? She needed to find him before Mother Pratt made a fuss about his absence.

First she must see to the refreshments.

Chapter Seven

>»>«<«<

James drifted away from the scrum of Livinia's friends as they debated the significance of the latest dispatches from France. Naturally, they had asked him about any progress. He could give them no new information. Had they guessed James had doubts about the success of the campaign? He hoped not, for the sake of the occasion and for their peace of mind.

According to Gwendolyn, Mrs. Pratt's son would soon be joining the fight. He'd noticed how the light within her dimmed when the conversation turned to the war. He would not spoil her party with idle speculation nor heated discussions about what ought to be done. In this parlor, heavy with the scent of perfume and bath powder, of shaving cream and fresh flowers, they must remember the foundation on which their civilization was built: Civility and kindness, generosity of spirit and friendship.

"Are you all right, Uncle?" Gwendolyn was at his elbow, looking lovely and exuding the charm that was her birthright.

"As you can see, I am quite well."

She turned her gaze up at him with eyes the color of the ocean. Her mother had looked at him that way a long time ago. The memory was sweet, he wouldn't deny it.

"Then I have no need to worry?"

"I am pleased to be here, if that is what you are asking. It's a splendid party."

"I am glad you think so." She kissed him on the cheek. Such displays of affection were part and parcel of social occasions, and he was delighted when Gwendolyn bestowed them on him.

As a rule, he hardened his heart to attachments of any kind, thought it best, especially after Gwendolyn's mother had married his brother.

Emotions interfered with discipline.

Tonight, he made an exception to the rule. By Jove, he would enjoy himself.

With a swish of her dress, she moved off to the next guest, and his heart ached to have her go. If circumstances had been different, if fate had only intervened, she would have been his daughter.

His gaze fell on the photograph on the mantelshelf of a much younger Livinia with her family. How content she looked as she stood next to a man who must have been her husband.

The cheerful family portrait brought a tightening in his chest. His mother and father had never shown the slightest affection to each other or to their children. Their home life had been stressful. The other lads at school had always been so excited about the holidays arriving, but

James had dreaded returning home to a chilly reception and a cheerless household.

"My son and his family, as you well can see." Grandmother Pratt had come up behind him. "Charles and Livinia were an arraigned match, but I assure you they were very much a devoted couple."

"The photograph demonstrates that very well," he replied.

"They had four beautiful children together," she continued. "I couldn't be prouder."

"A grandmother's pride is precious to children," he said.

Grandmother Pratt beamed. His comment had done what he'd intended.

The memory of his own grandmother flickered and died. She had been stern and uncompromising. Her family pride had been measured out in small doses and infrequently.

James had no doubt Grandmother Pratt saw him as a threat. He was flattered the old girl thought he could turn Livinia's head. She had nothing to fear. Even if he had taken a liking to Livinia Pratt, which he conceded could be easily done, he must be realistic. The fight overseas demanded his attention. He was committed to vanquishing their country's enemies. There was no room for anything or anyone else.

"Please accept my condolences for the loss of your son. My niece has explained the circumstances."

"A tragedy, to be sure. It's been over a year, but we all

still grieve."

"The heart has its own timetable," he replied.

Her cat-like gaze perused him. "You are quite different than I was led to believe."

"I hope you are not disappointed."

"Indeed, I am not. You're much more pleasant than you have been described."

James winced. His reputation for being a curmudgeon had reached Grandmother Pratt's ears.

"I'm sorry if my character has been found lacking."

"Unjustly, I might add."

He bowed slightly. "You honor me with your praise."

"Yes, I see that I have."

Grandmother Pratt sparred with words, but James was confident he'd taken the starch out of any opposition. Under the gaze of this lady's scrutiny, he'd managed to find favor.

"Now, if you would be so kind to escort me back to my chair," she said, "I see Livinia has finally brought us something cold to drink."

Livy returned to the parlor carrying a tray laden with glasses filled with freshly pressed cider. The harried maid, a girl from the village hired for the evening, attended the other guests mingling outside. Her guests were occupied in conversation, some serious, some not. All seemed to be enjoying themselves except one.

She noticed, with some concern, James stood alone by the fireplace.

"Where is our boy?" Grandmamma asked, taking a glass.

"I haven't seen him tonight," Livy answered.

"It's not like Wyatt to be late," Mother Pratt continued. "Where has he gone off to?"

"I don't know, but I will find him as soon as I've served these drinks."

Mother Pratt smacked her lips but seemed satisfied with Livy's answer. For the moment, anyway.

Livy served the rest of the ladies and then carried the tray over to James. As she approached, he stood taller, almost at attention. She found his solitude jarring.

What had happened? Had someone said something off-putting?

"Would you care for a glass of cider?" She held up the tray. "The apples come from our orchard."

He thanked her and took a glass. Livy watched as he downed half of it.

"What do you think? Does our local cider measure up to what you are used to?"

"I've never tasted better."

"I'm glad to hear you say so." And she was. She waited for him to say something, but an awkward silence followed.

"I hope you have found us to be agreeable," she said.

"Your family and friends have been most welcoming."

"And yet, here you are all alone." Livy couldn't abide

anyone being alone.

James affected a slight shrug. "It is my nature."

"I don't like talking about the war. I imagine you don't either."

"Not conversation suitable for cozy parlors?"

"That's not what I meant."

He arched a brow.

"All right. Perhaps I have tried to keep conversation steered away from the topic." She sighed. "I don't meant to sound shallow, but the war seems to be all we talk about these days."

"My dear Mrs. Pratt…"

"Please, call me Livinia."

"Livinia." He returned his glass to the tray. "We all need to sort out what's happening, to make sense of it all."

"I'm afraid we won't be successful."

He nodded. "A fear we all share."

She affected a smile. She appreciated his honesty. "When will it all end, James? When will the war be over?"

She'd asked a question he couldn't answer. Who knew how long this horror would continue? Still she needed to hear some words of reassurance.

"I cannot make any promises," he said. "I won't give you hope that might prove to be false."

Livy felt properly chastised. She'd wanted to show her support and despaired at how she'd botched the attempt. The major hadn't been fooled.

"Ah. This must be your son?" His gaze had shifted to a spot over her shoulder.

Livy turned and caught her breath. Wyatt had chosen to wear his father's evening attire and looked just like him.

Wyatt noticed her from where he'd entered the room and grinned.

Everyone to a man clapped him on the back and shook his hand as he made his way through the throng of well-wishers.

When Wyatt reached them, he was beaming. "Sorry to take so long, Mother." He turned to the group of neighbors and friends. "I'm so glad you all came."

They all talked at once, claiming him as their own. All except Mother Pratt, who waved frantically for him to join her.

"What's gone wrong with your tie?" Livy's throat tightened.

"I had the devil of a time getting it right."

"Let me see what I can do." Livy set the tray on a side table and made the adjustments.

"There, that's better," she said when she'd finished.

"Thank you." He stepped out of her reach.

Livy wasn't embarrassed her son turned away from her coddling. She supposed his need for independence was inevitable, even desirable.

She offered her son a glass, which he refused with a shake of his head.

"Wyatt, this is Major Gunnison."

"You must be the major everyone has been talking about," Wyatt said, standing at attention. "I'm Wyatt Pratt."

"I'm pleased to meet you."

"Sir." The boy saluted and clicked his heels together. To see her son acting so grown up gave Livy goose flesh.

Major Gunnison extended his hand. "Not necessary to salute, lad. We are not in uniform."

Wyatt's grin widened as he shook the major's hand enthusiastically.

Livy watched with maternal pride. This was not the nervous boy at the dinner table who'd spoken so earnestly about joining the army. He was a man wanting to become part of Major Gunnison's world.

"I'll soon be in the fight," Wyatt said.

"That's most likely where you will be," Major Gunnison replied.

"No," Livy said sharply. "Nothing has been decided yet."

"Oh, but it has," Wyatt told her.

Livy cast him a stern look. Wyatt said no more.

"What is this? Did you forget your grandmamma?" The woman's voice cut through the room like a scythe.

"Never," Wyatt declared, and he left Livy's side and joined the bevy of ladies.

"Here he is," Iris said. "He's decided to join us old folks at last."

"I'm only too glad to do so." Wyatt bent down and kissed his grandmother on her outstretched hand.

"How very grown up you look tonight," she said, eyes bright.

The other ladies murmured their agreement.

He pulled down on his jacket. "Do you recognize Father's evening suit? Mrs. Heath saw to the fitting. The sleeves were rather too long but I dare say the rest fit spot on."

The elderly women tittered as if Wyatt had said something terribly funny.

"All the girls will be after you, mark my words." Iris chortled behind her gloved hand.

"I shall dance with every one of them."

Mother Pratt nodded in agreement. Wyatt was her golden boy, Livy never doubted, the champion of her heart.

"It will be my last dance for some time, I shouldn't wonder."

Mother Pratt's smile faded. "I'm afraid I don't follow."

"I dare say there won't be many opportunities for parties in the trenches." Wyatt affected a laugh, but nobody joined him.

Livy clenched her hands as she watched the drama unfold. She must keep her composure. An outburst would be unseemly. She couldn't fall apart in front of this gathering.

Mother Pratt's face darkened. "What, may I ask, are you talking about?"

There was a moment of hesitation as Wyatt cast his

gaze to the others. Of course, her son would be sensitive to his grandmother's distress. After a moment, he faced her with his mouth set in a grim line.

"I've enlisted in the King's army, Grandmamma. I am leaving for my training first thing in the morning. No doubt I will be sent to France in short order."

The woman paled behind her face powder, and she turned a hostile look upon Livy.

"What is the meaning of this?" Mother Pratt looked ready to spit tacks; her expression was that severe. "Why wasn't I told? Why have you left such an important announcement to this moment?"

Her voice had risen to a feverish pitch.

Livy held her tongue. She would let Wyatt explain.

"I didn't mean to distress you," Wyatt said. "Time I joined the other lads from the village to fight the Hun."

Mother Pratt shrank back. A wealth of emotions and every fear a mother could have were wrapped up in the old lady's expression.

"Now that I'm nineteen, I'm eligible," he hastened to explain further.

Wyatt had chosen the moment wisely. No one would object to such a lofty decision. They would applaud him and rightly so.

Mother Pratt was on her feet. The other ladies joined her.

Livy's hands shook as she hurried to her mother-in-law's side. She must intervene before the evening was spoiled by a bitter argument and the hurt feelings that would surely be the result.

She'd come to the realization when Wyatt saluted the major. They'd talked of the day when Wyatt would take over the running of the farm. That day would have to be postponed. His birthday party had become his farewell party.

"Wyatt has such a strong sense of duty to his family and his country," Livy said, her voice more steady than she felt. "I'm very proud—as you must be."

"Very proud," Iris said.

"Yes, indeed," Gertrude agreed.

Mother Pratt cleared her throat. Her demeanor was mercifully calm. She couldn't very well object to what Wyatt had just told her, not in front of the other guests. She looked at Wyatt as if seeing him for the first time.

The other ladies gathered close around her. It was a familiar sight. These women—who'd seen their share of grief and pain, of hard times and defeat—always were quick to rally around someone in their hour of need.

They presented a formidable wall of disquiet, and panic flashed in Wyatt's eyes.

Livy took him by the arm to steady his nerves.

"I'm perfectly all right, Mother," he pulled out of her grasp. "If you ladies would excuse me."

He hurried from the room. Livy took a deep breath and let it out slowly. Her son had become a man with a man's sense of duty and honor. If he remained on the farm, he would be forever a compliant boy, and he'd never become who he needed to be.

"I'm sorry for Wyatt's rudeness," Livy said, as she knew she must.

Her mother-in-law's thin smile broke the tension in her face. Livy was relieved and didn't know why. This was only a skirmish. She'd no doubt there'd be more words spoken in anger and frustration in the days ahead.

Livy left the parlor and saw her son pacing in the kitchen garden. She hastened to join him.

"Thanks awfully for the party." Wyatt stopped abruptly and shoved his hands into his pockets.

"I'm sorry your announcement did not go as well as you'd wanted it to," she said. "You should have told your grandmother earlier, and in private."

"I'd hoped Grandmamma would be more understanding."

"She is in a state of shock."

Wyatt frowned. "She mustn't be."

Livy could not bear to see him so miserable. "Don't be cross with her. It will take all of us some time to adjust to the news."

"She thinks I am a child."

"Which is the privilege of her generation."

"Vexing, to be sure."

Livy thought about putting her hand on his shoulder and then held back. "I've not seen you more grown up."

Wyatt stood up straighter and smiled. He would be all right.

"You're leaving in the morning?"

"First train for London," Wyatt replied.

She patted him on the cheek. "Sooner than I would've liked, but I wish you well."

"Thank you, Mother. Your support means a great deal to me."

Livy returned to the parlor without him. The ladies had resumed their seats and Gwendolyn had joined them. All the gaiety had gone out of the evening. All of their expressions had turned gloomy and the conversation bore dark undertones.

There were so many young men who had already gone. Everyone seemed to have family or knew of someone in the fight, and they gave full voice to them now. There were the ones who had fallen: the butcher's son killed at Liege, the schoolmaster taken at Neuve Chapelle, the brother-in-law of Mrs. Dill dead in Anza Cove. The numbers of dead and wounded were growing, with no end in sight.

Livy searched for James and found him talking with a group of men where, thankfully, he wouldn't be able to hear the ladies' commiserate.

Gertrude and Iris fell into a conversation about the high price of sugar. Gwendolyn and the vicar's wife had put their heads together, leaving Livy to converse with Mother Pratt.

Mother Pratt leaned over and whispered in Livy's ear. "Let's hope this damnable war is over soon."

Livy felt weak and inadequate to reply. The war couldn't be over soon enough.

"I saw you talking to Major Gunnison. I hoped you

two would get along," Livy said.

"It's the very least one can do," Mother Pratt echoed in a mocking tone.

Livy despaired. The woman's contentiousness was exhausting.

"You were always so common," Mother Pratt continued, ice forming on every word. "While I have no doubt the major is a gentleman, I question the wisdom of clinging to him as if he was a post."

Livy cringed. Wyatt's announcement had naturally upset the woman, and her anger had found a target.

"I have done no such thing," she replied.

"Didn't I see you entering the room earlier this evening arm in arm?"

"He is our guest and an honored one, I might add."

Mother Pratt huffed. "Don't you think you overplayed your role as hostess?"

"Not a bit. I rather enjoyed myself."

"Such behavior is unbecoming, Livinia."

"I see no reason to be unfriendly," Livy said simply, tired of the woman's constant accusations.

Mother Pratt's face reddened, and Livy fancied she saw steam come out of her ears. Livy rarely contradicted the women but she wouldn't apologize. James Gunnison was an attractive man and she wouldn't pretend to have not noticed.

Livy wondered if Mother Pratt's complaints revealed a deeper fear: Livy's devotion to her late husband might soon be replaced.

The very idea Mother Pratt would think such a thing amused Livy.

Livy didn't offer any more explanations. She'd not been disloyal to Charles' memory. No one could replace him in the affections of her children.

Let the old woman stew in her own juice.

Livy took a deep, steadying breath.

"Where is Elizabeth? She hasn't done me the courtesy of an introduction to her young man," Mother Pratt said, conceding—for now.

"She must be outside with her friends."

"Indeed," Mother Pratt replied. "It appears your children have developed some very poor manners."

"They are independent, to be sure. In that regard, they take after their father."

Livy stood and excused herself from the other ladies and headed out of the room, unwilling to listen to the old woman's complaints a moment longer.

James stood in the doorway. He'd finished his conversation and looked ready to call it a night.

"I'm going outside," she told him. "I am in need of some fresh air. Would you care to join me?"

"Indeed I would."

As she had hoped, James didn't refuse her request. A gentleman never did.

Livy grasped his arm. Fie to anyone who objected. She didn't cling to him as Mother Pratt had suggested.

As they passed through the doorway, the two little whirlwinds ran by them.

"Girls, say hello to our guest," Livy said. "This is Major Gunnison."

They stopped and stared at the major. To Livy's dismay, their ribbons had come undone.

"Major Gunnison, these are my youngest, Winifred and Grace."

"Pleased to meet you," they said in unison.

"As am I," James replied.

"Where you are going in such a rush?"

"Elizabeth sent us away," Winnie said.

"She didn't want us bothering her," Grace added.

It wasn't a nice thing for a mother to hear.

"Go inside and find Mrs. Heath," Livy told them. "She's made lemonade."

The girls curtsied and then scrambled to be first through the doors.

"Slowly," Livy said.

They took slow, deliberate steps as they entered the house.

"I'm afraid they are rather rambunctious," Livy said.

"To be expected." James smiled. It was a generous thing to say.

They continued down the slate pathway. The back garden was filled with younger guests chattering and laughing. Old Tom had done an admirable job constructing a platform for the musicians. After dinner, there would be lively music played again at Fairview Farm.

She breathed in the fresh air, calming a bit. She was in a highly excitable state and needed to sort out what had happened in her parlor.

Why had she let Mother Pratt rattle her so? There hadn't been a shred of doubt the old lady would be upset by Wyatt's announcement, but Mother Pratt's criticism never failed to leave a nasty mark.

James had come to her rescue in a way. They stood shoulder to shoulder, strangers and yet companionable. She liked him despite his formal manner. She supposed such mannerisms were ingrained in an officer and couldn't be helped.

Livy searched for Elizabeth. To her relief, she saw her with Mr. Morehouse at her side, talking to another couple. She would not disturb them.

"There's my oldest daughter, Elizabeth," Livy said. "I see she is agreeably occupied."

"A very pretty girl," James replied. "She favors you."

"Thank you." His compliment was unexpected. She dared not look up at him. She did not want him to see how much a kind word after her spat with Mother Pratt affected her.

He directed his gaze to the view. "I am impressed with your farm."

"It's my late husband's doing. He made a great many improvements." She looked out at the barns, the fallow fields and hills beyond. The view was impressive. She never tired of looking at it.

"His dream was to be a gentleman farmer."

"It appears he was a success."

"Oh, he was," she replied. Charles was devoted to the

farm and his children. Maybe, even at times, to his wife. She'd always been a distant third.

"I love Fairview. I will never leave. When the war is over, Wyatt will take over, of course. The farm is his. Elizabeth will find a good man to marry, preferably from a local family. The little girls will grow up and find husbands of their own."

"Wyatt will have big shoes to fill," he said.

His flattery was welcome. Major Gunnison was a gentleman of the first order.

"I hope all that we've planned comes true."

"You are uncertain?"

"With this war…" She sighed. "The war has changed everything."

How easy he was to talk to, she decided. It was as if she'd known him for years.

"To be honest, I wish I could've persuaded him to postpone his enlistment until he finished school."

"His heart was in the fight. A man must face his duty."

"You think me selfish."

"I'm no judge of such things."

"My greatest fear is he will be hurt or worse." Her voice squeaked.

"You share the concerns of every parent."

She felt compelled to continue. "I cannot bear to think of him in the trenches subject to all kinds of deprivation—cold meals, drenching rain, and sleeping on the ground. And the danger. You know what he will be up against."

"The trenches are where he will most likely be." The major stripped off his gloves and held them against his hip. "Cold meals will be the least of his worries."

"Exactly." She waited for him to provide some comforting words, but none were, apparently, forthcoming.

An awkward moment followed. She shouldn't have burdened him with her troubles. He had enough of his own.

"What about your future?" she asked. "The war cannot go on forever."

"I'll stay in the Army." He leaned against the railing. "I always wanted to be soldier, even as a lad."

She had never met anyone who wanted a career in the military. She couldn't fathom what his life must be like.

"I know it is selfish of me, but I cannot bear Wyatt becoming a soldier."

"His country needs him at these most trying of times."

"Yes, I understand all of that..." A tear escaped. She couldn't help herself. She could not be weak at this critical time. Any failure of her composure would be contemptible.

"My dear Livinia." He pulled a clean handkerchief out of his pocket and handed it to her.

Livy took the white linen and dabbed at her eyes. "Goodness. What's come over me?"

"You are frightened."

"Please forgive me."

"There is nothing to forgive."

She was grateful he'd not chosen to be abrupt or impatient.

"I know we must be brave," she said, "only I'm not sure I can be."

Additional tears spilled down her cheeks. She had held back the floodgates since Wyatt made his announcement. If she didn't pull herself together, she would soon be a puddle.

"Let me fetch a glass of water," he said.

"No. I just need a moment." She blotted her face and returned his sodden handkerchief. "I'm so embarrassed. You're here to have an enjoyable evening and I'm blubbering like a baby."

Ashamed she'd fallen apart in front of an officer, and a major at that, she returned her gaze to her guests mingling in the back garden and decided she must do better.

Her son would be a soldier soon. She would need every ounce of courage at her disposal in the days ahead.

"I'm satisfied the Elizabeth and her guest are adequately chaperoned," she said. "Let's go back inside, shall we?"

With a heavy heart, she led the way.

Chapter Eight

>>><<<

James didn't know how to console Livinia. Nor could he spare her what the future held in store. Most certainly there would be more tears forthcoming in the days and weeks ahead.

Wyatt would soon be in the thick of it. The war would become an intimate part of Livinia's daily life. Newspaper accounts and letters home would tether her to the fight. She would follow the reports from the battlefields, the triumphs and failures. She would scour the lists of dead and wounded. There would be no escape from the sorrow each day would bring.

Her son would come home a changed man.

If he came home.

A girl dressed in a black maid's uniform entered the parlor carrying a gong. She rang the instrument, and all heads turned in her direction.

"Dinner is served," she announced in a meek voice. She bobbed a curtsey and retreated.

Despite how the evening had progressed so far, James had to admit he had a keen appetite.

Gwendolyn's husband escorted Livinia. He was glad to see she'd recovered her composure. No one would think, to look at her, that only minutes earlier she'd been crying. Her tears had dried, and she was the happy hostess again.

James offered his arm to the wily grandmother. She accepted with a thin smile. "I suppose this is your doing."

James resigned himself to Mother Pratt's contentious temperament, a woman who could wither an adversary with a glance.

"If you're referring to your grandson enlisting in the army," he replied, "I had no part in his decision."

She scoffed. "Certainly your presence in the community lent some urgency to his joining."

"I'm not sure what you mean."

"He sees a gentleman and an officer and wants to be like you."

"I think you are mistaken. I pride myself on being in service to the King, but I carry the scars of war. Hardly the ambition of the young."

She narrowed her eyes. "You know perfectly well what I mean, Major. Everyone wants to be a hero."

"You give me too much credit," James said.

"I'm afraid your modesty will not save you," the woman said with a sharp edge to her voice, "and I will hold you responsible if anything happens to my grandson."

She'd made her position known. James didn't blame her, nor did her comments come as a surprise. Women didn't understand the business of war, nor were they required to. If James could've assuaged their fears with platitudes, he would've done so, but there was no point in talking about what Wyatt was about to do in glowing terms.

He'd no doubt Grandmother Pratt had little tolerance for muddling the truth. He'd no wish to put her back up any further by suggesting Wyatt's time in service would be a cakewalk.

He would leave such rhetoric to the politicians.

Grandmother Pratt was fiercely protective of her brood, as was Livinia. He commended their loyalty and commitment to family. Young Wyatt was a lucky man.

They followed Livinia and the others and entered the dining room.

James held Grandmother Pratt's chair, and she eased into it with a rustle of bombazine. His presence was forgotten as she swiftly engaged in conversation with the elderly man next to her.

He found his own name card placed surprisingly at Livinia's left. He'd not thought his position so elevated. Vicar Collins and his lovely wife sat on her right.

Not that he was complaining. Livinia was a woman any man would be honored to have by his side.

He pulled out her chair and she thanked him. She looked stunning in all this candlelight in her green dress, which deepened the color of her blue eyes.

She sat down gracefully. Her hair, piled elegantly on top of her head, exposed her long neck. Sapphire earrings caught the light and sparkled as she spoke to the white-bearded vicar.

With the ladies seated, the men took their places. Even as he settled in the agreeable room with candles flickering and good food in the offering, James couldn't relax. What was he doing here? It grated on his soul to be celebrating while others made do with bully beef and weak tea.

Tom had been pressed into service to pour the wine, which he did competently.

Wyatt shot to his feet and raised his glass. All eyes turned to their host.

"To God, King, and Country." Wyatt raised his glass.

Amid the scraping of chairs and throats clearing, they all stood and repeated the words.

"To God, King, and Country."

James looked at Livinia. Her eyes gleamed as she watched her son. He saw no trace of unhappiness or uncertainty.

He was certain everyone at the table was patriotic and would do what was required of them to win this war. What they faced would necessitate a great deal of sacrifice. They all seemed willing. Would their efforts be enough?

Livinia looked his way as if sensing his gaze upon her. His pulse quickened. He dismissed the sensation as reckless. He could not ask her to align her stars with him.

They returned to their chairs amid boisterous chatter.

"Don't you agree, Major?" Livinia said, her eyes glittery in the candlelight. Such radiance reminded him of his youth.

"I beg your pardon?"

"Pastor Collins and I were reminiscing about the old days," Livinia said.

"Here's to a better time." The old fellow picked up his glass and drank his wine.

Yes, James thought, as he picked up his own glass. The night would be fanciful and amusing, and they would drink to a time long past. But hardly better.

He remembered his courting days. He'd been in love with a beautiful girl. She'd been feckless and insecure, opting to marry the brother who had inherited the stately home and large family fortune.

James looked down the table and saw Gwendolyn, a picture of her mother, immersed in conversation with a gentleman with substantial side-whiskers. His niece had learned the skills necessary to be successful in social situations. She'd been educated by expensive tutors. Her wardrobe included French-made gowns. She'd enjoyed the benefits of the best parties and balls—things he couldn't have afforded on an officer's salary.

James returned his attention to his hostess, who was staring at him.

"She's a lovely girl." Livinia had a way of looking at him that was quite unsettling.

"Yes, a credit to her family." He grimaced.

"Is there something wrong?"

"It's my knee. The discomfort doesn't last, I assure you."

"Maybe a doctor should take a look at your wound. Our doctor in the village is excellent."

"I'm perfectly capable of managing without the help of a doctor." His response was spoken with unquestionable authority.

The light in her eyes dimmed.

Of course he must apologize for the sharpness of his reply. She was not a raw recruit.

"Forgive me," he said. "I forgot the company in which I'm being most agreeably kept."

An uneasy silence followed. He needed to reassure her that he had everything under control.

"You don't have to worry about me," he said, looking at her, a woman with tender feelings.

"I think I exist in a state of perpetual worry," she said, which he'd no doubt was the truth.

Young Tom brought in a soup tureen and served up steaming bowls of leek soup.

The vicar smacked his lips as he ate. "How long do you expect to be with us, Major?"

"As soon as my leg heals, I'll return to my men."

"The battlefield awaits, does it?"

"Weren't you up to London this summer?" Livinia addressed the vicar, skillfully changing the subject. "The major was born and raised in the city."

"You don't say?" the vicar replied.

Before he could launch into a description of his most recent visit, Mrs. Collins interrupted. "A Londoner, are you? I've never been farther than Tonbridge."

"My wife doesn't like to travel." The vicar emptied his glass. Tom stepped up quickly to refill it.

"I'm told the air in London is very bad." Mrs. Collins sniffed as if the stench of chimney pots, automobiles, and omnibuses had reached them.

"At times," James replied, putting down his glass.

The vicar's wife nodded and waited for him to continue.

The conversation faltered. He could think of nothing more to say. This happy occasion was a pretense, a fiction that all was normal.

They all were a decent lot and tried to make him feel welcome. Livinia most of all.

She looked downcast at her wine which she hadn't yet touched.

James must try harder, as any gentleman would, to pretend along with them that the battlefield was far, far away.

"Not that I have much opportunity to go up to London," the vicar started, filling the lull. "When the bishop calls a meeting at Lambeth Palace, I must obey."

They turned his attention to the vicar, who had a story to tell.

Chapter Nine

>>><<<

J ames refrained from patting his stomach although, if he'd been alone, he would've done so. He hadn't eaten so well in ages.

After dinner, the party moved to the back garden. Fairy lights lit the way. An excellent orchestra had been set up at the far end of the lawn and played Austrian waltzes. Couples glided by, some danced expertly, others watched their feet. James leaned against a post, remembering a time when he'd liked to dance and had been thought quite good.

He regretted that he couldn't ask their hostess for one waltz. He hadn't forgotten what it was like to hold an attractive woman in his arms.

He wandered down a path away from the noise. The evening temperature had dropped. He'd hoped to return to his troops before the snow covered the trenches, but unfortunately he would have to stay in England for a while longer. He could not yet put his full weight on his leg, and after some time, the pain became too great to remain standing. In addition, he tired easily. What use was he in such a condition?

Of course, his replacement would be as diligent, as resourceful. James had no quarrel with the new man's dedication. Except he should be there. He'd trained those boys, led them through bombardments of mortar shells and constant sniper fire. He would continue to do so.

Peals of laughter beckoned him back to the parlor. He delayed returning. He'd rather not be making idle conversation just now.

He heard a cry and the plea of a lady to be left alone. The sound came from behind one of the barns which hid the occupants from view.

He turned his back, intent on minding his own business and returning to the party inside the house, but another cry, even more desperate, stopped him.

Something about the urgency and youthfulness in the voice urged him to investigate. Something was amiss. Something he could not ignore.

He hurried as best he could. The barn wasn't a great distance, but the grass was slippery with dew. His footing wasn't as stable as he'd like it to be, but he made haste.

Shadows hid the couple. He took a moment to adjust his eyes and realize he'd come upon Miss Elizabeth Pratt in the clutches of the older man he'd seen her with before dinner.

James cleared his throat. When the brigand turned his attention to the sound, she shoved him away. The man didn't appear to be vexed about James's arrival, and greeted him with a smile. His smile was most unpleasant.

James saw, with alarm, the sleeve of Miss Elizabeth's gown had been torn and her hair had come down from its pins. He should turn away to spare her any embarrassment, but he did not.

"May I be of assistance?" he asked her.

"Bugger off." The man grabbed Miss Elizabeth by the wrist, pulled her to his chest and held her in an embrace.

Miss Elizabeth whimpered, her eyes filled with terror.

James had met many a young man full of themselves and eager to prove their mettle.

This was another kind of man.

James took a step closer, not in the least intimidated. Still, he must proceed with caution. No telling what this blackguard was capable of if provoked.

"I believe this is where I say it's time to bid your farewells and depart," James told him.

The scoundrel's eyes widened, and his smile faded into a villainous sneer. "I have no intention of doing any such thing."

"You give me no choice but to insist."

Had this brigand thought he would succeed in his disgraceful plan? Had he counted on no one defending Miss Elizabeth's honor?

"Yes, Redding, you must go," Miss Elizabeth said, at last able to pull away successfully.

He snorted. "You country girls are such prudes. You lack sophistication, Elizabeth. I thought so from the beginning."

The girl gasped.

James wished he could have spared her feelings. Thankfully, only her feelings would be injured.

The bounder turned away from Elizabeth and departed. The girl made no protest to stop him. Instead she attempted to fix her sleeve.

"It's hopeless," she said.

"Tuck the loose end… here, let me." James managed to put the sleeve back in place temporarily. No casual observer would guess how the sleeve had arrived to such a disreputable state.

"Thank you." She avoided looking at him. "You must be Major Gunnison. I'm Elizabeth Pratt."

"I know."

"I was showing my friend the oast barns."

James was certain her companion wasn't the type of man with whom Elizabeth should be keeping company, but he kept his opinion to himself. He didn't wish to add to her humiliation.

She pinned her hair back into place. "You won't tell Mother?"

"You can rely on my discretion, of course."

She lifted her head to meet his gaze. If there had been any doubt in her as to his intentions, it had been erased. "Thank you. I appreciate you are a gentleman."

James wouldn't let her off the tenterhook so easily. "*You* must tell her, however."

She shook her head. "Mother would never understand."

"Do you really think so?"

"She never liked Redding—Mr. Morehouse—in the first place."

"For good reason, as it turned out."

She frowned.

"Do you find your mother's protective nature that disagreeable?"

"No." She looked away. "Only she can be overbearing at times."

James could appreciate her dilemma. Elizabeth had made an unfortunate choice. Who would want a mother to know?

"That's the conversation you must have with her," he said quite simply. "Woman to woman."

She lifted her chin. "I suppose you are right."

He offered her his arm. "Come along. Let's go inside."

She hesitated. Was it the authority in his voice or that he was practically a stranger? Probably a little of both.

Happily, she set her concerns aside and took his arm, allowing him to proceed. She had pluck, this girl, and had recovered her poise admirably.

Nothing seemed improper to those who were dancing. In fact, he rather fancied they considered him a father figure to the girl, escorting her thus.

When they arrived at the French doors leading to the parlor, Elizabeth turned and kissed him on the cheek.

"You are a dear man," she said without a trace of sarcasm.

"It won't do my reputation any good for you to say so to the others."

She squeezed his arm and let go. "If you'll excuse me. I must see to my dress."

He watched her hurry away, a girl in many ways still.

With Wyatt gone, they would be on their own—women and youngsters to fend for themselves. The very idea disturbed him.

A long case clock rang out twelve. The soreness in his knee reminded him he'd done enough for one night.

His niece and her husband met him in the foyer.

"There you are," Gwendolyn said. "We've been looking for you."

"Are you ready to leave?"

"Yes. Silly me. I'm usually the last to leave a party." She laughed. "I'm worn through."

"I'll have the car brought around, old boy."

James scowled. The husband was no more than a handful of years younger, and yet he persisted on labeling James as geriatric.

"Awfully good of you. I'll only be a minute to say goodbye to Livinia."

"Livinia, is it?" His niece winked and smiled at her husband.

James had no idea what she found amusing.

"How wonderful you're on a first-name basis with our neighbor," Gwendolyn said. "I'd hoped you'd get along."

"She's been a first class hostess," James answered rather belligerently. His niece needn't be so ambitious.

"Only just a hostess?" She patted him on the cheek.

Young Tom appeared with an armload of wraps and

assisted Gwendolyn with her cape.

"You won't have to look for her." Gwendolyn put on her motoring hat and tied it under her chin. "She'll be right back. She went to look for her oldest daughter."

James signaled to Tom to bring his hat, top coat and stick. As he waited, Livinia emerged from the parlor.

"I can't seem to find her," she said.

"Elizabeth has gone upstairs," James said.

"Are you sure? How very unlike her to leave her guests."

"Indeed."

"Would you know the whereabouts of Wyatt?"

"I'm afraid I don't."

"Give them our regards," Gwendolyn said.

James donned his coat with Tom's help and took his hat from him. Ronald returned to announce the motor was ready.

"I'm sorry you are leaving so soon," Livinia said.

"I'm catching a ride with my niece."

"We'll be in the Daimler." Gwendolyn gave her husband a nudge toward the open door. They descended the stairs and took their places in the back seat of the motor.

Livinia walked with James to the first step.

"If I asked how you knew where Elizabeth disappeared to, would you tell me?"

"I'm not at liberty to say."

"I see."

She stared ahead. The night air brought color to her face.

"I didn't expect you'd come, but I'm glad you did. It meant a great deal to Wyatt to have you here."

"He's a fine lad."

"Thank you." She looked at him and tilted her head slightly.

By Jove, it'd been a long while since he'd kissed a lady.

"I had a splendid evening," he said.

"We hoped you would," she replied. "You melded well with my neighbors and friends. I do believe you were quite the hit."

"You've all been very welcoming. I enjoyed myself immensely."

"It meant a great deal to me that you came," she said.

He acknowledged her feelings with a nod and questioned the appropriateness of his own feelings, on the steps of the lovely lady's home, yielding to her display of affection as if he were a schoolboy.

"Gwendolyn and Ronald are waiting." He steadied his stick on the step. "Give my regards to your mother-in-law."

"I shall." She watched him with her lovely eyes.

"Thank your cook. The dinner tonight was excellent."

"Mrs. Heath will be pleased that you liked her cooking." She smiled. "We are becoming proficient in preparing meals without a joint of beef."

James had no doubt Livinia would continue to make do in these trying times. He put on his top hat and buttoned his topcoat.

"Would you like to come to tea one day soon?"

Unfortunately, he must refuse. "In all likelihood, I will be leaving in a day or two. I must return to my regiment as soon as possible."

"I will be sorry to see you go. Perhaps another time? When you are here visiting with Gwendolyn and Ronald perhaps?"

"I will considerate it my good fortune to see you again—when the conflict in Europe is over."

Livinia put out her hand and he took it, held it. Gwendolyn was no doubt watching, but he didn't care.

"Until me meet again." She gave his hand a squeeze and let go.

James descended the steps, wondering if he'd made a terrible mistake. He shouldn't have told her he would be back.

Not even for the sake of politeness.

Chapter Ten

>»>«««

L ivy waved as the Ashers and James Gunnison drove
away, her spirits restored. The evening hadn't been
as merry after Wyatt had made his announcement, but at
least she'd recovered her composure. She must continue
for the sake of her family and friends. In the days ahead,
she must carry on not only for Wyatt, but also for all the
young men in the fight.

She was disappointed James would be leaving so soon.
She'd become overwhelmed with gratitude as she held his
hand. In the midst of this horrible war, they'd begun a
friendship she hoped would go further.

The temperature had dropped and her breath came
out in little clouds. She rubbed the goose flesh on her bare
arms as the motor disappeared around the curve in the
road. Happy in a way she'd forgotten how to be, she
returned to the house.

She didn't know what to make of James's puzzling
familiarity with Elizabeth's whereabouts.

Her guests continued to mingle and conversation was
bright with laughter. They'd shaken off their worries.

Talk of battlefields had been set aside, at least for one star-lit evening.

Mother Pratt and the local women were gathered around the fire in the parlor gossiping. They wouldn't miss Livy for a few minutes.

She hurried up the stairs. Mr. Morehouse had already left, and she had been relieved to see him go. He'd not been a popular addition to the evening's festivities.

Why had Elizabeth disappeared to her room? Something had happened. Something that involved James. Livy suspected he'd been drawn into one of her daughter's dramas. She shuddered to think Elizabeth would be so crass.

Was this something related to why Mr. Morehouse had left so suddenly, without so much as a by-your-leave?

By the time she reached Elizabeth's bedroom door, she'd worked herself into a state of reprobation. She should have monitored the couple's comings and goings more closely. If anything had happened to her daughter, Livy was to blame.

James had been so calm when he told her where Elizabeth could be found. Surely he would have been agitated if something terrible had happened to her child? He would've found Livy immediately and insisted the constable be called.

The constable? Livy shuddered. Nothing that drastic had occurred. Only James's poise and equanimity kept Livy from bursting into the room unannounced. She took a moment to compose herself. It wouldn't do to upset

Elizabeth with hasty accusations.

Muffled sobs came from behind the door.

She knocked. "Elizabeth, it's your mother."

A fragile voice bade her to enter.

Livy opened the door, dreading what she would find. Her daughter sat on her bed in her dressing gown, wiping her face with a handkerchief. Her beautiful dress lay in a heap on the floor.

Guilt and foreboding gripped Livy by the throat. "What is the meaning of this?"

"You were right about Mr. Morehouse," she said, looking up. The yellowish light made her eyes appear like green glass. "Have you come to gloat?"

"What has happened?" Livy fought to keep the hysteria out of her voice. A fresh wave of regret nearly toppled her. "He didn't...?"

Elizabeth shook her head. "Fortunately, the major interfered before he could tear my gown from my person."

Livy collapsed on the bed. Her gratitude to James Gunnison knew no boundaries.

"He lured you to a quiet place," Livy said.

"Yes, behind one of the barns. He said the farm intrigued him and he would like to see more. It seemed so very innocent." She covered her face with her hands and began to sob. "I didn't know what kind of man he was."

Livy put her arm around Elizabeth's quaking shoulders and hugged her tenderly.

Elizabeth stemmed a fresh flood of tears with her

handkerchief. The ordeal had taken a heavy toll.

After a few minutes, she stopped sobbing and laid her head on Livy's shoulder.

"If I could have spared you this trial, I would have," Livy said.

"I am all right, Mother." Elizabeth sniffed and sat up, blowing her nose into the limp handkerchief.

The experience had been frightful, Livy had no doubt, but the worst was over.

"You are being very brave," she said.

"I am a Pratt, and no Pratt stays down for long."

"I'm very glad to hear you say so." Livy released her. How happy she was that her daughter had found her inner strength.

Elizabeth sighed heavily.

Livy wouldn't lecture. There was no need to press her point. What she'd like to do is rail against Mr. Morehouse. What good would it do except to humiliate her daughter further?

Instead, she stood. "I must get back to our guests."

"You'll understand if I remain in my room?"

"Of course. I'll tell Grandmamma when she asks, and she will, that you've got a migraine."

Elizabeth's eyes brimmed with fresh tears. "Thank you, Mother."

"Not at all, my dear. This is what mothers are for."

As Livy closed the door behind her, she took a deep breath. What a toad Mr. Morehouse had been this evening. How could one prepare children for such betrayal?

Tonight, her daughter had learned an important lesson. It was essential to know whom she could trust.

Livy descended the staircase with a heavy heart. They both owed James their gratitude. Livy shuddered to think what might have happened if he hadn't come along when he did.

Thankfully, he'd kept Elizabeth's troubles private and not betrayed a confidence. His discretion had saved a girl's reputation.

Livy was indebted to him and would be sure to thank him personally the next time she saw him. When that would be, she couldn't say. He'd be gone in a day or two, he'd said. How long until he returned? A month? A year?

Who could say in these uncertain times?

Chapter Eleven

❯❯❯❯❮❮❮❮

L ivy woke with a start. She'd not gone to bed until the
early hours of the morning, waving off the last of
their guests. When blessed sleep did come, she hadn't even
dreamt. What a luxury to have her nightmares at bay for
one night.

The sun peeked through the cracks of the heavy
drapes. She rose from her bed and opened them. The day
was already bright, the sky an uninterrupted blue. The
lindens and elms dabbed with red and gold added their
color to the scene.

Today was no ordinary day. Today, Wyatt was leaving for the war.

She washed up in cold water and hurriedly dressed.
Most certainly Mother Pratt would have a word or two
this morning to remind Livy that Wyatt's enlistment could
be stopped. There was the farm to consider and work to
be done.

Livy wouldn't interfere any longer with Wyatt's decision. Instead, she would be a model of support.

The job of soothing all of their fears rested on Livy's

shoulders. Wyatt did not need a chorus of weeping females at his departure.

This was her mission, more than ever, to keep spirits high, to put hope ahead of despair. Wyatt must take with him the memories of a happy family at all cost.

Livy put on her sensible shoes. The children would be waiting. They would be excited about the ride to the station since they would take Mother Pratt's precious motor car.

Mother Pratt would not stoop to riding in the wagon.

Elizabeth met her in the breakfast room.

"You are up early," Livy said.

"I fixed breakfast so you could sleep in."

Indeed, she had. The pots had been scrubbed and hung back on their hooks and the plates put away in the cupboard.

"Would you like a cup of coffee?"

"Yes, please." Livy sat down at the kitchen table. She could not recall the last time she'd had the extravagance of being waited on at breakfast.

Elizabeth poured her a cup of coffee.

"I want to talk to you," Elizabeth said, "without Grandmamma's interference."

"Of course." Livy selected a piece of toast from the toast rack.

Elizabeth filled her own cup and sat opposite.

Livy was embarrassed for her daughter, for the humiliation she'd endured last night, but if she wanted to talk about the incident, Livy would certainly listen.

Livy spooned thick marmalade on her toast and took a bite as Elizabeth stirred her coffee. She seemed very composed for someone who'd been through such a terrible ordeal. She took after her father in that regard.

"Mother, I've decided to sign up for nurses' training with the Voluntary Aid Detachment."

Livy chewed her toast, her anger building. Elizabeth could've waited before making such a declaration. Why had she picked this morning?

"Can we talk about this tomorrow or the next day— any day but today?" Livy swallowed. "Your brother is leaving for his training. We must focus on him."

Elizabeth frowned. "What is there to discuss?"

Livy must tread with a light step. Elizabeth wasn't willing to wait. Any quick objection would only fuel the girl's determination.

"I am happy you have an interest in voluntary work," Livy said instead. "We must all do our part. As soon as you're finished with school, we can make inquiries."

"I'm not going back to school."

"I thought you wanted to become a teacher?" Livy couldn't imagine what her daughter must be thinking. "Have you given any consideration to what you'll be giving up?"

"I have done so. A great deal, in fact," Elizabeth protested. "I will return to my studies as soon as the war is over."

Livy was at a loss for words.

Her daughter tensed her shoulders. A wrinkle appeared on the bridge of her nose. "You think me impulsive, but I assure you I am not. The nursing corps is terribly understaffed. There's an article about the shortage of nurses in this morning's newspaper."

"Surely you are too young?"

"The account in the *Telegraph* states that women my age can join if they have their parents' permission."

Livy couldn't let her daughter be so reckless. "If you wish to quit your studies, you may. You are needed here at the farm. You can help the war effort by feeding our troops."

Livy despaired. She'd made the same speech to Wyatt and look how well that'd turned out.

"But, Mother…"

Livy swiped at her mouth with her serviette. "I've made up my mind."

"I am old enough to make my own decisions."

"Is that so? Only last night you were ready to run off with some rake."

Elizabeth blanched. She put down her cup and rose from her chair. "Are you going to remind me of that unfortunate incident for the rest of my life?"

"Of course not." Livy hadn't meant to lash out with heated words but honestly, the girl should think through the consequences of her decisions before she acted on them.

"I made a mistake." The color rose in Elizabeth's face. "We all do. I don't know why you must insist on perfection. No one can meet your standard."

With a huff, she rushed away. In her hurry, she almost collided with Mrs. Heath bringing more eggs from the chicken coop.

"Oh my," Mrs. Heath said as she hugged the basket.

Elizabeth did not apologize.

What have I done, Livy wondered. She hadn't meant to alienate Elizabeth, but the girl was being unreasonable.

Livy feared she had only made things worse.

Mrs. Heath offered to pour her another cup of coffee. Livy declined. She didn't want coffee or toast or breakfast.

She wanted her old life back.

The two little girls were the first to meet up with Livy in the parlor followed by Elizabeth, who thankfully didn't need to be coaxed and prodded into coming along. Much to Livy's chagrin, Mother Pratt arrived dressed in black, looking grim.

Wyatt was the last to join them. He wore his country tweeds. His hair was longer than Livy would've liked, but the army would make quick work of his unruly locks.

"I say, is it to be an expedition?" Wyatt affected a laugh as he put on his flat cap.

"Will you be embarrassed if we are all standing on the platform waving goodbye?" Livy asked.

"Not at all, Mother."

"It's not too late to change your mind," Mother Pratt

said.

Wyatt turned to her with a boyish grin. "I'm afraid it is. I signed a piece of paper. I made a promise to serve my country."

Livy was proud of him. He showed no fear or doubt. She would do the same.

Mother Pratt's chauffeur brought the Daimler around to the front steps and they sorted themselves out. Wyatt sat in front with the chauffeur. Livinia took the seat behind him. Grace sat on Elizabeth's lap next to her. Her mother-in-law took the seat by the window. A rug was secured around Mother Pratt's legs. Winnie wedged herself between them, and they were off.

The village bustled with commerce at this time of day. Those who recognized Mother Pratt's motor waved. Most of them knew, of course, what a momentous day this was for the Pratt family.

The chauffeur stopped the Daimler in front of the stone steps to the train station. A crowd had gathered on the platform. The train had arrived, spewing steam. There wouldn't be time for a lengthy farewell.

Wyatt didn't wait for the chauffeur to set the brake before he opened the door, ready to spring from his seat.

"Hurry, girls." Livy opened her door and climbed down.

Wyatt undid the strap securing his case to the boot and placed it on the ground. He removed his cap. "This is goodbye, I'm afraid."

"You will be careful." Livy had promised she

wouldn't be emotional, but a mother must have assurances.

"Yes, you needn't worry," he replied.

"You will write?" Elizabeth asked.

"Every day."

"If you need anything…"

"I will be well provided for, Mother."

The train blew its whistle.

"I must go." Wyatt kissed them all on the cheek. He'd reserved the last kiss for his mother.

She received his kiss with eyes squeezed shut, and then reached out and pulled him close. He was solid muscle and bone. She'd no doubt he was strong enough for the task ahead of him.

"Take care of yourself," Livy said.

He pulled away. "I will be all right."

"Off with you, then." She made no attempt to wipe the tears from her eyes.

Wyatt dashed away and climbed aboard the moving train as many on the platform shouted their goodbyes. At last, he popped his head out a window and waved. Livy stood helpless as if turned to stone.

The train had gotten up a full head of steam and chugged down the tracks. Wyatt disappeared inside.

"Come along, Mother." Elizabeth threaded her hand around Livy's coat sleeve.

Livy strained for one last look before she let herself be led away.

After Wyatt's departure, a somber mood descended on them as they climbed back into the motor.

Mother Pratt spoke of trivialities—the weather, the latest fashion in London. Livy half-listened as the countryside whisked by them. When they arrived at Fairview, the girls went to their rooms. Mother Pratt and Livy settled in the parlor in front of the fire.

"There's nothing for it but to keep a brave face," her mother-in-law said repeatedly.

Livy didn't need to be reminded. She intended to keep up a brave face, even a hopeful one, although her heart was close to breaking.

"Thank you for not causing a fuss. Criticism would have only made Wyatt anxious and unhappy."

Mother Pratt bristled like a hedgehog. "Of course I kept my opinions to myself. What do you take me for?"

Livy didn't wish to speak harshly, but the words were there on the tip of her tongue ready to escape.

"A caring grandmother," Livy replied instead.

Mother Pratt sniffed. "Hand me my needlepoint, will you? I find at times like these one must keep oneself busy."

Livy picked up the hoop and silk thread from the divan and brought it to her. She had not missed the old woman's strained expression when Wyatt boarded the train. Mother Pratt wore the same expression now.

Livy needed to escape. "If you'll excuse me, I think I'll

go for a walk." There was no need to explain where she was going.

Mother Pratt did not meet her gaze. "There's rain forecasted for the afternoon."

"I won't be long." Livy departed before anything more could be said. Indeed, before any further conversation suffocated her.

Chapter Twelve

>>>*<<<

Livy pinned on her hat and put on her wool coat. The war was tearing her family apart, limb by limb. She didn't know how to fight this enemy. She only knew she must. So much was at stake.

She started off filled with trepidation. The fields had been denuded of their ripened crops and the trees would soon drop their leaves. The hops were ready to be harvested and hung to dry in the oast barn. Thank heaven, the crop had been abundant this year. Apples waited to be picked and honey needed to be put up into jars. She waved at old Tom, who stood at the whetstone sharpening tools. She couldn't be gone long.

How would she manage?

By counting her blessings, for a start. Fairview Farm was more fortunate than some. Almost all of the food they raised went to the troops, but there was enough to spare. With so many young men gone to the war, Livy relied on old men from the village, youngsters, and her own determination to get things done.

She wondered if it would be best for them all to sell

the farm to Ronald Asher? He'd make her a good offer. There would be plenty of money for her and the girls to go into town where they'd be closer to school.

The very idea of leaving Fairview seemed foreign to her.

She'd been a farmer's daughter and a farmer's wife. Now she was a farmer's widow with four children to raise and protect. What the future would bring them Livy could not guess, but she would carry on the best she knew how.

Ronald Asher couldn't have Fairview. Wyatt's legacy wouldn't be sold.

When she reached the main road, she quickened her pace. She loved this stretch of road, especially at this time of year when the oaks and elms, the blackberry hedges and rosehips took on the palette the cold weather had hewn. These were vistas meant for wandering.

A jumble of dark clouds portended cold weather ahead. The air had the bite of winter. Each year she looked forward to the change of the seasons, the cold that turned noses red, the sound of geese flying south, the highly anticipated advent season with the smell of holly and juniper in the parlor.

She loved the earth turning white, the first footprints in the new snow, and the warmth of a fire to come home to after a day's work was done.

A frisson of trepidation reminded her that this winter would be different. She must brace herself for whatever may come. She wasn't a pessimistic person, but the future seemed filled with darkness.

She reached the edge of Asher Wood. The stand of ancient oaks blocked the sun, but the shadows did not frighten her. She and her friends had played here as children. Sometimes Ronald Asher had been allowed to play with them, but most often he had not. His duty had been to his studies, for the Ashers' vast estate and wealth were to become his to steward when his father died.

Smoke curled from the chimney pot of the stone cottage once occupied by the Ashers' gamekeeper. The place had always enchanted Livy, with hollyhocks poking through here and there in the front garden, like a cottage in a fairy tale. To her knowledge, no one had lived here for years. This morning, the hollyhock stalks—bitten by frost—were piled in a corner. The prolific weeds had been reduced to a smattering. James had been busy in the garden, which surprised her. She hadn't thought a Londoner would have any interest in gardening.

She would like to pop in and say hello. She owned him her thanks and appreciation for last night. Perhaps this wasn't the time. Her world was crashing down around her and it'd be unfair to burden him with her troubles.

He had enough to contend with at the moment.

Time to turn around and head home. She did an about face, gravel crunching under her shoes. She hadn't gone more than a few steps when she heard a crash and a string of oaths.

"Oh, dear." The sound had come from the other side of the cottage. What had gone wrong? Should she investigate?

"Hello? Major Gunnison? Are you all right?" Livy called out. She waited and listened, wondering if he'd heard her.

She decided to err on the side of caution and find out if the major needed help. She hurried up the path and opened the gate. The door to the cottage was ajar. She called out another hello. No one answered.

"Major? Are you there?"

Again, she received no answer and feared something terrible had happened.

She continued up the walkway, which had been swept. When she reached the door, she peeked inside the cottage. The room was empty.

The décor was simple and sparsely furnished—a fireplace with a wood fire burning, a cozy chair, and a small table holding a stack of books. The arms of the chair were worn through in places and in need of an antimacassar.

Where could he have gone?

Livy left the cottage and proceeded with caution around blackened vines and piles of brush to the back garden. As she rounded the corner, she wondered if being here was such a good idea. She would be intruding on his privacy, upon which—according to several accounts, he insisted on in no uncertain terms.

In for a penny, in for a pound.

She found him struggling with an overturned wheelbarrow. He wore baggy trousers and a loose-fitting wax jacket, not at all what she expected to see.

"Hello," she said, almost tripping over an exposed root.

He looked up and frowned.

"Yes, it's me." When his gaze connected with hers, her heart thumped as if occupying a hollow drum. Not an unpleasant sensation, but the intensity surprised her. "I heard you call out while I was taking a walk. Do you need some help?"

His frown deepened into a scowl. "No, I have everything under control, Mrs. Pratt."

His tone was off-putting. She didn't deserve a rebuke for a perfectly reasonable inquiry.

He righted the barrow, then picked up a rake, a hoe, and a shovel. He did so under a great deal of effort, the pain of each movement reflected in the twists and turns of his face. She made no move to help as she would've done with a neighbor or a friend. He had, after all, everything under control.

"Well?" He straightened.

Obviously, her presence irritated him. She would make allowances. She'd seen this before, a man trying to be strong, hating he could be weak.

"I'm satisfied all is as it should be."

He scowled, clearly not amused.

"You've done a wonderful job with the back garden," she said.

He took out a handkerchief from his back pocket and wiped his forehead. "I thought a bit of work outdoors desirable. One must keep fit."

"There's no shortage of work in the country, I'm afraid."

"Quite."

"This cottage has seen better days. I remember when roses climbed along the back wall. Pink, they were. They've all gone now." She sighed. "And you should've seen the hollyhocks. Quite tall and impressive. I believe they were my favorite."

"Is that why you're here? To admire my gardening skills?" He stowed his handkerchief in his pocket but he did not look at her.

Livy should leave. James was in no mood for company. Such a contrast to last night when he'd charmed her and her guests.

Had she given too much importance to the attention of a handsome gentleman? Had she confused her own gratitude with something else?

"I thought you'd like to know we've just been into town to the train station," she said. "Wyatt is off to his training."

"In good spirits, I trust?"

"Remarkably so." Her lower lip quivered. She couldn't help herself, her emotions were very close to the surface.

"Is there something else?"

His question vexed her. She could forgive rudeness but not unkindness.

"Yes, in fact, there is." She softened her gaze. "I don't know what I would've done last night if you hadn't been there."

"Come now, Mrs. Pratt. You were surrounded with good friends and family."

"You know what I mean. I'm talking about Elizabeth."

He bowed slightly. "I'm happy she told you."

"How fortunate for Elizabeth you arrived when you did."

"I did what anyone would've done."

"I am grateful nonetheless," Livy said earnestly.

"If allowed, I could talk about my children for hours."

"Understandable," he said. "They are commendable children."

"Thank you." His compliment pleased her.

Major Gunnison narrowed his eyes.

He was dismissing her.

She accepted the truth of the matter. Last night he'd done what was expected of him. Now that the major had revealed his true character, she didn't like him very much. In fact, she didn't like him at all.

"I must be off. I don't want to get caught in the rain," she said. She should've known better, she should've listened to what her neighbors were saying.

"Goodbye, Mrs. Pratt."

"Goodbye," she said over her shoulder, affecting a smile, trying to hide how foolish she felt.

Livy didn't stop, aware she was running. She skidded across a patch of stones and caught ahold of the top of the gate before she fell.

The gate was stuck against dry earth. Annoyed it proved to be such a formidable obstacle, she used her fist and pounded it open.

A tear started. The emotions she'd held back broke free. More tears spilled over and ran down both cheeks. She made no effort to wipe them away as she hurried down the road.

James gritted his teeth. Filled with unhappiness, Mrs. Pratt had turned to him for support and guidance. She shouldn't have. There was nothing he could do. Absolutely nothing.

He couldn't spare her from the pain love inevitably brings. This was reality at its cruelest.

In his defense, he had warned her, had warned them all he needed to be left alone. This war—the war to end all wars—demanded his undivided attention.

He'd overslept this morning, the first time in years. Eating too much had wrecked havoc with his digestion. Pulling weeds had seemed a good activity, better than idleness, but he couldn't even finish the job.

None of this was Mrs. Pratt's doing.

Bloody hell! Why couldn't he have been more civil? All the good lady had wanted was some cheering up. Cheering up wasn't something he did, granted, but why had he been such a disagreeable old reprobate?

True, he was good at pushing people away. Forming

attachments had never been easy for him.

Had the war jaded him so that he could no longer carry on a conversation in polite society? Had the battlefield made him cruel? He hated to think so, but what other conclusion could be drawn?

James picked up the handles of the barrow and proceeded to the shed. As he traversed the uneven ground, he stumbled and the barrow slipped from his hands.

"Stuff and nonsense," he roared. He bent over in pain, rubbing his knee.

Ever so gingerly, he put weight on the offending leg. Not too bad, he decided, but he'd done enough for one morning. He plucked his hat out of the wheelbarrow and staggered to the cottage and the comforts of a chair by the fire.

Livinia had dropped her handkerchief on the path. He stooped and picked it up. The linen smelled of lavender, sweet and feminine. The scent reminded him of last night on the front steps of the Pratt home when he'd held her hand and said goodbye.

Damnation!

These were memories best forgotten. A soldier must not give in to sentimentality. Such things were better left to poets.

He was not the type of man who needed a partner anyway. Hadn't he managed all these years on his own? He would continue to do so.

James tucked the handkerchief in his pocket, and headed to the front door.

Chapter Thirteen

>>>—«««

A maid showed Livy to a sunny morning room, and she removed her gloves in anticipation of a good cup of tea and some gossip. The week had flown by, and she'd been pleased when an invitation to tea had arrived from Asher Hall.

The invitation hadn't been extended to Mother Pratt, however. She made no excuses to her mother-in-law.

Livy and Gwendolyn had much to discuss.

As she settled on the sofa the door opened, and Gwendolyn swept into the room in a pale mauve dress cinched with a green belt. She wore her thick, dark hair swept up in a charming mound of waves and curls.

Her hostess's face brightened as she reached out and grasped Livy's hands. "Livinia, how good to see you on this lovely day."

Livy kissed her on the cheek and caught a whiff of expensive perfume.

Asher Hall had been in her husband's family for seven generations, but Gwendolyn had done wonders modernizing the place. The Hall was one of the first homes in Kent to install electric lighting, which took some getting used to—the glare hurt the eyes and sharpened the features.

Gwendolyn was also one of the first to have a telephone instrument installed. How delighted she'd been to demonstrate the efficiency of calling the city with only a few clicks and clanks. Now they all had telephones—couldn't live without them, Livy would dare say. Many in the village wondered what modern wonder would be next.

Gwendolyn invited Livy to sit down and ordered tea be brought up. Her butler bowed and left the room.

"I hope I haven't kept you waiting," Gwendolyn said. "I just finished a letter and wanted it to go out with the morning post."

"Not at all." Livy waited until Gwendolyn took a seat opposite. "I was so happy when I received your invitation."

"I wanted to have a little chat."

Livy was immediately curious as to what Gwendolyn needed to chat about.

Gwendolyn straightened her skirt and folded her hands in her lap. "Has Wyatt gone to his post?"

"Not to a post yet." Livy affected a smile, trying to show a cheerful countenance. "He's still in training but I don't know for how long."

"Ronald and I wish him well."

"Thank you." Livy spoke with gratitude. She didn't mention the lump in her stomach that hadn't yet shifted since Wyatt's departure.

"A pity Uncle is so slow to recover," Gwendolyn said. "He's anxious to return to the front."

"I've been to your gamekeeper's cottage to see him," Livy said.

"Have you? How delightful."

"I shan't go again."

Gwendolyn caught her lower lip in her teeth. "I apologize if my uncle was very rude."

"To be sure." *And a bit too grumpy for my liking.*

With laughter bright in her eyes, Gwendolyn spoke. "I say, I don't know what I'm going to do with him."

"I intruded on his privacy, and we'd all been warned," Livy told her.

"Fiddlesticks, and I thought the two of you were getting along so well at Wyatt's birthday party."

The party—it seemed so long ago—had been an evening she wouldn't soon forget. "Your uncle can be charming when he's of the mind to be."

"Do try again," Gwendolyn replied.

"He insists on his solitude." Livy said, understanding his need for peace and quiet. "I must respect his wishes."

"A preference that I hope is temporary."

So this is what Gwendolyn had in mind when she invited Livy for a chat: a little matchmaking. Livy hid a smile. The girl believed all the major needed was companionship to soften his rough edges. Livy was of the opinion the man was set in his ways and not inclined to change.

"Why the cottage?" Livy asked. "I must say the place is rather run down."

"Nothing but a rat's nest." Gwendolyn sighed. "When we received a note asking for the use of the cottage, naturally, we said yes. He's family, after all, and a war hero, I gather from reading the newspapers. Of course, he would never boast. Even if he wasn't family, we would've helped him. We all must do our bit."

At that moment, a soft knock on the door caught their attention. The door opened and her butler entered carrying a tray laden with their tea and biscuits.

He placed the tray on the table and departed. When the door closed behind him, Gwendolyn picked up the teapot and poured.

"Is your uncle's injury improving?" Livy asked. "He believed he would be leaving before now."

"Apparently not." Gwendolyn picked up the sugar tongs. "Sugar? Cream?"

Livy worried that the wound might be more serious than he'd believed. Gwendolyn didn't seem concerned and she wouldn't be either.

"Goodness, wherever did you find sugar and cream?"

Gwendolyn winked. "We have been most fortunate to have found an ample supply."

"In that case, I'll have one sugar and a spot of cream, if you please."

Gwendolyn gave her a sugar cube and a generous amount of cream and handed her the cup.

"I wondered but didn't dare ask how did your uncle become injured?"

Gwendolyn frowned as she added three lumps of sugar and a dollop of cream to her own cup. "I gather Uncle took on a bit of shrapnel when a Mills bomb exploded in the trenches."

"A Mills bomb? Isn't that one of ours?"

"Precisely."

"How terrible."

"A tragedy, to be sure. Several of our men were killed, according to *The Telegraph*, but more would've been killed or injured if Uncle hadn't taken quick action to evacuate the area."

Livy could picture the scene—the shouting and confusion—when seconds meant the difference between life and death.

Not only had James been hurt, but he'd also lost men to a horrible mistake. She'd judged him too harshly. "He must feel responsible. It explains his attitude."

Gwendolyn shrugged. "I am not unsympathetic. Only when a soldier comes home, he's expected to leave the tragedy of war behind him."

Livy didn't think it was that easy but held her tongue. She would be a poor guest to be argumentative.

"Even so, your family must be very proud."

Gwendolyn sipped her tea before she replied. "To be honest, Father never speaks about him. Uncle is as much a stranger to me as to you."

"How unfortunate."

"When Mother died, almost a decade ago now, Uncle came to the funeral," Gwendolyn continued. "There was a great deal of tension between Father and Uncle James that put others in the family at odds with each other."

Livy understood only too well. "A death in the family is trying."

"Father was so desperately sad. We all were."

"Naturally."

Gwendolyn's expression changed. "There was a terrible row between my father and Uncle that night at the house. I never found out what they'd quarreled about. Uncle left without a word to anyone. We hadn't seen him until now."

She sat up straighter. The memory had hurt her, but she recovered remarkably fast.

"I'm sorry," Livy said. She truly was, but couldn't imagine how brothers could allow themselves to become estranged.

"Have you called your father to let him know the major is here?"

"I haven't." Gwendolyn leaned forward and picked up the sugar tongs. "Uncle doesn't want company anyway. As you have found out."

"Hopefully, he will change his mind about joining your ranks as his leg heals."

Gwendolyn shook her head. "I'm afraid Uncle James has made the Army his career. He's always preferred his command over his family."

A big admission, Livy decided, which had caused a great deal of hurt.

"Ronald believes Uncle James is finished as far as the Army is concerned." Gwendolyn took another sip of her tea. "I wouldn't dare suggest he quit, of course, but it's another thing that might be bothering him."

"Thankfully, he is close by," Livy answered, "where you can keep an eye on him."

Gwendolyn nodded. "I have grown rather fond of him."

She was encouraged by the girl's affection for her uncle. Perhaps she would be the instrument of a long-overdue reconciliation.

Gwendolyn put her cup down on the tray. "Is your tea all right?"

Livy looked at the cup in her hand. She hadn't taken a sip. "Yes, of course."

"Good." She smiled. "Now let's talk about your day."

Livy leaned back against the comfort of the velvet covered sofa, the fragrant tea smoothing out the weariness of a busy morning.

How glad she was to have this conversation. She must make allowances for James's behavior. These were extraordinary times, and he had a great deal of responsibility.

Perhaps the old rules no longer applied.

———— ∽ ————

James heard a commotion and went to the doorway. A hay wagon pulled by a pair of draft horses lumbered passed, heading in the direction of Fairview Farm. The men and women riding in the wagon were his father's age. A second wagon followed carrying boys in their early teens.

He'd avoided the workers all week even though all available men, women, and children had been called on to harvest the crops withering in the fields and put them in the barns for winter. What could a man leaning on a stick do?

As they passed, they took off their hats and greeted him by name. Young Tom who worked for Livinia must have told them who he was.

James raised his hand and waved, and they all waved back.

"Do you have room for one more?" he shouted.

A bearded man nodded and pulled the team to a stop.

James set his stick against the wall and shut the door. They waited as he pushed through the gate and made his way to the road.

"Time to put the hops in the barn," the man explained.

"I'll do my best." James climbed onboard and plopped down next to the older man.

"Name's Martin," the man said. "Tom Martin. That's my grandson in the back wagon. He's a Tom as well."

"We have met," James said. "He made an excellent footman at Wyatt Pratt's birthday party."

The old man grinned.

"My name is James Gunnison."

"So I've been told. You're the major who's home from France convalescing."

"That's right."

"Mrs. Pratt will be needing all the workers she can get," Tom said. "Even with your leg and all, she'll find you something."

James wondered if his arrival would be met with disdain. He'd not acquitted himself very well the last time they'd met.

They hadn't gone very far when James spotted hollyhocks growing against a stone fence. They'd not yet been touched by frost and looked splendid.

"Stop," he said, and Tom Martin pulled on the reins and spoke to the horses. James jumped down, shuddered as the pain in his leg immobilized him, and then hobbled over to the flowers. He broke off the stems until he had a handful. They smelled like honey.

Tom Martin raised a brow as James climbed back to the box.

"They're for Mrs. Pratt," he explained. "I understand she happens to have a preference for the bloom."

"Right you are." The old man chuckled.

When they arrived at the hop-garden, James wanted to be part of the harvest and yet he stood apart, not quite sure what to do. He found Livinia working in the rows of hops. A boy walked on stilts picking the cones off the vines, and Livy collected them in a basket.

She wore a red kerchief on her head and her fair skin glowed with exertion. She looked surprised when she saw him but her expression welcomed him.

"Hello. How good to see you up and about," she said

and she put down her basket.

To think James might've missed this wondrous sight if he'd stayed home, a woman in her prime looking radiant. "I'm here to help."

"How very kind of you. We are short-handed this year. There's a great deal yet to do."

He held out the bouquet, bedraggled from the journey.

"Hollyhocks. Goodness."

"I behaved badly the other day. Please accept my apologies."

She took the flowers and inhaled their scent. "I intruded on what must be a very trying time for you. You were right to shoo me away like a pesky fly."

"My dear Mrs. Pratt..." He didn't continue. He felt awkward and the apology needn't be drawn out any further.

Besides, they'd spoken truthfully and courageously. Nothing more needed to be said.

James picked up the basket. He could jolly well tote a basket for a lady.

"Do you know anything about hops picking?" she asked, walking by his side.

"Only what Tom Martin has told me. I hope you won't ask me to put on a pair of stilts."

Her eyes lit up as they had the night of her son's party, displaying that fire within, the passion she had for all she did. "I have another job for you. You can put the hops in the oast barn to dry."

"I am at your service."

"Oh dear. You sound very serious."

"I want to do a good job."

Her eyes continued to sparkle. "Yes, I believe you do."

By Jove she was a handsome woman.

He'd worried that he'd made a muddle of the first friendship he'd had in a long time with a lady. He set his concerns aside. Livinia seemed willing to forgive the grumpiest of dispositions.

They reached the round barn with the feather-shaped vane. The interior was hot and dusty. Rows and rows of hops had been hung up on racks and filled the room with their earthy and slightly bitter aroma.

James put down the basket, took out his handkerchief, and wiped his brow. The work would be arduous and demanding, but he would do what was required of him. He could do no less.

Livy watched as James stripped off his jumper, unbuttoned his collar, and loosened his tie. Sweat darkened his shirt which clung to his skin, revealing the hard planes of his chest.

Mrs. Tilbury had been watching also and with a wink and a nudge, put Livy to shame for starring.

"There's a nice distraction for ye," Mrs. Tilbury said.

"Quite, and we've got work to do," Livy replied.

"There's no harm in looking." The old woman shook her head and continued her work.

James pitched in for all he was worth. He wouldn't

take a break, not even for a glass of water.

The man wanted to be useful, Livy mused, but his health must come first. Convincing him to slow down, however, would most likely lead to an argument. So she didn't ask him to take a break. She would, under no circumstances, embarrass him in front of the others.

They worked side by side, hauling the heavy baskets into the oast barn and hung them up on racks. They toiled for hours, until the shadows lengthened and the air turned cold.

Livy watched James guardedly for signs of discomfort but saw none. His injury seemed to have healed.

Which meant he would be leaving soon. She wanted him to be well again, to be the man he needed to be, even if it meant his inevitable return to the battlefield.

"Looks like we've got most of it," Tom declared and he rubbed the back of his neck with his handkerchief. "A good crop this year, Mrs. Pratt."

It was a good crop, she decided, and all promised to the Army.

"Very well." She pulled off her gloves. "I'll have Mrs. Heath send out freshly-pressed cider. We all could use some refreshments."

Big Tom left them alone in the barn. The last rays of sunshine turned the withering hops golden. Particles of dust floated in the air. Livy should make her excuses and carry on to the house, where she could wash up and run a comb through her hair.

She didn't want to let go of this moment.

James shifted his stance. His face was red, his hair unruly. The faint suggestion of a beard made him look like a rogue. Not at all the man who'd presented himself at the top of the stairs at the farmhouse the night of Wyatt's party.

She found herself drawn to him with a force that threatened to crumble her resolve.

"Won't you come up to the house for supper?" She smiled. She hadn't forgotten her manners. "It's simple fare, to be sure."

He frowned. "Regretfully, I must decline."

His company had become a precious jewel to her. There was nothing obvious and yet she believed what she felt was mutual.

"Thank you for your help," she said.

"You don't have to thank me," he said.

Livy took a step closer.

"I must be going." He averted his gaze. He was worn through and not about to admit it to her.

"Another time, perhaps?"

He bowed as any gentleman would.

"Goodbye, James."

"Goodbye."

She watched him walk away, limping slightly, and climb into old Tom's wagon.

Chapter Fourteen

James heard someone fiddling with the latch on the front
gate and clutching the armrests, pushed himself to his
feet. He'd overdone it yesterday and paid the price with
aching limbs and a knee that just wouldn't cooperate.

By Jove, putting in a day's work felt good. He'd be
back in shape in no time.

"Major?"

James peered out the window. Livinia had returned.
He regretted their parting yesterday. He'd thought it for
the best.

Relationships could be tricky and even unreliable. The
inner voice warning him to be cautious had played over
and over in his thoughts, reminding him of the past,
warning him nothing lasting would come of this.

Blowing out both cheeks, James surveyed the room.
He could not entertain a lady in a state of upheaval. He
picked up Pettigrew's excellent biography on Nelson from
the floor and set it on the mantelshelf. He removed the
linen serviette he'd discarded and the lap rug he'd used
this morning to cover his legs and set them on a hook

behind the door.

Breadcrumbs littered the seat of his chair. He brushed them off. He'd eaten his breakfast here since there was no need to adhere to the rules of etiquette when living alone. No reason to put on a proper jacket and tie or to make polite conversation, to pretend civilization still existed when the entire world was in turmoil and had for all intents and purposes gone barking mad.

A gentle tap on the door snapped him to attention.

"Major Gunnison, are you home?" Her voice was full of cheer, her disposition like a cloudless day.

"Major? Are you there?"

Satisfied all was in good order, James answered her knock, this time without his customary scowl. He realized too late he was wearing the jumper that had a hole at the neckline.

"Hello. It's me again," she said.

"Livinia."

The cold had inflamed her cheeks. Her eyes sparkled with good will.

As she stepped over the threshold, his whole being became alerted to his needs.

She held up a glass jar to show him what she'd brought. "After all your work yesterday, I thought you could use some harts-horn jelly."

His gaze shifted to the offering. She held out the jar, an elixir to help him mend.

He took the gift. "I have been well provided for during my stay."

"It's what we do in the country, look out for each other."

He nodded. He shouldn't have expected any less. He owed her his thanks and so much more. He searched for the proper words, but they didn't come.

She lifted her chin. "Very well. I should be going."

He couldn't let her go. Not yet. "Perhaps you'd like a cup of tea?"

Her look of relief was immediate. "If it's not too much trouble."

"No trouble at all."

"Then I would love one." Her face brightened. He would like to gather her in his arms. Indeed, he could think of nothing else.

"I can't stay long," she said, pulling off her gloves and stuffing them into her pockets. "There's work to be done. Thanks to you and my neighbors, the harvest is progressing as it should be."

"A monumental task," he said.

"Work on a farm is never done," she replied with a sigh.

He took her coat, hat, and muffler and hung them on a peg. She removed her hat and patted her hair—combed into a soft knot at the nape of her neck. Then turned her attention to the fire. Reaching out to the heat, she warmed her hands.

Steady on, soldier.

"If you'll excuse me, I'll put the kettle on." He retreated into the kitchen.

He set the jelly on the cupboard shelf and moved the kettle from the back of the stove to the heat.

"Bah!" The pain in his knee intensified.

"Excuse me, did you say something?" Livinia shouted from the other room.

"No, Livinia. Everything is under control."

He found two earthenware cups in a cupboard, chipped but serviceable. They needed to be washed. Regrettably, the cupboard held no proper saucers for the cups. He added them to the tray.

Blast! The water jug needed filling. He grabbed ahold of the earthenware jug and pushed open the kitchen door. The wind had picked up and blew cold air into the room.

James hurried to the pump and filled the jug quickly. He returned to the kitchen pleased with himself. Placing the two cups in a tin pan, he poured water over them and dried them with a piece of sacking. The two cups, two spoons and teapot he placed on a tray.

All was organized at last. All he needed was hot water and he'd be ready.

The throbbing in his knee returned with a vengeance. James gasped. This time the pain didn't subside. His leg buckled underneath him and flailing his arms for a handhold, he crumpled onto the slate floor.

As Livy waited for James to return, she looked around the small room. He'd cleaned up from her last visit when she'd peeked in the doorway and found the room in disarray. She took it as a sign of healing. When one was ill, there was no energy or will to be tidy. It gave her satisfaction to see the cottage and the gardens looking in such a good state.

She sat down in the single chair. The objects in the room were not personal. The deer head mounted above the mantelshelf looked like moths had feasted on it. A large trout attached to a board needed dusting. She saw no photographs or mementos of any kind. Only a single book perched on the mantel.

She stood and went to see what he was reading. A tome on another war. She did not open it but returned to the chair and sat down with a sigh, reminded of his purpose. He trained men to fight and die for their country.

The very idea sent her spirits into a tailspin.

The kettle started to whistle. It wouldn't be long now before she would have her cup of tea and they could have a chat. What would they talk about? His family, perhaps? Gwendolyn had mentioned some kind of rift in the family. Would he confide in her?

The whistling continued and then turned into a shriek.

"James?"

Livy rose to her feet. She should let him fulfill his duty as a host, but she wondered why he didn't take the kettle off the hob.

"Are you all right, James?"

Receiving no answer, Livy decided to see if he needed help. The kitchen could be a foreign land to men.

When she arrived, she saw him sitting on the floor, his

back against the wall. He was very pale and perspiring.

"What has happened?" She shoved the kettle off the heat and knelt next to him.

His mouth was twisted in a frightful scowl. "My leg."

"Let me help you into the other room," she said.

He refused to take her hand and struggled to put his feet underneath him. After several attempts, he was able to push himself off the floor.

Livy didn't doubt her strength—she could shift the most stubborn of cows while milking—but she should have realized James would not or could not accept any assistance.

He moved slowly. By the time they reached his chair, beads of sweat had broken out on the bridge of his nose and he was breathing heavily.

As he lowered himself into the seat, he groaned.

"I'll find Gwendolyn. She can ring the doctor." She made no attempt to hide her fear.

"No," he said forcefully. "No. The pain comes and goes. I only need a few minutes and I will be fine."

"I must insist."

His gaze darkened. "Livinia, I know you mean well, but I assure you I don't need any help."

His reprimand stung. Her offer had been clumsy, but she couldn't have imagined such a strong response.

James clenched his teeth. His lips had gone alarmingly colorless.

"I'll get you some water." She hurried into the kitchen and found a glass. Thankfully, the stone pitcher was half full, and she filled the glass to the top.

"Here we are," she said. James took the glass, gulped the entire amount, and set it down.

His pain was greater than he let on, she'd no doubt. How stubborn of him to pretend otherwise.

"I'll go make the tea. If you don't mind me saying so, a cup will put us both right."

She'd hoped to lighten the mood and to put a smile on his face.

She was rewarded.

Livy returned to the kitchen.

This would not do, she decided. How could she convince James he needed medical attention? She added the hot water to the teapot and gave it a stir. She picked up the tray and carried it into the room.

"Nothing like a cuppa." She put the tray down on the table.

"There's a chair in the kitchen, I'll get it." He grabbed hold of the chair's arms, making ready to stand.

"You'll do no such thing." She put a hand on his shoulder and he sank into his seat.

Livy returned to the kitchen and found a wicker chair. She dragged it into the sitting room and placed it next to him. Taking her seat, she began to pour.

"There, that wasn't so difficult, was it?"

"What are you talking about?"

"Letting me take over."

His stiff upper lip twitched. "I am not a child."

"No, and you shouldn't act like one."

He huffed. She was glad he understood exactly what she meant.

Livy handed him a cup full of steaming tea, regretfully without sugar or milk. He didn't object. She poured one for herself. As she watched the curls of steam, she took a deep breath. He'd given her such a scare.

The room was cozy and warm. With the wind whipping through the trees and a storm brewing, she strove for a quiet domestic scene in which they both could be comfortable. She would not let anything intrude on their quiet time together. Conversation would be reserved for happy memories only.

James, thankfully, relaxed a fraction. His pain seemed to have subsided. How long he would go on like this wasn't for her to say, only he must come to the realization and soon that he needed a doctor.

"You must find country life rather dull compared to the city," she said.

"To be perfectly honest, I'm enjoying my stay here," he replied.

She would do what she could to make sure this contentment he'd found in the gamekeeper's cottage continued.

"I understanding Gwendolyn is your brother's daughter."

"Yes."

"He lives in London?"

"He does."

His short replies could only mean one thing. She'd

intruded on his privacy by asking about his family. She'd asked questions he wasn't willing to answer.

"I went to London once when I was a girl," she said, carrying on as if she hadn't noticed. "Father took us to the Colonial and Indian Exhibition."

He sat forward, knocking against the side table and almost upsetting his cup. The excitement of the fair shone in his eyes. "I was there."

The change in him was remarkable. "We had such a good time," she said. "I will never forget all the wonderful exhibits that we saw. Every one was so exotic, so marvelous."

"Do you remember the lions?"

"How could I forget? They frightened me so badly I had night terrors for months after."

He picked up his cup and took a sip before answering. "I remember my father commenting about darkest Africa. I want to go there one day. Perhaps I will after the war is over."

She smiled. "Perhaps."

"How about you? Have you ever wanted to visit the dark continent?"

Livy laughed. "Not me. I'm a homebody through and through."

He grimaced and almost spilled his tea.

"More pain?" Livy had to ask.

"Only a twinge," he said.

She saw how he struggled to be brave, to not show how he was hurting. They were alike in that way.

They both stared into the crackling fire, sipping tea and reminiscing about a time long past.

James grasped the sides of the chair as a new wave of pain coursed through his leg. What had started out as a twinge intensified a thousand-fold.

Livinia put down her tea and stood. "You need a doctor."

His first instinct was to tell her to mind her own business. He was used to having these bouts of soreness. Obviously, he'd gone and done too much in the past few days. Why hadn't he been more careful?

"All I need is some rest." Air whooshed out of his lungs as the pain took possession of his body.

She persisted. "Did your London doctor give you anything for the pain?"

"Tablets. Only a few left." He could barely get the words out.

"I think you need one."

James couldn't answer. Searing white heat made it difficult for him to take a breath.

Livinia pulled the ottoman in front of him. Ever so gently, she placed his offending leg on top.

"Where is the bottle your pills came in?" She looked around the room.

"There are only a few. I'm saving them for an emergency."

"We have a very good pharmacy in the village. Take what's left today and I'll get you some more."

He gestured at the closed door of his bedchamber and she went into the room.

Picking up the glass, he gulped down the rest of the water and slammed it on the table.

She returned with the brown bottle. "Show me your hand. I'll go into town and have this bottle refilled. Is there anything else I can do to make you more comfortable before I leave?"

"No, thank you. You've done enough."

"I've done very little." She shook the last of the pills into his hand and covered him with the rug. "You stay put until I return."

James downed the pills. They tasted bitter and he could use some more water.

Livinia anticipated his need. "I'll be right back."

She returned from the kitchen with the stone pitcher.

"Drink up," she said as she filled his glass.

He obeyed her command. Livinia was a lady of compassion—which was to be commended—but he hated her seeing him like this.

She picked up the glass. "Another?"

James shook his head. "I've had enough."

"Perhaps you'd be more comfortable in bed?"

He would loath being caught in bed at this hour. "Not necessary, I assure you."

"You do not look well at all."

"It will pass."

Livy pocketed the empty bottle. "Come along, Major."

"I'm perfectly content in my chair," he protested, to deaf ears, apparently.

"Don't be silly."

"I don't need you to coddle me."

"Is that so? Perhaps it would do you some good to be looked after for a change." She grabbed hold his arm.

In the face of such persistence, he yielded. "I suppose the bed would be more comfortable."

He sat forward and stood with her help. She was surprisingly strong for a woman her size, bearing a great deal of his weight.

If only the lads could see him now.

"Steady." She put her arm around his waist.

Unnerved and frustrated by his weakness, he took the first step.

She held on. "Very good, you're doing splendidly."

He scowled. Her voice was authoritative. She'd taken charge when he jolly well could walk on his own.

He opened his mouth to tell her this, but she interrupted.

"You're going to have to depend on me, whether you care to or not, Major."

She'd pulled rank and he gave in.

Leaning against her, he inhaled her scent, summer flowers, which awakened his senses and put him in a better state of mind. She grabbed a handful of his jumper, her arm acting like a brace.

James hobbled to the small room that served as his bedchamber. He'd kept the door closed to keep the heat in the parlor and the room was cold.

Livinia shivered.

"Sit." She released him to his bed.

James sat and kicked off his carpet slippers. He was ready to collapse but waited as she pulled down the counterpane and the blanket. He would give her high marks on efficiency.

"Have a lie down," she said as soon as she'd finished.

He fell back and pulled the covers up to his waist.

"You'd make an excellent Sergeant Major," he said.

"I'm glad you think so." She turned her head in the direction of the door. "Did you hear a motor car?"

James had not, but a knock on the door confirmed her suspicions.

"I'll go see who is here," she said.

James sunk lower in the covers, hoping whomever had arrived wouldn't stay long. The trip to the bedroom had exhausted him. He'd no wish to entertain any further.

He heard the latch click and the door open.

"Livinia, what are you doing here?"

Gwendolyn. James sat up. He couldn't let his niece see him flat on his back.

"My dear, I don't want you to worry, but would you be so kind to go into the village to fill this prescription for pain tablets?"

"How bad is he?"

"He's resting. I will stay with him. He shouldn't be left to his own devices."

"I must see him."

His niece was at his bedroom door. He attempted a smile.

"Uncle, are you in very much pain?"

"Only a temporary condition, I assure you."

"We'll get you more medicine straight away."

Livy appeared beside her. "He needs a doctor. You must telephone Dr. Bainbridge in the village."

"I do not need a doctor." His voice boomed in the small room.

"You must," Gwendolyn said, ignoring his plea. "The local doctor is excellent. He will help you."

"There's no need," he said.

Neither appeared convinced.

Mercifully, the two women left. He put his head back on the pillow, his last ounce of energy deserting him.

"I'll stay and make sure he remains in bed. Have your cook send some soup," he heard Livinia tell Gwendolyn.

"Yes, Livinia. An excellent idea. Nothing like chicken and leek soup to put a man on the mend."

"Would you be so kind to telephone Mother Pratt? She'll worry about me not returning in a timely fashion."

"Yes, of course. I will let your family know," Gwendolyn replied. "What you are doing is very charitable. Thank you for staying." The door closed and the latch engaged.

James stared at the ceiling and pouted. Is that what he was? A charity case?

Livinia returned. "I know you object, but I decided to take the matter into my own hands. You need a doctor and are too stubborn to admit it."

"All I need is some peace and quiet."

"Which you will get. Now stay in bed."

"On whose orders?"

She smiled. "On my orders."

There was no doubt.

Without further admonitions, she left him alone. He could hear her humming in the kitchen. How could he be expected to get any rest with that noise?

He took a breath to lodge a complaint, but let it go. Such behavior had all the hallmarks of a first-class curmudgeon, and Livinia Pratt deserved better.

Chapter Fifteen

✦≫≫≪≪✦

"He's resting comfortably," Dr. Bainbridge told Livy. She'd waited in the sitting room as the doctor did his examination.

"I'm grateful," she replied.

"I've given him some morphine. He'll sleep for several hours." The doctor's forehead was deeply creased.

When had he gotten so old? Livy wondered.

"What brought on this attack?" she asked.

"Over exertion, I should think." He opened his case and stuffed his stethoscope inside. "There's a great deal of swelling around his knee and some purulent drainage from the surgical wound."

"Oh dear, I fear I'm responsible. I invited him to my house last Friday night for a birthday party for Wyatt. We were so pleased when he came. And then just yesterday he came with Tom Martin and helped with the harvesting of the hops."

"Don't blame yourself. I suspect the major isn't the type to sit still for very long."

She was well aware of this. "Will he get better?"

The doctor frowned. "Difficult to say."

She'd hoped for a more reassuring prognosis. "How bad is the infection?"

"Any infection can be serious. The leg won't heal until it's dealt with properly."

Livy didn't want to imagine what would happen if the infection spread. "What else can be done?"

"I'm leaving a bottle of Dakin's solution." Dr. Bainbridge put on his hat and wrapped his scarf around his neck. "The wound needs to be cleaned every four hours."

She helped the doctor with his coat.

The doctor picked up his case. "He'll need a nurse. I'll arrange for a woman to come from the village."

Livy had a better idea.

"That won't be necessary. I'll stay and take care of him tonight."

She would not leave him in his hour of need. Her family could manage without her for one night.

The doctor who'd delivered her four children and kept them in excellent health gazed at her with affection.

"Very well, Livy. Watch for more swelling and discoloration. You'll have Mrs. Asher telephone me if there's any change?"

"Of course, Doctor. Gwendolyn is bringing some tablets from the village for the pain. Do you think they will be enough?"

"If not, he will need another injection of morphine. Do you think you could give it to him?"

Dr. Bainbridge knew full well that she could. Livy had

been the one to administer the morphine injections those last days of her husband's life.

She walked with him to his motorcar. A light rain had begun to fall and she held an old umbrella—found in the corner of the kitchen—for them both.

"What if the antiseptic solution doesn't work?" Livy shouldn't be asking, but she was afraid. No medicine had been able to save Charles. She'd watched helplessly as he'd wasted away until death relieved him of his suffering.

"His only option will be to have a surgeon see to his knee."

"An operation?"

"He may not have any other choice."

The doctor opened the door of his motor and stowed his case on the seat next to him. He cranked the engine and his automobile sputtered to life.

Dr. Bainbridge climbed inside, his face mottled from the effort. "I'll be back in the morning."

She thanked him. Her world was a place where the people were dependable. This was the way it should be.

"Hopefully the Dakin's solution will clear the infection and he'll be on the mend in no time. I've asked for Gwendolyn to send down some soup as well."

The doctor nodded. "I'm sure hot soup will help."

He shut the door and motored away.

Livy knew what she must do and said a prayer for strength and healing.

She hurried back to the cottage and shut the door. The umbrella dripped on the slate floor and she left it open in the corner to dry.

She wasn't sorry to have asked Gwendolyn to call out the doctor. James had met his match in stubbornness.

From the doorway of his bedchamber she could see he slept. The morphine had worked its magic. His breathing had steadied, the gentle rise and fall of his chest satisfied her that he didn't suffer.

She added more coal to the stove, and the grate glowed with renewed warmth. The days were getting shorter. She checked her watch. Half past four o'clock and the room was already bathed in shadows.

Exhausted, Livy sat down in James's chair in front of the fire, pulling his lap rug around to cover her feet. The old chair smelled of tobacco. Even with stained armrests and a lumpy, worn cushion, she settled comfortably into its depths. Rain pattered on the slate roof. Most likely it would continue through the night.

She was here to care for James, and she wouldn't abandon him. His need was immediate—although she was sure he wouldn't agree. When he woke, she would try her best to keep him in good company until he could cope without her.

Of course, she'd stretched the bounds of propriety staying here alone with him, but it seemed silly to ask someone to come from the village when she could manage.

After all, she was not a maid and the major was not a bounder, at least she did not imagine him to be. He did become loud and demanding at times, but that was mostly bluster, in her opinion. She'd seen glimpses of who he was behind his military bearing, and she found him to be a man who could be depended on.

Livy closed her eyes and relaxed for the first time all week. She could use a bit of a catnap as well. The work of the past few days, especially, had been draining.

A motorcar came to a stop outside the cottage and Livy jumped to her feet. As she opened the door, Gwendolyn's butler walked briskly up the path, head bowed against the wind-driven rain, carrying a covered iron pot.

He stood under the eaves, big raindrops dripping from his bowler.

"Mrs. Asher sends her regards," he said. "She wants you to have this soup."

She took the pot from him. He removed a packet from his coat pocket and set it on top of the lid.

"The major's medicine," he explained.

She thanked him. "I'm sure the major will be grateful."

The butler tipped his hat and hurried back to the motorcar, slipping as he reached the door.

"Do be careful," she called out.

Holding on to his hat, he righted himself. "Thank you, Mrs. Pratt. Most clumsy of me. Cheers."

Livy closed the door with her hip. The pungent smell of leek soup reminded her that she'd not eaten since this morning, and only then a bit of toast. Her stomach squeezed tight as the aroma filled the room.

She would wait until James woke. No doubt he'd be

hungry. They could dine together and share stories of happier times. The very idea made her smile. She put the soup on the back of the hob and returned to his chair.

Sleep had her in its grasp when Livy heard a voice. At first she thought it was a dream. She sat up. The red glow from a dying fire reminded her of where she was—in the gamekeeper's cottage. She'd fallen asleep under the watchful gaze of the deer's head and a stuffed trout.

James must be awake. She checked the clock on the mantel. Six o'clock already. She'd hoped the morphine would last longer, but he had the pills now for the pain. Hopefully they would bring him relief and he wouldn't need the stronger injection. Morphine could play tricks on the mind and bring on bouts of indigestion, as she'd found out with her husband.

Livy rose from the chair and lit the candle on the mantelshelf. The flame bent and twisted with each breath but didn't go out. Shielding the flame with her hand, she tiptoed to the open door of his room.

What she saw alarmed her. James was writhing in his bed, mumbling.

"I see you are awake. Your pills have arrived. Do you want one?" She set the candle down on the small table next to him. She reached over to touch his forehead, hoping his fever had broken, but he grabbed her wrist. His fingers dug into her skin, shocking her more than hurting her. Alarmingly, his grip was so strong, she couldn't pull away.

"What the devil is wrong with you? You'll divulge our

position with that bloody light." He raised himself on one elbow. His breath came in gasps. The flickering light revealed the contortions in his face. "The enemy will lob a mortar round right at this spot."

Livy blew out the candle. He seemed to have confused her with someone else and believed they were hunkered down in the trenches.

"I didn't know," she said, her throat tight, her mouth dry.

He released her and slumped back on his pillow. "You must be more careful."

"Everything will be all right," she said gently. "The light is out. They will not see us."

He turned his head to the sound of her voice. The room was dark and the wind howled outside.

"I'm thirsty." His voice was barely audible.

Livy held the glass of water to his lips. A few drops spilled on his shirt. She hadn't realized her hand was shaking.

He drank a few gulps. Leaning over the side of the bed, he spit out what he'd consumed, retching as if he'd been poisoned.

Livy held on to his arm so he wouldn't pitch over. When he was through, he wiped his mouth with the back of his hand.

"This water isn't fit to drink." He was breathing hard. "You know it must be treated with chloride of lime."

"The water is clean," she assured him. "I have drunk some myself. There is no contamination."

She helped him to lie back down. Using her own handkerchief, she patted the corners of his mouth and dabbed at his chin.

"Now, have some more," she said.

He shook his head vigorously. "We must share what little clean water we have."

"There is plenty," she said.

"Give what is left to the lads."

Livy didn't know how to persuade him to drink more. His stomach must be roiling. "A cup of tea, then?"

"Don't be daft. We can't boil water. The enemy will see the smoke from the fire."

"You needn't worry about a fire. I will take care of the preparations without alerting the enemy."

He closed his eyes. What he'd experienced in the trenches haunted him and wouldn't let him sleep.

Mother Pratt had wondered if the major suffered from a case of nerves. This was very much on Livy's mind. She hadn't noticed any evidence up until now, but these night terrors were very real to him.

What should she do? She was so frightened.

The sour odor of the counterpane permeated the room. She removed the vomit-soaked coverlet and brought the rug from the sitting room and spread it across him. He seemed to settle into its warmth, his breathing quiet now.

Livy put the glass within easy reach. The floor was wet. She would need a mop.

"No, no," he bellowed.

She hurried to his side. "What is wrong?"

He kicked and thrashed about violently. The rug slid off the end of the bed to the floor.

"Rats," he cried out. "So many."

"I don't see any." She kept her voice calm.

"There are hundreds of them. Thousands."

"I've had a good look, Major. They've gone."

"They were biting my toes." He exhaled. "I must keep my boots on. Where are my boots?"

"I will look for them." She picked up the rug and covered his feet. "Where did you put them?"

He stared at the ceiling, the boots forgotten.

Livy brushed the perspiration off his hot forehead with the heel of her hand. He was burning with fever. She should run to Asher Hall and have Ronald call the doctor. James needed medical attention, but she couldn't leave him. Not like this.

"These are only night terrors," she whispered. "They will soon go away."

There was no answer, no indication he'd heard her. Thankfully the nightmare seemed to have subsided.

She returned to the sitting room feeling woefully inadequate in the face of these memories that held him in their terrible grip.

The counterpane lay in a heap. She picked it up and tossed it out the back door. As she shut the door, James was shouting.

"Steady, lads. Use your handkerchiefs."

She hurried back to his room and found him sitting up

in bed.

"See that yellow mist coming our way?" He shook his finger at the single window. "Poisonous gas."

"Oh, dear."

"Where are the gas masks? We don't have enough. We never have enough." His fist came down on the nightstand. "There's nothing to be done once you've inhaled it."

Livy felt helpless, but she had to do something. She yanked the heavy muslin across the window. "That should stop the gas from coming any closer."

"Cover your mouth and nose immediately, do you hear me?"

"Yes, I will." She trembled in the darkness. "I have a handkerchief. I have pressed it against my mouth."

"Very well." He fell in a heap and coughed. "I've seen men clawing at their faces. The gas burns the eyes, but worse, melts the lungs. Men drown in their own spittle in three or four hours."

The horror of what he'd described was too terrible to bear, and she fought back tears.

"How many?" His breath rattled in his throat. "How many were lost."

"You rest," she said, insistent. "We will assess the damage in the morning."

"Very well, Sergeant. Wake me in two hours. I will relieve the watch."

"Yes, sir." She let go of his hand and pulled up the rug to cover him.

"The town was burning when we arrived. There was nothing to be done."

Livy reeled. She didn't want to hear any more, but that was not an option. There would be no escaping. She must stay and listen.

"Which town?" she asked and sat down on the bed.

"Ypres, in Belgium. Great columns of black smoke fouled the air." He sniffed as if smelling the char. "One does not forget the odor of burning flesh."

"I can't imagine," she said.

"The loss of life was terrible. There was nothing to do but give the order to bury the dead."

Livy'd seen the photographs in the newspapers. She'd never forget the images of the hollow faces of those who'd lost their homes, the terrified mothers clinging to their children, the men weary and in despair. She had seen the photographs and had wept.

"That's all you could've done," she said softly.

"There were men who wanted to go home then. They'd had enough."

Livy despaired. "The brutality is beyond the will to believe it."

He turned to look at her. "You have to put on a brave face for the lads."

"I know what you mean. Others depend on you to be strong."

He battled a ruthless enemy and intended to win. Her heart filled with admiration for his courage, his bravery in the face of such adversity.

She could love this man.

"You rest now." She stood and straightened the rug and tucking it around him.

"I'm not always a curmudgeon, you know."

Tears welled in her eyes. She let them spill over. He was back with her in this small room, in England. "I find that difficult to believe."

"Do you, Livinia?"

Livy dried her eyes. She was of no use to him in this state. She must call upon her reserves of strength and courage. She could not fail him now.

Livy tucked her handkerchief back in her pocket and grasped his hand. She could feel his pulse, beating strong and true. His skin was cold and clammy, which she decided was good. He had been in the grips of a fever, and something much more terrible.

"Go back to sleep," she said. "We'll talk more in the morning."

He closed his eyes and seconds later was snoring.

Chapter Sixteen

J ames woke up in the pitch-blackness of a night in the grasp of an angry god. The rumbling of thunder and flashes of lightning sounded like big guns mounting an offense.

Only a storm, he realized, and he took a couple of deep breaths to quiet his pounding pulse. He was warm and dry and safe. His bed had been stripped of its counterpane and blanket and he'd been covered with the gamekeeper's rug. The stone jug and a water glass had been placed within easy reach.

Most certainly, this was Livinia's doing. The dear lady had taken care of his needs and eased his burden. She'd sat by his side during the night and had been there when he awoke from a terrible dream.

He would never be able to thank her enough. Such kindness and concern affected a tired, old soldier despite his protests to the contrary.

How distressing she'd had to see him helpless and disoriented. What must she think of him?

He struggled to sit up. The room began to spin and a

powerful nausea churned his insides.

Blast!

James fought to keep control of his stomach's contents as he swung his legs over the side of the bed. Fortunately, his carpet slippers were there and he stuck his feet in them. The pain in his knee had not left him completely but he managed to stand.

A new wave of nausea assailed him.

Biting his fist, he shuffled out the back door. The rain had stopped but the wind buffeted the trees and was bitter cold. Mercifully, he reached the loo in time.

Emptying his stomach made him weak, and he sat down on the wooden seat. This is no good, he thought. I cannot continue like this. I am no use to anyone in this condition.

After he'd rested for a few minutes, he recovered his dignity and stood. His legs held him, and his strength returned to a reasonable level. This infection would not defeat him.

James made his way back to the cottage, navigating the pathway slick from the rain, fearing he might fall. He reached the door without incident and shuffled to his bedchamber.

The glass for water was empty. He filled it and drank. The cool liquid took away the vile taste in his mouth but did not quench his thirst.

He hobbled back into the sitting room. The fire had burned to embers, casting the room in a fiendish glow. To his shock and surprise, there, sleeping in his chair, was

Livinia.

She looked so peaceful, and yet the chair could not be as comfortable as her own bed. She'd used her coat for a blanket.

What was she doing here? Why had she stayed?

Her small hands clutched her coat close to her chin. A lock of rebellious hair framed her face. Even in the dark shadows, he could see the delicate curve of her cheekbone and mouth.

She'd scolded him yesterday, gave him a direct order to go to his bed and stay there. And then Gwendolyn had arrived and the two—interfering busybodies both— conspired to keep him off his feet.

James wasn't angry. Instead he felt an overwhelming emotion he'd kept at bay for a very long time. Too long.

Of course, he would tell her how grateful he was. What he felt was more than gratitude. Why in the devil was expressing all that was in his heart so hard?

Seeing her here pleased him, but he'd no right to ask for her affections. He'd nothing to offer but a murky future. The outcome of the war was far from certain. Even if he did manage to survive, he would have only a small army pension and the gratitude of his country to offer her.

He returned to his bed and sat down. Slumping back against the pillow, he listened to a tree branch scraping against the window glass. The sound vexed him. He must do something about it.

The pain intensified. He could use some more morphine, but he feared becoming dependent on pain killers. Gwendolyn had promised to bring him some tablets from the local pharmacy. He would like one now.

He sat up with the greatest of care and heard Livinia stirring in the other room.

He waited for her to appear in the doorway, all smiles and loveliness. She would reprimand him for getting out of bed. He would protest that he was perfectly capable of managing a walk to the parlor.

They sparred like they'd been a couple for decades. He chuckled. War had a way of speeding up the timetable for relationships, he decided, although he wasn't sure if that was a good thing. He preferred the days when a gentleman courted a lady, but those days were behind them. They didn't have the luxury of a slower pace with a war raging in Europe.

At last Livy arrived carrying the tray with a steaming pot.

"You're up early." She smiled. "It's not light out yet."

"Good morning. I've had a good rest, thanks to you."

"It's the least I could do for a neighbor, and I dare say, a friend." She set the tray on the table next to his bed. "How are you feeling?"

"Much better."

He was rewarded with another smile. It'd been a long while since he'd started his day with a smile and he counted himself lucky.

James shifted his legs to the floor and pushed his feet into his carpet slippers. The heavenly smell of East India's finest roused him.

"Where are you going?"

"Into the other room. I want to sit in my chair."

"You'll do no such thing." She removed the tea cozy. "You're to remain in bed until the doctor examines your wound and gives the go-ahead."

James scoffed but stayed in bed. He felt like a slacker as she folded the rug at the end of the bed and fixed his pillow so he could sit comfortably.

"Now sit back and have some tea."

He'd obeyed, albeit reluctantly. To refuse would have been a colossal show of ingratitude.

She poured him a steaming cup. A tinge of pink colored her cheeks, making her look younger. He found the color agreeable. Most agreeable, indeed.

"The doctor should be here any minute," she said and handed him the cup.

"He needn't come again." He avoided her gaze out of habit.

"We are fortunate to have such a dedicated doctor in our village," she said.

"There is nothing more he can do."

"That is for the doctor to decide."

James frowned. "Very well. I see I have no choice."

She ignored the comment and put her cool hand on his brow. "It appears your fever has broken. What a scare you gave us all."

"I feel much better," he said, pretending her touch didn't matter.

"Your pain tablets arrived. Would you like one?"

He shook his head. "I do not." He wasn't about to admit to her that he wanted one.

"Are you sure?"

"My dear lady, if I should need any more medication, I will have one." He met her gaze. He'd expected to see revulsion in her expression, but there was nothing of the sort. Her gaze was like a loving embrace.

She awakened a yearning in him, which he must do his best to resist before he did something they'd both regret. A soldier must maintain discipline at all cost.

"You've been outside?"

"Yes." It was futile to hide anything from this woman. "The medicine didn't agree with me."

"The doctor said the morphine would make you sick to your stomach."

"It has done so." James did not elaborate but finished the last of his tea with two gulps.

"Hopefully you won't have to take any more. Would you like some more tea?"

"Yes. Thank you."

She poured more tea into his cup. Her movements were practiced—a lady taking care of the morning ritual. It was something he could do perfectly well for himself, and yet, if she left, he would miss her company. He had to admit, being on one's own was not all it was cracked up to be.

"A soldier isn't used to such an indulgence."

"Is that so?" She handed him the cup. "You needn't

worry. Your secret is safe with me."

She watched as he drank. He was self-conscious with her here and he could very well have decreed a cup of tea was all he needed.

He didn't. Time he made amends for his bad behavior. Time he showed his appreciation.

"Now tell me what else you'd like for breakfast," she said.

"The tea will be sufficient," he replied.

"Gwendolyn sent down some wonderful smelling soup. Perhaps you will feel well enough to try some later?"

"Perhaps." He drank some more of the tea. "Thank you for all you have done."

"How could I do any less?"

"Last night couldn't have been easy."

"We managed, didn't we?"

"Still, I must apologize for any inconvenience." He put his cup down on the tray. "I'm sorry if I was difficult."

"You have no need to apologize. You were not yourself."

He winced. His behavior during the night must have been reprehensible.

"What happened to the counterpane?" He probably shouldn't ask.

"You were sick."

"I don't remember." *What else didn't he remember?*

Livinia sat down on the bed. The intimacy jarred him.

A woman shouldn't be sharing a man's bed, especially a man she barely knew. And yet her action seemed as natural as any person wishing to give comfort, which was all it was.

"You were beset by night terrors," she said.

He shook his head. "I apologize."

"There's no need to apologize. I was only too glad I could be here. Would you like to talk about them?"

She intended for him to unburden himself. He couldn't take the plunge. Best to err on the side of caution.

She grasped his hand. There was no hesitation in her, no doubt. The warmth of her hand provided a connection to a willing heart.

"You were in the trenches," she prompted.

Caution be damned. He gave in to her appeal.

"I have the same terrible dream every night," he said. "I don't seem to be able to escape."

"Understandable. All that you've experienced, you won't soon forget."

"I am sorry to have put you through such an ordeal."

"I know you are." She gave his hand a gentle squeeze and released him. "I'm sturdy enough. Indeed, I surprised myself."

"I am grateful," he said.

She favored him with one of her smiles. It was more than he deserved.

"You understand why I must return to my lads as soon as possible. They depend on me."

"Yes, I think I do. Our soldiers need leaders with your

courage and fortitude." She stood, looking pensive. "As soon as the doctor arrives, I will be on my way."

She turned her attention to the window and threw open the draperies. The room filled with light. Frost marred the window, shooting icy fingers across the panes.

"How delighted the children will be to see the first frost." She touched the glass. "There will be snow arriving before we know it."

She'd changed the topic. Enough had been said about last night, and they would move on.

As Livinia left the room, she couldn't help but wonder at the change in him. He'd actually let down his guard—a little—admitting to her he had these frightful dreams.

Shaking her head, she went back to the small kitchen and set about washing up. What a terrible night he'd had reliving the terrors of being in the trenches. Soon Wyatt would face the same beastly conditions, would experience the same crippling nightmares.

She shuddered.

The screech of metal on metal alerted her to the arrival of an aging motorcar. Wiping her hands on a cloth, she headed out of the kitchen for the front door.

James stood in the doorway of his bedchamber dressed in his trousers, a clean shirt, and necktie.

She frowned. What was she to do with him?

Livy opened the door to a bright, clear morning. It

was that way sometimes after a bad storm.

Dr. Bainbridge looked apologetic as he pulled out his handkerchief from his pocket. "Good morning, Livinia. Major." The doctor wiped his nose and had a good blow. "Excuse me. This cold air makes my nose drip."

"Hello," she said. "Do come in."

James remained in the doorway.

"Your patient is waiting eagerly for you to examine him." She cast James a look that warned him not to be disagreeable.

Dr. Bainbridge removed his hat and coat. Livinia took them.

The doctor set his kit on the side table. "Have a seat, sir, and let's take a look."

James had been a spectator until that moment. He grunted a hello and flopped down in his moth-eaten chair.

"Easy does it," Dr. Bainbridge said as James rolled up his pant leg.

Livy glanced at his knee and was shocked by what she saw. The knee had swollen to twice its normal size.

The doctor inhaled sharply. "I don't like the looks of this."

"Nonsense. I've had this swelling before." James unrolled his pant leg. "It goes down eventually. I'll be right as rain in a day or two."

Dr. Bainbridge raised a brow. "The antiseptic hasn't been as effective as I would like. I must say, I didn't think the infection was this advanced."

"Nonsense."

Livy despaired. His hostility was quite annoying. He was unwilling to admit to a failing of any kind. Did he think the good doctor would be persuaded to ignore his condition by such bluster?

The doctor opened his case. "I'll give you another injection, but I'm not confident resting your leg will be enough. I fear gangrene may be the source of the infection."

"Impossible. The wound was thoroughly cleaned at the field hospital." James huffed. "You doctors are a pessimistic lot. Just do what you will and we'll see an improvement in no time."

Dr. Bainbridge didn't reply as he prepared the syringe. No doubt he'd met resistance before from a reluctant patient.

Livinia had been hovering close at hand, ready to be of assistance, but for the sake of privacy, she left the room for the kitchen. The injection would be to the thigh, which necessitated James dropping his trousers. Not that she was unfamiliar with that part of a man's anatomy. She felt a blush creep up her neck and burn her cheeks anyway.

When she returned to the sitting room, the doctor was waiting by the fire. James remained in his chair, his expression grim.

She handed Dr. Bainbridge his hat and coat.

"Walk me to my motor," the doctor said as he put them on.

Livy followed him outside and shut the door behind

her. The cold air made her shiver.

When Dr. Bainbridge reached his motor, he turned to face her. "Major Gunnison must see a surgeon at once."

"Oh I agree. The possibility of gangrene can't be ignored," she said. "Unfortunately, the major is opposed to the very idea of more doctors and hospitals visits."

"This is where you must influence him."

Livy didn't know how she could. "He's very determined resting here at the cottage is all he needs for his condition to improve."

The doctor pinched the bridge of his nose. "I fear that's no longer an option. No doubt bits of shrapnel remain in his leg. They must be removed at once."

"Yes, I understand. Can you do such an operation?"

"He must go to London. The surgeons there are better equipped. He cannot delay, his condition will only get worse."

Livy caught her breath. The doctor need not explain further. "I will do my best."

Dr. Bainbridge smiled. "I know you will."

He cranked the engine, and the motorcar started. Pulling on his gloves, he climbed into the driver's seat. "I'll call Mrs. Archer and have her send down some ice. That should help the swelling for now."

"I will tell him," she replied. Livy marched back to the cottage, her orders clear.

Chapter Seventeen

James braced himself for a lecture as Livinia closed the door. He hadn't been able to persuade her all was satisfactory. Certainly, the doctor hadn't been fooled.

She would not let him off the hook so easily this time.

Firmly ensconced in his chair, he focused on the fire. Arguing with the lady served no purpose. Nor would he retreat to his room in anger like a child.

"What were you thinking, getting out of bed?" Her mouth was set in a frown as she put on her coat.

"I do not want to stay in bed. I am not an invalid."

She regarded him with eyes blinking rapidly as she pinned on her hat. "The doctor believes you belong in the hospital, and I must say, I agree."

"I'm aware of his opinion. And yours."

James did not want her to think he was ungrateful, but he must be firm. "I am done with beds and hospitals and to be frank, coddling. As soon as I have this pain under control, I intend to return to my men."

She regarded him with her mouth set in a frown. "Dr. Bainbridge believes you've bits of shrapnel in your leg.

The shards must come out."

He huffed. "The doctor is a good sort, but he's had no experience with wounds of this nature. I dare say the occasional broken bone and delivery of babies are his forte."

Her gaze was quite fierce. "You cannot ignore the swelling, the infection."

"Believe me, I do not. The tablets will take care of the pain and I assure you I will soon be on the mend."

"Ah, so now you are an expert in medicine?"

"Enough to know there's nothing that can be done."

"Is that so?" She raised her chin. "You puzzle me. How can a man who doesn't hesitate to confront a ruthless enemy be afraid of doctors?"

"What? You don't know what you're talking about!" His voice sounded like thunder in the small space.

Livinia stood her ground. "That's the only conclusion I can come to."

James quelled the fury inside him. He knew what she was doing. The woman was tenacious to a fault and meant to goad him into seeking help. He must insist she let go of this notion that surgery was the answer.

"I know you mean well," he said, meeting her gaze, "but I have everything under control."

"Discipline?"

"Precisely."

"I fear your precious discipline will not help you this time."

He clamped his mouth shut. What more could he say?

She was being emotional. Furthermore, nothing he said convinced her he could very well managed on his own.

"You are very stubborn, you know."

"So I've been told."

Her face betrayed her disappointment. She'd without a doubt expected him to acquiesce. She would be better off to direct her abundant reserves of caring to those who needed it.

"I will leave the telephoning of the doctor to you," she said at last. "You can tell him your decision. I warn you he will not be happy."

"He will understand."

"Perhaps." She sighed. There was a mix of emotions in her sigh, but an acceptance, hopefully, that he would be all right.

"I value your friendship," she said.

Her declaration pleased him. Her good opinion mattered.

"Your friendship means a great deal to me as well," he said. "As a friend, I ask you to let me sort this out."

He struggled to stand. She hurried to his side and put her arm around his waist. Her strength made him feel helpless. He tried to pull away from her as soon as he was securely on his feet. Without success, as it turned out.

There was no restraint in her. She wrapped both arms around him and held him close.

Women were impulsive creatures, he'd found in his experience, and gave hugs and kisses freely and generously. No discipline at all. And yet his as they stood together his armor fell away. He didn't even try to pretend her closeness meant nothing to him.

He'd never been one to give in to impulse, and yet he did something totally unplanned. He hugged her back. A team of horses couldn't have stopped him.

Her heart beat with his—a strong, capable heart. His voice choked in his throat—no words were adequate to express what he felt. The dark places he'd yielded to over the past couple of weeks were flooded with light.

James rested his chin on the top of her head. Her soft hair, the sweet smell of lavender, the sound of her breathing, her warmth against him added to his sense of well-being.

The moment could not have been sweeter, and yet it could not last.

She looked up at him, her eyes glistening. "I have feelings for you, James. I know it sounds foolish—we've only known each other for a few weeks—but I've come to think of you dearly."

"Livinia, are you sure you're not confusing the sentiment with the compassion you have in abundance for so many?"

"Quite sure." She lifted her chin, an invitation for a kiss. He obliged. The kiss was cautious, as if she was fragile and might break.

"I beg your pardon," he said. "I'm not very good at this sort of thing."

Her eyes reflected a wealth of good things. "I dare say we both need practice."

He was tempted to try again.

"How glad I am we have found each other in the midst of this terrible time," she said.

"A terrible time indeed." Much to his regret and contrary to his deepest desire, he disengaged himself. "You must agree, this is not a good time for us to think of ourselves. Relationships are an encumbrance to a man in my position, and you have the farm and your children to consider."

He went and stood by the fire.

Livinia looked so alone, so abandoned. He was a cad for letting his feelings go this far. "I'm going back to the battlefield. I have do my duty, Livinia, and so must you."

The brightness in her dimmed. "I hoped we could help each other get through this terrible war."

"I am sorry."

She averted her gaze. He'd hurt her and was deeply sorry.

Livinia took a pair of gloves out of her coat pocket. "So that is how it is?"

"That's the only way it can be."

She jerked on her gloves. "Of course you are right. Perhaps when the war is over."

"Yes. After the worst is behind us." Wishing to avoid further admonitions, he sat down in his chair, his back to her. Easier this way, he decided. He could not let her see how he ached to hold her again.

"I'd better be going," she said, her speech clipped, her tone filled with regret. "I can stop in the morning if you'd like."

"You've indulged me enough." He hated that she would leave yet he could not encourage her. "I will be all right."

She opened the door. "Your lunch is warming in the kitchen," she said as cold as the wind invading the room.

"A hot meal will be appreciated."

"You will rest?"

"Of course," he said firmly.

She left, and the room felt empty without her.

James hobbled to the window to catch one last glimpse of her. Her hair, entangled by the breeze, whipped around the brim of her hat. Her complexion was the color of the last roses.

How he wished circumstances could have been different. He could not give in to his desires. Emotions were unreliable and only served to interfere with the discipline required of him.

"Blast." Her parting wounded him deeper than any of the Hun's ordinance ever could.

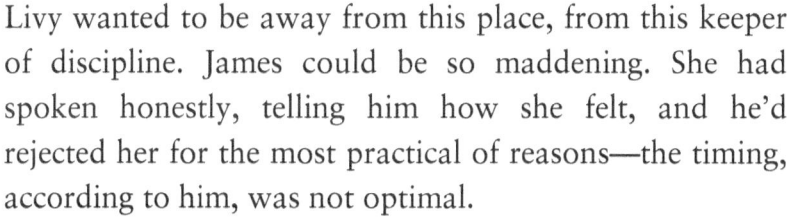

Livy wanted to be away from this place, from this keeper of discipline. James could be so maddening. She had spoken honestly, telling him how she felt, and he'd rejected her for the most practical of reasons—the timing, according to him, was not optimal.

When was a good time to fall in love? For surely love

was what she'd felt in his embrace.

A claxon blared. Gwendolyn arrived driving her new Daimler and skidded across a patch of gravel. She'd brought the children and Lady. The girls waved. Livy affected a smile even though she was still angry. Angry at a man who reminded her of duty. Angry at the war that called him away when she needed him.

"Why are you here?" Livy asked as they spilled out of the motor and gathered around her.

"Grandmamma said we could," Winnie replied.

The girls searched Livy's face. Had they guessed her distress? Did they believe they were the cause?

Livy gave them both a hug. "I'm very glad to see you."

"Don't be cross with them," Gwendolyn said. "I insisted. I stopped by Fairview only to discover you were still here at the cottage. The girls and I decided Uncle could use some cheering up."

James could use a great deal of cheering up, Livy decided, but he was determined to be unhappy with his lot and that was the end of the matter.

"We'll all be late for Sunday services," Livy told them.

Gwendolyn scoffed at her objection. "There's plenty of time. I'll return you to the farm in the motor."

"We promised to pray doubly hard if we could come," Grace confessed.

Livy dreaded going back into the cottage but she couldn't confide to Gwendolyn why, especially with the girls present.

Seeing the children had tamped down her anger and their arrival reminded Livy she was needed at home. She shook off her temper for their sake and relented. "You may call on the major to say hello, but then we must hurry home."

"Dr. Bainbridge telephoned me and explained the situation," Gwendolyn said. "I've not brought ice as requested. There's none left from the summer stores."

"Ice was meant to help with the swelling." Livy shook her head in dismay. "There must be some that could be done."

"Oh, but there is. I've called for some blocks to be sent down from London. They should arrive tomorrow."

"Your uncle needs more than ice. Dr. Bainbridge believes the major should consult with a surgeon, but he refuses."

Gwendolyn didn't appear at all disturbed by this news. "Let me talk to him."

"A good idea. He listens to you."

The girls scampered down the path, the dog at their heels. Livy could've called them back, but she didn't.

Gwendolyn unloaded a large hamper and followed the parade to the cottage.

Livy didn't have to knock. James opened the door as they approached. She searched his face for a reaction. Thankfully, he didn't look too vexed at her return.

"Look who's here," Livy said. "You remember Winifred and Grace."

Livy would not apologize. This was an invasion and

James had every reason to be cross, yet she sensed the children's laughter and exuberance would be a tonic.

"Hello," they said in unison.

"Hello," he replied.

"Uncle." Gwendolyn kissed him on the cheek. "We thought you'd like a bit of company. It's a beautiful morning. Did you see the frost?"

"I've been resting," he said.

Livinia pierced him with a look he was beginning to recognize. James amended his greeting. "Yes. Yes. A splendid morning."

"I wanted to make sure you were all right," Gwendolyn said.

He narrowed his eyes and blocked their entry. "Which I would be if I wasn't expected to answer the door."

Oh dear, Livinia thought. Have I pushed him too far? She took a deep breath, unsure what she should do.

James had been watching the cheerful domestic scene from the window. The two little girls were two miniature versions of their mother in wool coats in a most becoming blue color trimmed with rabbit. Their hats had been fashioned to cover their ears, but feathery curls stuck out at the brim. At the end of the ties were two pompoms looking like snowballs.

Gwendolyn wore her mink—lined motoring coat and wide-brimmed hat tied under her chin. They were a welcome sight, he wouldn't deny it.

Livinia had come with them. They'd already said their good-byes, as painful as that had been. And as necessary.

"Aren't you going to invite us in?" Remarkable how Gwendolyn framed her requests as a question when she'd no intention of taking no for an answer.

He stepped aside, outnumbered. He'd had a rough night, but he could not bring himself to send them away. He could manage two children and some light conversation.

They filed across the threshold, including the dog. The little girls squealed with delight when the cur jumped into his chair and began to dig at the upholstery.

"See here," James said in a commanding voice.

The dog leapt into the arms of one of the girls and began to bark. The girl turned a petulant face to him. "He meant no harm."

James realized he'd spoken more harshly than was required with children.

"Major Gunnison needs the chair for himself," Livinia said over the noise. She motioned for him to sit. "Girls, you must settle down at once."

Livinia took control of the situation admirably, James would be the first to admit. He sat down.

The girls flanked him on both sides.

Gwendolyn beamed. "We've brought you something good to eat."

It was on the tip of his tongue to tell her he wasn't hungry, that Livinia had already amply provided a bracing cup of tea, but he quelled his objections.

Instead, he responded as any gentleman would. "How very good of you."

His response sealed his fate. They unbuttoned their coats and untied their hats and left them in a pile on the cane chair. Apparently, they intended to stay.

Gwendolyn pushed his book aside and set the hamper on his side table.

The dog found one of his carpet slippers and carried it off, no doubt for a chew.

"Lady, give that back." The little girls cried in unison and gave chase—running around his chair screaming and laughing.

James wasn't used to this kind of familiarity—it came so natural to these girls, as if they were in their own home.

"That's quite enough." Livinia's command interrupted their game. She picked up the dog and extracted the slipper.

Livinia did not admonish them further. As it turned out, there was no need. They settled down and became the sweetest of girls with angelic faces.

James sat back in his chair. He'd almost forgotten what children were like: Noisy and contentious, going off in all directions at once.

He'd not been allowed such liberties as a child. Instead, he remembered sitting quietly in the parlor with his invalid mother. Father hadn't allowed him to speak unless he'd been spoken to.

These were not memories the Pratt children would have.

"No harm done," he said and couldn't believe he had been so agreeable.

Livinia handed him the slipper. "Best you keep these on your feet."

"Yes, Mrs. Pratt."

The girls giggled and all was sorted satisfactorily.

"What has your cook sent?" Livinia proceeded to unpack the many wondrous items Gwendolyn's cook had made.

"Oat porridge," Gwendolyn explained when Livy held up a tin. "Cook always says oat porridge will cure every kind of ailment."

Livinia showed him a pie she'd plucked from the depths of the hamper. "Oh, how wonderful. This game pie is still warm from the oven."

James sniffed. The smell was mouthwatering. How very odd, when only minutes before, he couldn't stand the idea of food.

"You must have a slice of this pie," Livinia picked up the hamper and carried it into the kitchen.

"A feast fit for a King," Gwendolyn said, following her.

Which left James with the girls. They giggled again. Apparently, this was their reaction to everything. Their cheeks were rosy and their eyes shone with wonder. They'd seen porridge and pies before, of course, but opening the hamper had been fun game for them. Now they stared at him.

Thankfully, Gwendolyn returned before any questions were asked. "Livy thinks you should eat in here." She removed the book to the mantelshelf and dragged the side table closer to him.

"He needs a fork and knife," the older child told her sister.

The girl skipped away. She returned with the utensils and a jar of honey. Her mother carried a loaf of bread and a slice of pie on a plate.

"Gwendolyn, you've thought of everything," Livinia said as she put the food on the small table.

They buzzed around him like bees around a hive. He'd never known this kind of attention and would have to say it wasn't as bad as he might have imagined. Except for the beast, who poked his nose in every corner of the room, looking for mischief, no doubt.

They watched him in earnest as he buttered the bread. The jar of honey was open. He added a teaspoonful and spread it around with the back of the spoon.

Their gazes followed him as he took a bite.

"Is it all right?" the youngest asked.

It seemed terribly important to them that he enjoy his meal, so he stifled any comments he'd been harboring about the dog and cleared his throat.

"I must say this is the best honey I've ever had."

The girls broke out in delightful grins.

"I'm glad you like it," Gwendolyn said. "We have our own hives."

"Would you like to play a card game when you've finished?" One of the girls reached into her pocket and pulled out a packet.

"We can't stay, girls." Livinia spoke firmly. They frowned. He hated to see their disappointment.

"Perhaps another time," James replied. That seemed to satisfy them both.

Livinia picked up their coats and hats, scowling. He'd made a promise he couldn't keep.

"The doctor rang us up again this morning." Gwendolyn shot her uncle a stern look. "He's very concerned about your knee."

Ah, so that explained the real reason for this unorthodox visit. The good doctor sought reinforcements in his campaign to convince his patient to seek additional medical treatment.

"He needn't have bothered."

"I think you should tell me why you refuse Dr. Bainbridge's advice." Gwendolyn waited for a reply with arms folded.

"The doctor was most emphatic the major seek a surgeon's opinion immediately," Livinia added. "Dr. Bainbridge believes your uncle should go to London at once."

Both women looked at him for an explanation.

He snorted, but for naught. He was surrounded. "I do not wish to see any more doctors."

"Don't be so obstinate," Gwendolyn said. She put her arm around his shoulder and gave him a kiss on the cheek. All that was harsh and mean drifted away. The soft brush of soft lips, a whiff of French perfume, the tenderness of Gwendolyn's feelings put him in a better place.

James took a calming breath before he spoke. "Your doctor is an overly cautious man. I've had these bouts before and they right themselves. All I need is some peace and quiet."

"At the very least, you could move up to our house," Gwendolyn said, "where we can look after you properly."

He didn't need incessant pestering at the big house. He'd managed perfectly well in this cottage.

For some reason, Livinia smiled. Even her eyes smiled, which perplexed him. He'd done nothing to merit her good will and yet there she stood, looking like she could see right through him.

He could think of any way around her request. "I will consider going back to London. The city appears to be the only place where I will get any rest."

"Thank you." Gwendolyn squeezed his arm.

He was relieved she didn't insist he leave right this minute.

"Girls, we must be going," Livinia said.

"Do we have to leave so soon?" Grace asked.

"We have been here long enough. Now, I really must ask you to put on your coats." She helped them with their warm clothing. "We will be late arriving at church as it is."

He started to get out of his chair.

Livinia stopped him with a steady hand. "You, sir, must stay right where you are and keep off that leg."

Gwendolyn flanked him on the other side. "Promise me you will."

He promised. To do otherwise would've been churlish and ungrateful.

Gwendolyn tugged on her gloves. "Uncle, I will be around this afternoon to see how you are coming along."

"That's a splendid idea," Livinia said. She didn't include herself.

"You will take your tablets?" Livinia was a lady, he realized, who left no stone unturned.

"I will follow the doctor's orders to the letter."

"Then I will leave you to rest." She ushered the two children and their dog out the door.

The motor's engine rumbled and doors slammed. The party of well-wishers left, and soon all James could hear was the ticking of the mantel clock.

It'd been quite a morning, he reflected. He'd found the children's natural ebullience fortifying.

The empty room disturbed him. He missed Livinia—her feminine presence—even her constant nagging.

Stuff and nonsense.

Thank goodness they've all gone, he decided. Much better this way. He shoved the bread, heavy with butter and honey, into his mouth and chewed.

Chapter Eighteen

→→→⫸⫷←←←

"Grandmamma says you were very wrong not to come home last night," Gracie said from the back seat as Gwendolyn raced down the road.

Winnie nodded solemnly next to her, holding Lady in her lap.

"Did she?" Livy wasn't surprised Mother Pratt had jumped to conclusions about what had taken place in the cottage last night, but she shouldn't have speculated in front of the little girls.

"I'm very sorry to have caused you to worry. I asked Mrs. Asher to ring up Grandmamma and tell her the circumstances."

"Oh, she did," Gracie said.

Gwendolyn nodded. "Your mother-in-law was very concerned, as you would expect."

Livy couldn't imagine why. "Then you know the major wasn't feeling well and needed someone to stay with him."

Both girls took the explanation in stride.

"Elizabeth told us a German soldier shot him," Winnie said. "That's why he limps and walks with a stick."

Livy wondered how much she should tell them. She felt protective of their innocence. "He wasn't shot. A bomb exploded and pieces of metal cut his leg."

"Will he recover?" Gracie asked.

"His injury is not healing as it should," Livy replied. "His recovery may take a while longer."

"How long, do you think?" Gracie seemed most anxious about the major's wound.

"With proper medical care, not so very long." Livy hoped her optimism wasn't misplaced.

"He won't have to walk with a limp forever, will he?"

"I don't know, my dear."

"Will he go back to the war when he's well?" Winnie asked.

Livy found the question distressing. "Of course. That is his duty. He must do what is expected of him."

She exchanged looks with Gwendolyn.

"You mustn't worry about the major," Gwendolyn said cheerfully. "He'll return to the front in fighting form and protect us from those nasty Germans. He's a very good soldier, you know."

Thankfully, the girls did not ask any more questions. What Gwendolyn said was true, Livy realized. The country needed him.

They arrived at Fairview and Livy thanked Gwendolyn for the ride. The children jumped down from the motor. With Lady at their heels, they climbed the steps and disappeared inside the house.

"You were very good to stay with my uncle," Gwendolyn replied. "I would make a terrible nurse."

"I hope he will be better soon," Livy said.

"He's an awfully good sort." Gwendolyn spoke as if Livy needed reminding.

"I know."

"Do stop by and keep him company," Gwendolyn said.

"I don't think that's such a good idea," Livy answered. "Maybe he will rest better if we're not there."

"I suppose you are right." With a wave of her hand and then shifting gears, she was off.

Livy hurried inside the house. They'd only minutes to spare before it was time to leave for church. Grace and Winnie ran off to greet their grandmamma, who waited in the parlor for their return.

Livy followed. She had something important to say to her mother-in-law.

"Livinia, at last." Her mother-in-law gave her a quick perusal. "You gave us all quite a scare last night. I couldn't sleep from worry."

Livy sincerely doubted her mother-in-law had lost sleep over her absence. She didn't apologize.

"We brought Major Gunnison his breakfast," Grace said. "He was so pleased."

She turned to Livy for confirmation.

Winifred giggled. "Lady found one of the major's carpet slippers and we had a jolly good time trying to catch him."

Livy smiled at the memory of the major being circled by shrieking children and the excitable dog. His mood had improved, having the children there.

Mother Pratt turned to Livy. "Is that what you were doing, entertaining the major? I was led to believe the man has nearly recovered from his war wounds."

"Oh, he had been," Livy replied "but he took a turn quite suddenly."

Mother Pratt smirked.

Certainly Gwendolyn had told her about the infection? Why was she playing cat and mouse? here

"Gwendolyn called the doctor," Livy continued to explain. "Naturally, she was as concerned as I was. The doctor came and gave the major morphine by injection."

"I'm sure the local doctor did what he thought best, but why did you find it necessary to stay the night?"

"We both felt the patient couldn't be left alone."

"You have no medical training." Mother Pratt's face was twisted into a frown. Winning the lady's approval was never easy.

"While I have no formal training," Livy replied indignantly, "I have a great deal of experience with injections of morphine and caring for an invalid, as you well know."

Mother Pratt's mouth snapped shut. Being reminded of Charles's illness and prolonged suffering brought a sickly pallor to her complexion.

She didn't stay silent for long. "I fail to see how the little experience you might have justifies spending the night with a gentleman you barely know."

Both girls looked at her wide-eyed.

"What would you have had me do?" Livy asked.

"There were many others who could've taken care of him. His own people, for example."

"Gwendolyn and her husband don't have the experience I have. It didn't seem necessary to ask someone to come from town when I was already there."

"No, you took it upon yourself to take care of a man who is for all intents and purposes a stranger. In my day…"

Livy interrupted. "Propriety didn't seem as important as helping a neighbor in need. He required nursing care, which I was able to provide."

Livy wouldn't be shamed. She'd stayed because she couldn't imagine anyone being alone at such a critical time. There was no telling what might have happened if she hadn't been there when James relived his night terrors and almost pitched over in the darkness.

Mother Pratt stiffened. She was not used to being talked to in this manner, Livy knew, but she soldiered on. She could not let her mother-in-law cast doubt upon Livy's reputation.

"Besides," she continued, fighting to control the tremor in her voice, "I don't consider him a stranger. James is very much my friend."

Her mother-in-law's eyes narrowed. The lines in her face deepened. "What kind of friend, may I ask?"

"A good one, I'm proud to say."

Mother Pratt harrumphed. What a revolting sound, Livy decided, to come out of a person who professed to be a lady.

"Next you will tell me you intend to continue seeing the man."

Oh, if Mother Pratt only knew the half of what Livy was feeling!

"I will certainly help if I'm needed," Livy replied.

Livy would say no more in front of Winnie and Grace.

Fortunately, Mother Pratt made no further additions to her concerns. The spat between them was over for now.

"Where's Elizabeth?"

"Gone on to church," Mother Pratt replied. "Where we should be. Have you lost all track of time?"

"I have not." Livy let go of her anger, for both of their sakes. "If you'll excuse me, I'll go change."

Mother Pratt nodded. "Be quick about it. You'll make us late if you don't hurry."

After church services and a luncheon of roasted chicken, the two younger girls sat with their grandmamma in the parlor sewing a cross-stitch sampler while Livy did the washing up. Elizabeth had stayed in town to visit a friend and wouldn't be back until dusk.

They looked up when Livy entered the room. It was rare to see them so quiet. Under the guidance of the old woman, the girls were learning to be young ladies.

"Run along, girls. Your mother and I have important matters to discuss."

Clearly, Mother Pratt had more to say about Livinia's comings and goings and was not to be denied her time of judgment.

Grace and Winnie jumped to their feet and placed their sewing in a pile next to their grandmother. They ran to Livy and gave her a hug as if they hadn't seen her in ages. Did they sense Livy and Grandmamma were about to quarrel?

Livy petted Grace's hair. She did so love the energy of her youngest children, their wiggling bodies and their boundless enthusiasm.

"May we go out into the back garden?" Winnie asked.

"Heavens no," Mother Pratt said. "There is far too much mud. Go to your rooms and find more sedate occupations."

They looked up at Livy. She was too tired to fight their cause. "Do as you're told."

The little girls kissed their grandmamma on the cheek and skipped out of the room. Livy took a place on the sofa.

Livy was grateful they would not hear what she had to say, for she was not about to sit quietly and listen to a reprimand she didn't deserve.

"I did nothing wrong," Livy said, addressing Mother Pratt when the girls were far enough away that they wouldn't hear.

"I'm so very glad."

Livy didn't like the sarcasm in her tone. It wasn't necessary.

Mother Pratt stabbed at her needlepoint. "I don't mind telling you, when my son was alive he kept a respectable household."

Her mother-in-law was being unfair. Livy's ire took over. "Charles would've expected all of us to do our part with this terrible war raging."

"Within reason, surely."

"How have I been unreasonable?"

"Your behavior of late has confused all of us."

"You needn't be concerned." Livy knew what this was really about.

They all had suffered a great loss when Charles had died. Nobody had forgotten about him. He'd been a loving father, a wonderful man in so many respects, but he'd not been perfect.

Mother Pratt meant to intimidate, Livy knew full well, to bully her about her lack of devotion to Charles's memory and her marriage.

Nothing could be more false or unfair.

"I miss Charles very much," Livy said calmly.

"He wouldn't have tolerated such conduct."

"He was a Christian man and didn't turn away from helping others."

Mother Pratt's severe expression softened a tiny bit. "He was an excellent person in all respects."

"I will always honor his memory."

Mother Pratt shook her head. "And yet you are willing to drag the Pratt name through the mire with your wanton behavior."

Livy was close to tears. The woman could be cruel. The conversation had wrenched the last bit of strength from her.

Seeking escape, she stood. "Perhaps it is best we reserve our arrows for another time."

"Your children have all sorts of questions."

"I will speak to them."

"You had better. You know how young imaginations can run wild."

Livy took a deep breath to steady her nerves. Now she understood why Mother Pratt had relented and allowed Grace and Winnie to join Gwendolyn for a ride to the cottage. She'd wanted the children to find their mother in a compromising situation.

"If there's nothing more, I'm going upstairs." She could not tolerate being in the same room with the woman.

"Oh, but there is. I've had a rather disturbing talk with Elizabeth."

Livy's blood froze. She'd not thought Elizabeth brave enough to confide the difficulty with Mr. Morehouse to her grandmother.

She collapsed into the nearest chair and faced the old woman. "I'm surprised she told you."

"Of course she would tell me. The question is what are you going to do about it?"

Livy found the question perplexing. "What more can I do?"

"Forbid her to take such a drastic course of action."

Relief came like a spring thaw. They were talking about Elizabeth's decision to join the nursing corps, not her adventurous romance.

"She is determined," Livy said.

"Her emotions are unreliable. You cannot allow her to make her own decisions."

"I asked her to wait until she turned eighteen."

"Without success, it seems. Try harder. Of course, I made my wishes known." Mother Pratt sniffed. "Elizabeth ignored me."

"I'm very sorry. I'm sure she meant no disrespect."

"I'm not so very certain," she replied. "In my opinion, you are raising these children to be ill-mannered heathens."

The remark was unfair but Livy wouldn't fight any longer, not with someone who refused to listen. "I will speak to her."

"What have you done about her prospects?"

Livy sighed. She'd done woefully little. "I admit I've been neglectful."

"Before we know it, she'll run off with some unsuitable character from a disreputable family."

Mother Pratt had hit the mark remarkably well.

"I will try and do better by Elizabeth."

"Her future is by no means secure."

"She will be all right. She's hardly an old maid."

"When I was her age, I asked my father's permission when I wanted to go out of the house. He arraigned my marriage to a suitable gentleman. His choice worked out well. What is wrong with girls today? They act as if they'd a will of their own."

Livy suppressed a quick retort. Hadn't she wondered the same thing? "It's the war. Everyone is so unsure of what comes next. Elizabeth wants to help."

"Naturally. We all do."

"She wants to be a nurse."

"Nursing simply won't do. I blame you. You have set a poor example. My son would have never allowed his family to go off willy-nilly to empty bedpans or perform other such menial tasks."

"You don't know that for a certainty."

Mother Pratt carried on as if she hadn't heard. "My greatest fear is Elizabeth will turn into one of those radical women."

Livy wasn't sure what that meant. Did Elizabeth want to steer her own course? Did Elizabeth possess the courage to give her opinion? Was she ready to fight for what was right?

Livy hoped so. Their world was changing. Her daughter should not be expected to give up on demanding her voice be heard.

"She has her father's independent streak," she replied.

Mother Pratt blinked several times. Her son, a Londoner, had taken up farming against the wishes of his family. He'd been earmarked for greater things, according to his mother, but chose the country life instead.

His choice had been a bone in her mother-in-law's throat, and apparently continued to lodge there. Mentioning it, however, appeared to have put an end to any further speculation about Elizabeth's choices.

"If you will excuse me, I must go to my bedchamber," Livy said as she rose from her chair.

Mother Pratt looked up from her needlepoint. "There is one more thing I need to say before you go. The girls and I have been talking about their future."

The woman spoke with a haughty aloofness that never failed to grate on Livy's nerves.

Livy met her gaze. "I'm happy you have such a good relationship with them that they would share their dreams and desires."

"Which they have done." Mother Pratt pursed her lips. "Given the circumstances, I'd like them to come to London with me."

Livy remembered the eager faces of Grace and Winnie as they sat next to their grandmamma talking about the city. "Of course they can go. A holiday in London would do wonders for their education."

Mother Pratt exhaled. "I don't mean for a visit. I intend to take custody of the children."

The room was so quiet Livy first believed this was a dream.

"I beg your pardon?"

"From what I've observed, the girls are neglected."

Livy's stomach churned. Had she neglected her children? She'd been so occupied with the summer's harvest, and then Wyatt's departure, they'd not spent any time together in the last few weeks.

"What you are asking is out of the question," Livy said.

"Surely you can appreciate how difficult it is for me to tell you this." Her mother-in-law surveyed Livy from head to toe and frowned. "I've observed your household is out of your control."

Livy couldn't deny there were times she felt the same way. "As you know, Charles was the disciplinarian, and I admit the household did run more smoothly when he was alive."

Mother Pratt drove home her point like a stick in the eye. "I'm sure you'll agree I'm better equipped to take care of two growing girls. Think of all the opportunities they will have living with me."

Livy wasn't about to give in. "I don't agree at all. The girls belong here at home with their family."

"A family that is dwindling."

Livy cast her gaze out the window. "True, Wyatt has gone, and Elizabeth plans to leave shortly, but the girls and I will manage, and we will be here with open arms when the older children return."

"What of their schooling?"

"They are happy at the village school."

Mother Pratt sniffed. "What do they learn at this rural school?"

"What is necessary."

"They are better off in London where they can form good attachments in the best social circles."

"They have an abundance of friends."

"And what of this farm?" Mother Pratt continued. "Do you really think you can keep this place running?"

Livy had reached her breaking point. "I have lived here at Fairview all my life. I know how to farm perfectly well."

"I see you are determined. There is another concern, however. A concern that has just come to my attention."

The woman was relentless, Livy decided.

"Your relationship with Major Gunnison will cause some unsavory speculation."

"Only if you encourage and support it."

"Are you telling me there's nothing between the two of you?"

"What I am saying is what the major and I do is none of your business."

Livy heard the gasp. She'd not argued so strongly with her mother-in-law before, but the woman had pushed her to the edge.

"Just as I thought." Mother Pratt's voice was as crisp as a starched collar. "As a precaution, I shall make the necessary arrangements."

Livy could take no more. "You'll not have my children."

"We shall soon see, won't we?" Her mother-in-law glared at her. "You will hear from my solicitor in due time."

Livy prayed she wouldn't lose her temper. Why was her mother-in-law being so obstinate? Did she really think a mother would give up her children so willingly?

"Why do you think the law will help you? I am their mother. The law will favor me."

Mother Pratt's smile was not pleasant. "You forget my father was a barrister and my grandfather sat the bench. I am very well connected in the legal community, my dear, very well connected indeed. Heed my words. I will not fail."

Livy could no longer rein in her anger. "I think you had better return to London. The sooner the better."

Mother Pratt's head snapped back as if she'd been slapped.

Livy turned and left the room, but not in triumph. The woman had not made an idle threat. In the days ahead, she'd try to turn the girls against her and would continue to tell them her 'concerns.'

The devious woman meant to take Winnie and Grace away from their home, but she wouldn't succeed in such a scheme.

Livinia Pratt wouldn't be bullied any longer.

Chapter Nineteen

Mother Pratt left before breakfast, refusing even a cup of coffee. She didn't demand an apology, and Livy hadn't been inclined to offer one.

The wretched woman had kissed the girls warmly. "Remember what we talked about. When you come to London, we will go shopping in Piccadilly."

Gracie clapped her hands. "Can I buy a new dress?"

"Of course, my dear. You can have as many dresses as you want."

"We will have great fun, won't we, Winnie?"

Her sister didn't seem as certain. She accepted her grandmother's kiss and turned to look at Livy.

Livy smiled. She thought it important to show herself to be a mother who could be gracious and generous, even as she watched the children being bribed to go and live with their grandmother in a city bright and shiny with new things.

Elizabeth was last in line to say goodbye. Today her hemline was modestly at her ankles and her face bare of any cosmetics.

"You will come to visit me when you are in London?" Mother Pratt said.

Elizabeth kissed her on both cheeks. "Yes, Grand-mamma. I am looking forward to it."

Her reply seemed to satisfy her grandmother—for the moment, at least.

Livy and her mother-in-law stood toe to toe. There wasn't any pretense of affection, not even for the benefit of the girls.

"You'll be hearing from my solicitor," Mother Pratt said.

Livy grasped her hands together. She would not crumble in the face of such adversity. "I'd hoped you had reconsidered."

"I only need to take a look at these primitive surroundings to convince me, more than ever, these children should be brought up where their father had been."

"This is the home Charles and I made for them."

Mother Pratt tilted her head as if she was some exotic bird who didn't understand a word Livy had said.

"Then do what you must," Livy replied stiffly. "You will be wasting your money on the services of a solicitor. The law is on my side."

Mother Pratt raised her nose a notch. "Don't be so sure."

A stone-faced chauffeur opened the door of the motor car and Mother Pratt slithered inside.

The girls waved, and the Daimler started with a jolt, smoke billowing from the tail pipe.

They all shivered in the cold as the motor chugged away. Elizabeth rubbed her arms and hurried back into the house. Livy and the little girls were right behind her.

"What did Grandmamma mean about a solicitor?" Winnie chewed on her lower lip. Naturally, her girls would be curious about their grandmother's parting words.

"She wishes for you to come and live with her in London."

"Can we bring Lady?" Gracie asked.

"She means permanently," Winnie said too solemnly for her tender years.

Gracie looked at Livy and then back at her sister. "You mean leave Fairview forever?"

"Of course, you ninny. That's what permanent means."

Livy headed for the kitchen. "That's not going to happen."

"She's going to try, isn't she?" Winnie trailed after her.

"Yes," Livy replied, "but don't worry, she won't be successful."

"I should like to go to London, but only for a visit," Grace said behind her.

"And we shall one day," Livy said, trying to sound reassuring. "Only I won't allow the family to be separated. We must stay together."

Winnie crossed her arms. Rarely had Livy seen her defiant. How unfair to put both girls' lives in such turmoil. Livy must continue to show confidence she didn't feel.

Thankfully, her comment brought a full stop to their questions. Her emotions weren't fully in her control after this latest battle with Mother Pratt, and she didn't want to break down in tears in front of them.

She'd done her best to persuade the girls all would be well in the very near future. Had she said enough? What about her own misgivings that'd taken root in her heart?

As Livy prepared their breakfast, she thought about James, worried actually, lest he become entangled in this distasteful situation.

Livy handed the little girls a wire basket and they scrambled out the back door to collect fresh eggs.

"How can Grandmamma insist on having Winnie and Grace live with her?" Elizabeth arrived and put on her smock.

"She's lonely, I suspect."

"You won't let her take them?" She frowned as she set the table.

"Of course not." Livy poured herself a cup of coffee. "I think she misses your father."

Elizabeth scoffed. "We all do."

"We are a family and we will stay together." Livy spoke resolutely, "which includes your grandmother."

Elizabeth kissed her on the cheek. "Mother, you are such a foolish old dear. Of course we will stay together. How do you intend to convince Grandmamma?"

"Not so old," she said. "As far as what can be done

about a woman who can be trying, I haven't a clue."

Livy didn't ring up the solicitor the very next morning as she'd intended. Laundry day was at full throttle, and she couldn't neglect her duties at the farm any longer. Dear Mrs. Heath had been given an overdue day off, and so it would be Elizabeth and her sharing the dolly stick.

Besides, she was hopeful Mother Pratt's ambition of taking custodial care of her children would meet a chilly response from her advisors and the matter would be dropped.

When she arrived in the kitchen, Elizabeth had already boiled the first tub full of linens and was cranking them through the mangle. She'd become remarkably companionable since Mother Pratt's departure. They hadn't argued once.

They worked for several hours until exhaustion overtook Livy and she sat down on the cracked slate of the back step. The bed sheets—hung out to dry on the clothesline—snapped in the breeze.

Elizabeth stayed in the house to finish another load.

Livy couldn't help but wonder how James was faring. Gwendolyn was a good sort and seemed genuinely concerned about her uncle, but there a tendency in her to minimize the gravity of a situation. Livy knew all too well the how seriously infection could compromise a person's health.

Perhaps she should ring up Gwendolyn and ask if she would look in at the cottage, but then thought better of it. James needed his rest and she knew all too well he wouldn't sit still in her company.

Mother Pratt had no cause to be concerned about the major, and yet Livy had let her leave Fairview believing there was more than a friendship brewing between them. It'd been a cruel thing to do. Except her mother-in-law would believe what she wanted to believe.

What James had told her about duty was the truth of the matter. Their loyalties were required by others. There could be nothing more between them except friendship.

Livy should've made that clear to Mother Pratt.

Elizabeth came outside carrying the morning post. Her daughter waited eagerly for the postman every morning and afternoon and was growing impatient for her answer about the nursing corps.

"Anything from Wyatt?" Livy tried not to sound too anxious.

"No," she handed the stack to Livy, "but you know how he loathes to put pen to paper."

Livy picked through the letters. Her son had been gone for more than two weeks and they'd yet to hear from him. Livy, on the other hand, had written him a lengthy letter every evening since his departure and posted it promptly the next day. She would write another tonight.

What was this? She held up a snowy white envelope postmarked from London. She did not recognize the name

Biggs and Dolton, Esquires, on the return.

Elizabeth sat down and tucked her legs underneath her. "Who is the letter from?"

"I'm not sure." Except she did know. A letter from London could mean only one thing.

"Open it." Elizabeth didn't reach for the letter as she might have done in the past.

Livy broke the seal and opened the vellum. As she suspected, the letter was from Mother Pratt's solicitors. The words blurred as she perused the message. She looked up and met Elizabeth's gaze.

"Would you like me to read it to you?" her daughter asked.

"No, I can manage." She did so, her anger building. When she'd finished, the letter dropped from her hand to the floor. She made no effort to pick it up.

"What does it say?" Elizabeth asked.

Livy was flooded with outrage. She'd not given Mother Pratt enough credit for being vindictive. Nor had she thought the woman capable of such spitefulness.

She took a deep breath. "Your grandmother has filed a complaint in court concerning my competency in raising Grace and Winnie."

"You must be joking. There must be some mistake."

"The claim is my behavior of late is immoral. That I am unsuitable to be the children's mother."

Elizabeth snatched up the letter and read the vicious charges.

When she finished, she looked at Livy. Her cheeks had

gone quite pink. "Why would she tell such a lie?"

Livy inclined her head. The very idea Mother Pratt believed something unseemly had gone on between Livy and James was laughable. What she felt for him was not sordid or wrong.

"Because of the night I spent at the gamekeeper's cottage."

"You were nursing Major Gunnison. Nobody could fault you for helping him."

"Let's hope a judge is as understanding."

Elizabeth tossed the letter aside. "You must go and see Father's solicitor at once and ask him what you must do."

Livy straightened. She couldn't fall apart in front of Elizabeth. "Yes, I quite agree. I shouldn't have assumed the matter had only been a threat."

"I will go with you."

"Thank you, my dear, but I must handle this myself." Her breathing had steadied. The shock was beginning to wear off.

Elizabeth stood and began pacing. "You will have to ask the major to write a testimonial on your behalf."

Livy didn't want to involve him.

"Mother, did you hear me?"

Livy looked up. Elizabeth had stopped her pacing and was staring at her, concern marring her lovely face.

"I don't want to ask the major for his help in the matter," Livy said.

"You can't think he would not be forthcoming? He's really the most kindest and decent of men."

Ever since the unfortunate incident with Mr. Morehouse, Elizabeth had been the major's most ardent
admirer.

Livy shook her head. "I know he's honorable and I'm
certain he would champion my cause, but ..."

"What is it?"

"I'm loath to bring this travesty to his attention. It's
shameful."

"I'm sorry, Mother, telling him would be embarrass-
ing, but it must be done." Elizabeth put her hand on
Livy's shoulder. "There's something else, isn't there?"

Livy looked at her grown daughter, so capable, so
willing to steer her own course. They'd become confidants, which would strengthen their bond in the years
ahead.

"You will think me hopeless."

Elizabeth's eyes sparkled with affection. "You have
grown fond of the major, haven't you?"

"I suppose I have."

"Why do your feelings seem hopeless to you?"

"It is not a good time for such things."

"You mean romance?" Elizabeth smiled. "And why
not?"

Livy had wrestled with the question ever since she'd
left James to fend for himself. When he'd reminded of
how irresponsible and selfish it would be to fall in love,
she had quelled her desire.

"Mother, I asked you a question."

Livy must be brave. "He's got a job to do."

"Of course he does." Elizabeth sat down beside her. "Do you fear he isn't attracted to you? That your feelings aren't reciprocated?"

"I'm sure they are."

A tiny spark of electricity burst white-hot throughout Livy, igniting the panic and joy that comes from the realization love had found her again.

"Then it's settled. You must see him at once."

Livy smiled weakly.

Elizabeth grinned. "I'm so happy for you. You can't let him go back to the war without telling him exactly how you feel."

"I will think about it," she said, as if affairs of the heart were merely an everyday matter.

She couldn't lose the girls.

"Don't wait too long," Elizabeth said. Then she did something she hadn't done in a great while—she gave her mother a hug.

Chapter Twenty

>>>—<<<

The sun was sinking into the treetops when Livy set off for town in the trap with a stop planned for the gamekeeper's cottage. She didn't know exactly what she would say to James Gunnison. She would like to leave him out of this mess completely, but Elizabeth was right. Livy must ask for his help.

How would she even start?

A letter from the major would confirm what had happened. No one would question his authority or his integrity. Livy'd done nothing wrong, and a judge would have to agree.

As to the other question, Livy would leave to the future. She could not share her feelings with him, knowing he was opposed to giving in to his own.

Livy stopped the mare in front of the gate. She was happy to see smoke wafting from the chimney and a light in the window. She wondered which major she would find this day: The gruff man who pushed people away or the man who could be charming and at times even loving.

Anger had put her in a frightful state, and James

would be sure to notice. Coming here was an act of desperation; she would the first to admit. What would he think of her? What would he think of a family that inflicted such wounds on each other?

She should drive away from the cottage and carry on into town. She couldn't. But Mother Pratt's demands must be dealt with. Her lies must be quelled.

Her mother-in-law had never been an agreeable person. Livy had tried to maintain a good relationship with her for the children's sake, but this time she'd gone too far.

Who better than Major Gunnison to put an end to this charade? The major knew what'd happened that night, and no one would question his account.

Her nerves shattered, Livy opened the gate. Her hand shook as she closed it.

Frost crunched with each footfall. She clutched her coat tighter against a strong wind blowing from the north.

The cottage door opened when she reached the first step. James filled the doorway where he stood unaided. Despite her regrets about the purpose of her visit, her heart soared upon seeing him.

"How good to see you up and about," she said.

"Do come in out of the cold." He greeted her with a raised brow, curious, no doubt, why she'd returned.

Livy entered the cozy cottage, the fire radiating warmth. The tray with an empty plate and a cup sat on the small table next to his chair.

"I've interrupted your dinner."

"On the contrary. As you can see, I am done."

Her smile was tepid. She could do no better.

They stood only a few feet apart, two people brought together by extraordinary circumstances. She could not close the gap. Too many things kept them apart.

They'd exhausted social requirements. To talk next about the weather would be absurd. She refused to talk about the war.

Alas, this was not a social occasion as much as one of necessity. She couldn't avoid the purpose of her visit any longer and must speak now. Her words caught in her throat.

"May I take your coat?" he asked.

"No, I can't stay." She wrung her hands, deeply sorry for what she had to say.

"There's something I need to tell you," he said. "I'm leaving for London in the morning."

"You're leaving?"

"I have made an appointment for a consultation with the surgeon. I will be on the first train."

"What a pleasant surprise." She'd hoped he would change his mind and see a specialist.

Still, the news crushed her that he'd soon be gone.

"I hope Ronald and Gwendolyn are going with you."

"They are busy with their own affaires. To be frank, I don't need their help."

She shook her head in dismay.

He invited her to sit down. She started to demur but

the warmth in the room was quite soothing, and she dropped into the cane chair.

He did not join her but stood with his arm resting on the mantelshelf. Of course, he wouldn't show any discomfort while she was here.

How could she explain how her emotions thrashed about quite out of her control? James would be sure to consider such turmoil a personal failing.

For that reason especially, she needed to leave as quickly as possible.

"I've come on a delicate matter. I'm in need of your help."

"My dear Livinia, I am at your service."

"I hate to be a bother, and you can't imagine my embarrassment…" He shifted his feet. "Good lady, what is it?

Livy swallowed, tasting bile. "My mother-in-law is in the process of trying to take the younger girls as wards."

"Indeed."

"I can't let her. That's why I've come." A note of hysteria had crept into her voice.

"What is the basis of her action?"

"She cites my staying here with you overnight as an indiscretion."

He blanched. Livy didn't know if it was from shame or anger, or some other emotion.

"Surely everyone knows that her claim is preposterous," he said.

He was a gentleman of the first order. This obvious

slander had offended him.

"She'd filed in London, where I am not known," Livy replied.

"What can I do to help?"

Livy smiled out of appreciation and gratitude. He would help her fight this injustice. He was a man who could be depended on. How glad she was to have met him.

"Would you be so kind to write a letter to the court to support my character?"

"Of course. At once."

She'd the foresight to bring pen, paper, and ink with her.

He removed the tray to the kitchen, his limp more pronounced than ever. When he returned, he sat down in his chair. She had placed the items on his table. He picked up the pen and scribbled furiously. The petition to the court upset him, which endeared him to her as an ally. There would be no question of impropriety with him on her side.

When he finished, he signed his name with a flourish. "That should suffice," he said with the hint of a smile.

He blew on the ink, having no blotter.

"I'm very grateful." There was not much more she could say.

He folded the letter in half and handed it over. "If you need anything more, don't hesitate to ask."

"Thank you." She stowed it in her reticule and stood. "I'm on my way to the solicitor's office."

As James struggled to his feet, Livy caught a glimpse of distress in his expression, but only for a fleeting moment.

All was not well as he pretended, she realized. How very sad he could not trust her with his feelings.

"After your doctor's visit, will you return to the cottage?"

"No. I will go to my club until the wound heals properly. Then I must return to the front."

"You are to be commended for your dedication to the war effort. I will miss you."

He bowed his head. "My dear, Livinia…"

"Major," she interrupted. "We have come to know each other, and for that I am glad. You have your duty and I have mine. We should not disappoint those who depend on us, should we?"

She'd put the matter as succinctly as she could.

"I appreciate how very understanding you are," he said. "I will not forget your kindness."

"Then this is goodbye." She smiled, not with the smile she had greeted him with but with a genuine smile of appreciation.

He stuck out his hand. "I'm grateful we have become friends."

They shook as good friends do. His hand was warm and his handshake strong. She pulled away before she did something reprehensible to break their truce. She would not give in to her desires this time.

"I must hurry. The solicitor will be waiting," she said.

"Then I won't keep you a moment longer." He opened the door.

She stopped in the doorway. They were close enough to touch, and the floodgates would certainly be opened if he took her in his arms.

"Would it be all right for me and the children to write to you?" she asked.

His face brightened. "I would be delighted to receive your letters."

"Perhaps we can send a lardie cake or a tin of biscuits every so often?"

He bowed slightly. "A pudding will be a most welcome relief from bully beef and stale bread."

"We will be most faithful to your nutritional needs."

She would like to kiss him but held back. Much as she would like to express her love, she didn't. They must say their goodbyes in good humor. She did not wish their parting to end in tears. She held back to protect his well-being as well as her self-respect.

"I will not forget you, Livinia. Your courage is an inspiration."

"I don't know what to say except thank you." She did not consider herself courageous by any stretch of the imagination. Having her praises sung was unexpected but welcome.

"Goodbye," he said.

Surely the most terrible word in all of the English language, she decided.

"Goodbye." She departed, head held high.

James shut the door and sat down heavily in his chair.

Blast it all!

He missed Livinia, had felt nothing but emptiness since Sunday when they'd parted company, even though he'd learned to cope without attachments years ago.

Peace and quiet wasn't the elixir he'd thought it would be.

Meeting Livinia had been a revelation. A home could be a place of warmth and devotion. Livinia had taught him that much. He envied her, her children, her friends, this community.

To think her reputation had been compromised because of her kindness. His letter to the court explained the circumstances of that night she'd stayed with him. He'd stated in no uncertain terms his appreciation for all she had done.

He'd also had a letter in the post. The Army command had been blunt. The doctors agreed if there hadn't been any improvement in his injury, he must consider the possibility his career was over. Indeed, his commander strongly suggested he resign his commission.

The very idea he should give up all he'd known left him cold. He held out hope the Army surgeon could help, and so he would present himself for another examination. James couldn't retire with so much left to do. He couldn't end his career with a war going on.

James heard a noise and twisted around in his chair. He fancied Livinia had returned. The sound was only dried leaves stirred by the wintry air.

He resigned himself to staring at the fire.

He'd closed himself off from Gwendolyn and her husband for what reason? He thought he'd be a burden to them. Instead, he discovered Gwendolyn was a marvelous girl. Her affection made him happy in ways he didn't deserve.

It'd been so long since James had seen his brother. The last time they'd met ended in a terrible row. He remembered the day well. Gwendolyn's mother had been laid to rest.

James had vowed then he was through with the lot of them. He hadn't spoken to Robert since.

What had his pride cost him? He laid his head back against the chair. His damnable pride had cost him his family.

James wanted a long overdue reconciliation? How should be start? Livinia had left the ink and paper. He could write a letter and ask for forgiveness. It would not be an easy task. He picked up the pen. The nub wasn't as fine a point as he would've liked.

What should he say? He should inquire after his brother's health. Would that sound too presumptuous? Robert would think he was after his money. James didn't want his wealth. All he'd ever wanted was his high regard.

Should he tell him about his injury? No doubt Gwendolyn had already informed her father. There'd been no response, no inquiry about his condition. Nor had there been an invitation to visit.

Would his brother forgive him? The armor James wore to protect his feelings no longer seemed necessary. Time he shed it. He hoped it wasn't too late. He dipped his pen in the ink and started to write.

Livy was bereft James would be leaving in the morning. She may never see him again.

Hadn't she encouraged him to return to London? His recovery is what she'd hoped for, prayed for, and at the same time dreaded. She'd become possessive of him, as if he belonged here with her.

Nothing could be further from the truth. He belonged to the Army, to those young men who needed his guidance.

With James's testimonial safe in her reticule, Livy headed into town. She needed to interview her solicitor, the sour-faced Mr. Shakes.

The old mare plodded along in no great hurry. As Livinia bounced over the pockmarked road, she stifled her heartache. In time, her own wound would heal, she supposed, but that day seemed a long way off.

She arrived in town a half of an hour later. The streets were deep in shadows. Most of the shops were closed.

The solicitor maintained his office in a Georgian-style brick building on the High Street. She'd made an appointment by telephone and Mr. Shakes was only too happy to accommodate her, she'd been told by a secretary.

Livy had only met the solicitor once. He'd been so kind to come to the house to read her husband's will.

He'd told her then he was at her disposal. She'd thought it an odd turn of phrase but had appreciated the sentiment.

There was no room to park on the main road, so she found a convenient spot on a side street. She exited the trap, her nerves in an excitable state. She wanted this disagreement over and done with as soon as possible. Her children had suffered enough from the old woman's selfishness. Did she think Livy wouldn't fight to keep the family together?

A bell rang as she opened the door to the solicitor's office. A dark-haired woman dressed in a gray wool suit looked up from a typewriting machine. "How may I help?"

Since the war, many jobs that had been held by young men had been taken over by women. Livy didn't recognize her. She wasn't a local.

"My name is Livinia Pratt. I have an appointment with Mr. Shakes."

"Good afternoon, Mrs. Pratt. You are expected." The woman rose from her chair. "Won't you have a seat and I'll see if Mr. Shakes is ready for you."

Livy sat in the nearest chair.

The secretary walked down the hall. Her hemline was inches shorter than Livy had seen before, which made Livy feel dowdy and old. The receptionist opened a door and went inside.

Livy looked around her. This was all new territory for her. She'd never been involved with the business of the farm or any of the legal matters. Charles had taken care of the accounts and seen to the paying of bills. When he died, the farm's finances fell to her to manage and would continue now that Wyatt was gone. It was an area she found herself struggling, and yet she mustn't shy away from the challenge.

Heat radiated from a coal stove and she unbuttoned her coat. The woman returned, the heels of her shoes clicking on the wood floor.

"Mr. Shakes will see you now."

Livy smiled. "Thank you."

She led Livy to Mr. Shakes's inner sanctum. The good man was sitting at his desk when she entered, and he pushed back his chair and stood.

"Mrs. Pratt. How nice to see you." He didn't smile or extend his hand, acting very formal for a country solicitor, but Livy didn't mind.

"I'm very sorry to have kept you so late," she said.

He invited her to sit down.

Livy sat. Mr. Shakes did as well and folded his hands on top of his polished desk.

"I trust all is well at the farm?"

"Yes, very well."

"How may I serve?"

She opened her reticule. "I have a letter from my mother-in-law's solicitor. I think it's self-explanatory."

She gave Mr. Shakes time to read it. He finished with a downturned mouth and a gaze that wouldn't meet hers.

She took out James's letter next. "Do you know Gwendolyn and Ronald Asher?"

"I'm familiar with the name."

"They live at Asher Hall. Gwendolyn's uncle is staying at their gamekeeper's cottage while he recovers from a battlefield injury."

She took time to explain the evening James's knee had failed him. How Dr. Bainbridge had been called. She showed Mr. Shakes the letter James had written.

The solicitor wore a pinched expression as he read. Livy didn't blame him. This was a sordid matter which would repulse anyone.

"As you can see," Livy said, "there is no reason to worry about the welfare of my children."

Mr. Shakes cleared his throat and looked up at her at last. "Of course, Mrs. Pratt. What is it you want me to do?"

"I wish to nip this frivolous interference on the part of my mother-in-law in the bud."

He placed the two letters in front of him with an economy in his movements. "I will do my best, Mrs. Pratt, to protect your interests."

"Thank you."

"I will write these solicitors and tell them what you've shown me."

"I must make it plain that I do not wish for my children to live in London."

Mr. Shakes shifted in his chair. "Could this be just a misunderstanding? Perhaps she wishes only for the children to visit?"

Livy shook her head. "Mother Pratt was quite clear in her intentions. Her lawyers have not minced words."

"And yet I wonder if some accommodation could be made?"

"Why would I be so generous?"

"Wouldn't it be better to avoid a public spectacle?" He sat back in his chair. "Have you considered what a court proceeding might exact on your children?"

Livy grasped her hands together. Her palms were moist with perspiration. Her nerves were getting the best of her. She hadn't expected the case would go to court.

"I have seen families torn apart over far less," Mr. Shakes added. "My advice is to work out some sort of arrangement where your mother-in-law can have the children for school holidays and part of the summer. It's the best for all concerned, don't you agree?"

Tears burned in Livy's eyes. She wouldn't give in to the woman's demands.

"I don't agree. Far from it! My girls stay with me. They belong at Fairview." Livy sniffed, drew her handkerchief from her sleeve, and pressed it into both hands.

"If that is your wish," he replied.

"I know you will do what must be done to prevent the matter from going to court." Clutching her handkerchief, she rose from the chair, having said all she needed to for the moment.

"You will be hearing from me the next day or two," Mr. Shakes said as he stood.

"Thank you, sir. You have relieved me and my children of a great deal of anxiety."

He showed no expression in reply.

She left the office, feeling she'd accomplished very little. The solicitor had not been as intimidating as she'd believed, but his advice had been flawed. Mother Pratt was determined to have the girls. A compromise would not quell her ambition. Once they arrived for a visit, she wouldn't let them leave.

Would Mr. Shakes be able to convince the London solicitors to stand down? A country solicitor might not have the clout necessary to persuade a London firm.

If the case went to a judge, it would be Mother Pratt's doing, not Livy's. Mr. Shakes would be successful despite his reservations.

Of course, the children's sensibilities to the scheme should be a concern. Mr. Shakes *had* made a valid point. Livy did not want to involve the girls in any legal proceedings. The inevitable ugliness would scar them.

Satisfied she'd at least made a good start, Livy hurried to her trap.

Jenny nickered as she climbed aboard.

"Let's go home," she told the mare. She turned the trap around and headed back to the high street.

On the way, Livy reconsidered Mr. Shakes's advice. She would do well to remember her mother-in-law had lost her only child. The grandchildren were all of her son she had left.

Livy realized it was up to her to make sure this dispute didn't go any further. If she didn't take action, the family could be torn apart by this unfortunate incident.

In fact, a visit to the city might be the best solution after all.

Hadn't she enjoyed London when she was a girl? Her children would, no doubt, benefit from everything a big city had to offer, and both would be overjoyed to miss a few weeks of school once in a while.

"It just might work."

Jenny's ears flicked back and forth as if she agreed.

"I think it's sensible to leave for London as soon as possible." She gave the reins a shake.

Elizabeth and Mrs. Heath could manage the household chores for a few days, a week at the most. She didn't want Winnie and Grace to miss too much school.

Going up to London on the morning train posed a problem. James was leaving on that train. It might be awkward for them both. Perhaps she should wait another day?

Why should she wait? She'd left him on good terms. They'd forged a friendship that would continue with letters and baked goods. They would greet each other as neighbors do under similar circumstances.

Confident she and Mother Pratt would sort out their differences and all would be well again, Livy gave the reins a shake, eager to get home and tell the girls about her plan.

Chapter Twenty-One

⟫⟫⟫⟨⟨⟨

J ames Gunnison stood on the platform of the train station with the leather case his mother had bought for him when he'd turned seven and had been sent away to school.

He'd found goodbyes too grueling and was grateful Gwendolyn and her husband had not insisted on coming along to see him off. He'd not waited for his niece to send the motor either, but had asked young Tom Martin to bring around his cart.

As he'd shut the cottage door behind him, he'd realized how he'd grown fond of the place, even though the stay had been short and had not provided the rest he'd anticipated. His peace had been intruded upon by a parade of visitors, most notably the persistent Livinia Pratt.

He would miss her the most.

Someone calling his name broke into his thoughts. He turned and saw Livinia and her children climbing out the trap driven by her housekeeper.

Livinia looked so lovely in her squirrel-trimmed motoring coat and dark brown hat with dried roses bunched around the crown. What in the world was she doing here?

He removed his hat and stepped off the platform. "How good to see you." He meant every word.

Her gaze was direct, her mouth set in determination. He'd seen that look before, knew its meaning.

"As am I," she said.

The two little girls gathered around him. Their little dog, straining on her leash, barked.

"We are going to London," the oldest girl explained.

"You changed your mind about sending the girls to your mother-in-law?"

Livinia shook her head. "Nothing that drastic. We are only going for a visit."

"So you have reconciled."

Livinia nodded. "The family must stay together."

She shamed him with her courage. How long had he avoided his brother? How many years had passed before he'd written a letter meant to bridge troubled waters? Far too long, and yet he hadn't the daring to post it.

"Can we ride with the major?" Grace asked.

He held a crème-colored ticket.

"I'm afraid we can only afford a third-class ticket," she said.

James was moved by their downturned faces, their obvious disappointment the four of them couldn't travel together.

"May I offer to buy your tickets?" he asked.

"Please say yes," the girls said in unison.

"Given the circumstances," Livinia replied, "I must refuse."

He was fully aware of the circumstances of which she spoke. How would it look if she accepted gifts from him?

Propriety be damned.

James put his hat back on and gave the top a tap. "There's only one solution. I will join you in the third-class coach."

"Indeed?" She smiled. "I suppose that would be all right. I can't very well tell you where to sit."

"Jolly good," the children said and giggled. James fancied the girls had taken a liking to him.

By the time he exchanged his ticket, the train had arrived. James had to wonder why Livinia picked this morning to travel up to London. He did not believe in coincidences.

Admittedly, he was glad to see her, but it would be a job to keep up the pretense that his leg didn't bother him.

James opened the carriage door for Livinia and caught a whiff of lavender, reminding him of the night of Wyatt's birthday party. He'd learned something about himself that evening, about what made him happy. He'd Livinia to thank.

He picked up his case and followed. The bench seats were crowded with fellow passengers. Livinia and the girls found the last empty seat.

A stout lady dressed in black moved over to make room for him in the seat directly opposite them. He planted his stick in the aisle and sat down against the varnished wood. The effort brought sweat to his brow, and he took out his handkerchief and patted it away.

The pain medication should last another hour or two but the weakness was there, ready to bedevil him at the slightest movement.

"Grace and Winifred are very excited about seeing London," Livinia said.

He was glad she didn't ask him about his leg. He was tired of talking about his injury. "Then we should waste no time in getting there."

His response was met with a generous smile.

"Does your mother-in-law know you are coming?"

"I sent her a wire this morning." She looked wistful. "I hope my decision will be a pleasant surprise."

James realized this was her gift, the kindness she bestowed on those around her. He wasn't the only recipient.

The whistle blew. They lurched forward. The children cried out in their excitement and Livinia held onto her hat.

The noisy engine and clack of the rails made conversation a challenge. Livy stared out the window at the fallow fields and the gray skies threatening rain.

They arrived at Tonbridge, where they needed to change trains. The station was warm, with a fire blazing in the cast iron stove. They wasted no time to huddle around it.

Mostly farm laborers and elderly men filled the tables. The room smelled of tobacco and ale.

James ordered cider for himself, cocoa for Livinia and

the girls, and a bowl of water for the dog. After using the washroom, they gathered at one of the oak tables.

"This is rather an adventure," Grace confided in a whisper.

"Will it be much farther?" Winifred asked solemnly.

"We are about halfway," he replied.

She sighed. "Good. I don't mind telling you I've bounced about enough for one day."

"You are such a complainer," Grace said, piercing her sister with a scathing look.

"Girls," Livinia spoke firmly but without a trace of disapproval.

Both looked shamefaced.

"I admire how well you ladies are managing the trip," James replied.

The children gazed up at him with open affection.

The cider and hot cocoa arrived, and they clinked their mugs together, toasting each other's good health.

"Such a nice-looking family," an elderly lady said to her companion, a woman who could have been her daughter. The two swept by their table and nodded their approval.

James didn't correct her. They were a family, of sorts, if only for a brief time. He exchanged gazes with Livinia, who must've heard the comment. Her cheeks had turned rosy and her eyes were bright.

James would have to admit he was content in a way he'd never been before.

Livy was worn through when, at last, they arrived at Charing Cross station. The children had argued ever since the rooftops of the city appeared in the horizon. No amount of entreaties on her part had stopped them.

James insisted on accompanying them from the station to Mother Pratt's house in the fashionable neighborhood of Longrow Place in Belgravia. Livy couldn't very well tell him no. In truth, she didn't want to say goodbye quite yet.

What would Mother Pratt say when she discovered Major Gunnison had come with them? The girls would be sure to tell her. The old lady's conviction that Livy's behavior was reproachful and not suitable for the eyes of children would, most likely, be reinforced.

Livy would laugh at the notion, but indignation kept her from doing so.

Now that they were almost at her house, Livy was having second thoughts. Perhaps she should've been more prudent. Should she have told James goodbye at the station? It would have been an easy thing to do if she'd wanted. She'd never considered herself an impulsive creature, but taking the early morning train to London—knowing James would be on it—had been something she'd never have done with another man. Her decision could be misconstrued as chasing after the poor fellow. Except James hadn't been vexed to see her and he'd seemed to enjoy himself.

Livy suppressed a sigh. Her behavior of late had become reckless. Had she lost all her good sense?

The cab ride through the busy streets of London kept the girls enthralled. The sheer number of people on the streets mesmerized them.

Mother Pratt's elegant Georgian house peered down at them like a dowager duchess. A judgmental one.

Livy sat straighter. She'd not come for an argument, nor was she here to capitulate her duties as a mother. If the old lady meant to bully her, she would resist. She did not relish a confrontation, where words would be said that would land like fists and couldn't be taken back.

Hopefully, they could get along amicably for the sake of the children if nothing else. Livy would ask for a ceasefire. Would Mother Pratt agree?

If all went well, Livy would send the children for the school holidays. It was the best she could do. It was all she could do.

When it came time to leave for home, Livy must be firm.

James opened the cab's door and stepped down on to the cobblestones. The cold air made Livy shiver. He was at her door and opened it. She took his offered hand and exited. Thankfully, the pavement was dry. The girls had not worn their boots.

Mother Pratt's neatly kept garden was in sharp contrast to the country: Not one curl of dead ivy or withered flower.

Livy preferred swirling leaves as she walked down the

country road, black birds calling out from the newly mown fields, hollyhocks growing in wild abandon against an old stone cottage.

A wave of homesickness threatened to break her composure. She couldn't turn back now. When the door opened and Mother Pratt's butler clomped down the steps barking orders at the footman and maids, who followed him to take up the cases. He was older than Mother Pratt, but his voice hadn't lost its forcefulness.

"How good to see you, Mrs. Pratt."

"Thank you, Holbrook."

Hat in hand, James waited at the curb as the girls climbed the steps, the dog barking at their feet. When all seemed to be in order, the cases taken inside and the children attended to by the staff, Livy turned around to thank him.

"This is where we part company," James said.

"We are in your debt for accompanying us."

"I'm the one who owes the thanks. I enjoyed traveling with three ladies."

She laughed. "You are very kind to say so. The children can try the nerves."

"They are a delight," he replied.

Livy met his gaze. "When is your consultation?"

"First thing in the morning."

"I see. Would you keep us informed about the results?"

He hesitated. Her request was intrusive, but she wanted him to know she cared.

"You needn't worry," he replied. "These sort of injuries are easily sorted out."

"Just in case, let me give you my mother-in-law's phone number."

She opened her reticule and found a pencil and a pad of paper. She scribbled the number and handed it to him.

James stuffed the piece of paper in his coat pocket. She hoped he would call but wouldn't press. If he wanted her to know what could be done about his knee, he would.

She'd one more thing to ask. "When will you return to your duties?"

"If my consultation with the surgeon is successful, I will return directly."

She nodded. Even though she'd expected this answer, she wondered if he was being realistic. Dr. Bainbridge seemed to think the injury severe enough to require surgery. A short recovery time seemed optimistic.

"Livinia, I just wanted to say I appreciate all you have done."

"Sir, you've returned the favor many fold."

He bowed slightly. "I am glad to have been of some help."

She had more to say, but time had run out.

"I must be going," he said. "The cabbie is waiting."

"Then this is goodbye—again." She leaned forward and kissed him on the cheek. She'd not expected to be so forward, but the desire to show her affection could not be denied.

In other circumstances, they might have let their

friendship grow. Who knows? It might've even flourished.

He stepped back and tipped his hat. Had she embarrassed him? Or was he merely protecting her reputation? Or did something else cause him to hide his feelings? She felt sad in any case.

"The girls and I will write."

"I'll look forward to receiving your letters. You must tell me what is happening with your family."

"We will remember you in our prayers," she said.

"Thank you." He winced.

"Are you all right?"

"Yes, just a twinge from sitting too long."

Livy understood perfectly. "I hope you will come visit us at Fairview when the war is over."

"When victory is won."

She took that as a promise he would come home. They all would.

The first thing anyone saw when they entered Mother Pratt's house was Charles's larger than life portrait. Livy remembered when the portrait had been done. They were newly married, and his mother had insisted on having his picture for her entryway.

The pang of loss stopped Livy momentarily. She was reminded of what a handsome man her husband had been, and the power of his personality was evident in the portrait. He'd never suffered from self-doubt, a trait which she had found attractive.

So much had changed since his death. She was a widow and had sent a son off to war. Their oldest daughter would soon follow, and the two little girls were growing up fast.

And she'd found love again. She would have never predicted such a thing or believed it possible.

When the war was over, they all would reunite and the family bonds would be stronger than ever. What role would James play? Livy didn't know what the future would bring, but she mustn't be afraid.

Livy removed her gloves and her hat. A maid waited to take them from her. She was expected in the parlor but dallied. Hopefully, the conversation would revolve around the children and not Major Gunnison. Livy wasn't prepared to answer the inevitable barrage of nasty remarks, but she wouldn't try and escape them either.

Patting her hair and finding nothing out of place, she proceeded down the hall. A gas fire hissed from the hearth. Mother Pratt sat in her favorite chair. The girls were already drinking more hot cocoa from mugs.

"I trust your journey went well?" There was no warmth in her greeting.

Livy smiled. She suspected the woman had ice in her veins. Or something more lethal. "Very well." She didn't bestow a kiss on the cheek but instead took the chair positioned on her mother-in-law's left.

"Would you care for some tea?"

"Yes, please."

Grandmamma Pratt ordered the maid to bring another tray with a fresh pot.

The fire was warm and comforting. Livy would like nothing better than to stretch out her legs and soak in the heat.

"Have you heard from Wyatt?" Mother Pratt asked.

Livinia returned her attention to her mother-in-law. "Not a word. I'm sure he will let us know of his plans as soon as he is able."

"He must be very busy."

"We're hoping the army will give him a few days leave before they send him away."

Mother Pratt stared at her, her eyes shooting daggers. "You will keep me informed?"

Livy understood the depths of the old woman's concern. She shared the same paroxysms of fear.

"Of course I will. You are his grandmamma."

"I will continue to write letters." Mother Pratt spoke defiantly.

"Yes, we must let him know we are thinking of him."

"And pray."

"I am confident our prayers will be a source of comfort."

Mother Pratt remained stiff as a corset. "Where is Elizabeth, may I ask?"

"She stayed at Fairview. She's waiting for her acceptance letter from the V.A.D. You needn't worry. She's under the watchful eye of Mrs. Heath."

Mother Pratt did not reply. The sharp angles of her

face softened—a bit. Livy's answer seemed to satisfy her. At least, Livy hoped so.

Did Mother Pratt really think Livy had travelled all this way to fight with her? She had to admit her mother-in-law had cause to wonder. They rarely had a conversation that, of late, didn't involve a clash of wills.

Livy must waylay Mother Pratt's fears. They must, for the sake of the children, present a unified front.

"Major Gunnison came with us," Gracie said. Her upper lip was coated with cocoa.

Mother Pratt blinked. "Indeed?"

Livy would not be shamed. "The major has business here and was kind enough to accompany us."

"He's very nice," Gracie added.

The woman fixed her pale eyes on the girl. "It appears the major has ingratiated himself into your affections."

"I suppose he has," Livy replied frankly.

Mother Pratt shifted her gaze to Livy. Was she thinking of something to say in retaliation? Livy waited.

"Then I am grateful," she said, smiling.

Livy's insides twisted into a knot of barbed wire. Her smile could only mean she would use this new information against Livy.

"As you should be," Livy answered.

Mother Pratt's smile faded into the most appalling look of disapproval.

Livy had no regrets. She'd enjoyed James's company tremendously, and so had the girls. They would not pretend otherwise, even to humor an old woman.

Chapter Twenty-Two

→»»«««←

After a harrowing ride through busy streets, James arrived at his club a block off the Pall Mall on St. James Square. Doctors had cautioned him to be careful not to put weight on the leg until it was completely healed. Of late, he'd not heeded the warning. The discipline in which he prided himself had been lax and he paid the price.

That was neither here nor there. He wouldn't have traded his fortnight in the country for anything.

He'd come to realize, maybe too late, he needed Livinia in his life. He'd not been honest with her. He'd told her the war kept them apart, but that'd been a lie.

She thought him respectable, but he was nothing of the sort. The only way they could have a relationship is if he told her the truth.

The steward greeted him by name and took his coat and hat. He made his way into the parlor where several men sat ensconced in leather high back chairs. They looked up from their newspapers at his arrival.

He recognized a general from the Boer Wars. Well

into his seventies, General Winthrop was a lion of a man with a mane of white hair and eyebrows and whiskers reminiscent of steel wool.

The two men exchanged greetings.

"On leave, are you?" The general's voice boomed in the small room. James knew he'd gone partially deaf due to mortar fire.

"Yes, sir. Medical."

"I imagine you're eager to get back in the fight." The general coughed and cleared his throat.

"Yes, sir."

"The high command has made a botch of it, haven't they?"

James grimaced. The criticism of the war effort had become more vocal of late. "I assure you, sir, we are doing our best."

James was introduced to the other men in the room. They were retired military, put out to pasture. He'd no doubt every one of them wouldn't hesitate to take their uniforms out of mothballs if called up for duty. He shouldn't be here, able-bodied and in his prime.

He sat down in a chair near the fire in a state of despondency. The men returned to their reading. Certainly they'd noticed his limp, but no mention was made of it. These men did not talk about their infirmities. They'd faced injury and loss with uncommon courage and found no need to expound further.

James grew restless. General Winthrop's gurgling snore drove him to distraction. Nothing in the newspapers interested him at the moment. News of the battlefield was always grim and often inaccurate. No journalist could give a complete rendition of conditions at the front or the tremendous amount of casualties. Even the high command had difficulty keeping track of the number of dead and wounded.

What was to become of him if he couldn't carry out his own duties as an officer? The prospect of spending his days in front of a fire depressed him.

His thoughts turned to Livinia. She was a remarkable woman coming to London for many reasons, but foremost to keep her family together.

If she could face her mother-in-law, James could jolly well present himself at the hospital without a complaint.

Best to get this business of doctors over and done so he could return to his duties at quick march. In the meantime, he'd nothing to do but wait.

James dressed. He hadn't slept well. The city noises had woken him out of a fitful sleep. The sounds of petrol-powered vehicles in the street, the occasional backfire, voices shouting out in the dark served to remind him of his time in the trenches.

Satisfied his four-in-hand was tied correctly and straight, he shrugged on his jacket and secured his grandfather's half hunter in his vest pocket.

He dreaded the appointment. He'd much rather face

the Huns than the gloomy dispositions of doctors, but he'd waited long enough. The knee must be seen to—he couldn't function at his best with this pain.

A morning mist covered the ground and the streets were slippery. The dull gray sky portended of more rain and sleet. In other circumstances, he would've walked. The Royal Hospital wasn't far.

Instead, he hailed a cab and dove inside. The leather seat was cold and clammy. The traffic slowed progress, and he directed the cabbie to use the side streets.

James sat back and closed his eyes. The journey to London yesterday with Livinia, the lively children, and even the dog had pleased him.

He'd not believed domesticity to be for him, but he'd been privileged to have a glimpse of real family life, not what he experienced as a child, but in a household with love and respect. These cherished memories were something he'd take with him to the front.

"Here we are, Guv," the cabbie said. James opened his eyes. They'd arrived at the hospital.

James paid the man and descended into the street. A cold rain fell in sheets. A sergeant hurried by, holding on to his hat. A group of nurses huddled under an umbrella as they clambered up the steps.

James followed them, relying heavily on his stick. Pulling open the heavy door almost unbalanced him. The girls chattered as they passed through. They were very young. Soon Elizabeth would join their ranks.

The interior smelled heavily of carbolic soap. He made

his way down a dark hallway and climbed a set of stairs to the second floor. Pain sliced through his knee at regular intervals now, and he breathed heavily as he made his way down the corridor.

The doctor's consultation room was the last door. He paused, dreading the interview. He would have to admit all was not well with his wound, something he'd been reluctant to do. He could hear Livinia's voice urging him forward.

What was he afraid of? The doctor would give him some new kind of tablets, no doubt, and the matter would be settled. It was another lie he'd told himself over and over. Only a surgeon's knife would give him the relief he sought.

He pushed open the door. Two other occupants sat on a bench. They nodded a greeting. A woman was writing in a copy book at a small grey desk. She looked up.

James removed his hat.

"May I help you?" the woman asked.

"Yes, I've an appointment. The name is James Gunnison. Major James Gunnison."

She ran her finger down a ledger book and put a tick by one of the entries.

"If you'd like to take a seat, sir," she said, "the doctor will be with you shortly."

James dropped into the bench. The other men stared at him, but he didn't wish to talk. One of them had a bandage taped to the side of his head just above his ear. The other man's hand shook, a condition he tried to hide by grasping his hands together.

James thrummed his fingers across the scarred wood of his seat. The doctor's office was unadorned apart from a nearly empty bookcase. The stacks of folders and books that hadn't been returned to their place on the shelves were gathering dust on the floor. He found this highly irregular and in need of someone's immediate attention.

He sat back and tried to relax. His nerves, as a rule, never bothered him, but this morning he must admit to a degree of anxiety.

"Major Gunnison?" The receptionist's soft voice woke him from his reverie. "The doctor will see you now."

He grumbled that he'd heard her and pushed himself off the bench. His balance wasn't what he'd like it to be, and he plopped back down.

Blast!

The other occupants of the room averted their gazes. If he'd made them uncomfortable, they needn't be. He could very well manage the task of standing. This he did without further incident and picked up his stick.

The receptionist showed him to a small room where a corpulent man with thinning hair leaned across a metal desk and extended his hand.

"Major Gunnison, how very good to see you. I'm Dr. Wells."

They dispensed with the pleasantries and James was invited to sit down. A file, presumably his, was open on top of the desk.

"I understand you had your knee operated on to remove shrapnel."

"Correct."

"What seems to be the problem?" The doctor perused the file.

James squared his shoulders. He was an officer and was expected to tell the truth.

"There's some swelling—water accumulating on the knee—the surgeon who operated told me this might happen. Unfortunately, there's now a discharge, an infection, I'm told, which I've been trying to deal with by using Dakin's solution. With little success, I might add."

The doctor looked up and frowned. "And the pain?"

"The pain is a concern."

"Does the discomfort keep you up at night?"

"Yes."

The doctor stood. "Let's take a look."

James rolled up his pant leg.

Blast! The swelling had increased from yesterday's exertion and the area around the largest incision was a fiery red.

The doctor nodded. "We'll need an X-ray straight away and see what we've got. Do you have any questions?"

James did not.

"I'll instruct a nurse to bring you a gown and take you to a room where you can change. Then she'll collect you for radiology." The doctor clamped him on the shoulder. "We'll soon find out what seems to be the problem."

The man sounded all together too cheerful. James feared an X-ray would only be the start.

Chapter Twenty-Three

⇒⇒⇒✦⇐⇐⇐

"Livinia, you'll wear out the carpet if you keep treading back and forth," Mother Pratt said.

"I'm sorry." Livy stopped and settled into the green sofa with the serpentine back. The sofa always provoked fits of laughter from Elizabeth and Wyatt when they returned to Fairview after a visit with their grandmamma. Funny, what children latch on to, what takes hold in their imaginations. The curved back was so terribly ancient, in their opinion. So many things in this room spoke of another era.

Her mother-in-law returned to her book, a tome on the flora and fauna of southern Italy.

Livy had wanted to go with James to his appointment, but she hadn't dared to ask. Such a request would have been met with disdain. Much as he resisted doctors and hospitals, and her gentle coaxing to seek medical attention, he disliked even more for her to see him indisposed in any way.

He didn't want her to worry. How could she help but worry?

She glanced at the mantel clock for the hundredth time. James had said his appointment was first thing this morning. Certainly he'd have a clear picture of what he was up against by now.

"The children will be home for tea, I gather," she said.

"Yes, it was so kind of Cousin Rosamund to take them to the zoo," Mother Pratt answered. "Thankfully the rain has stopped."

"Grace and Winnie were so excited when she suggested the outing."

Mother Pratt looked up from her reading. "I'm happy you are discovering all the benefits living in the city can afford a young mind."

Livy ignored the implication. Would the woman never give up on her campaign to have the girls here in London with her? "I'm sure they will be well pleased with their day."

"Precisely." The word was spoken coldly.

Livy pictured icicles dripping from the woman's nose. It was not a generous image or a kind one.

"Perhaps we should talk about something else," Livy said.

The woman's face took on the expression of someone who'd been pinched hard. There was no pleasing her. Nothing Livy said, or did, seemed to be satisfactory.

Mother Pratt turned a page.

Livy struggled to keep her emotions under control. The woman could be so infuriating.

"The three of us are only here for a visit and don't

intend to stay long," Livy explained. "A few days, nothing more."

Mother Pratt's book closed with a snap. Her bosom rose and fell as did her mourning broach. She sat so rigidly, she appeared to have added inches to her height.

"Be reasonable. Surely you don't dispute that living with me here in London is in the best interest of the children?"

"Ah, but I do. Grace and Winnie belong at the farm."

"If you're concerned about Winnie and Grace changing school mid-term, let me put your mind to rest."

"Winnie and Grace will stay at the village school where they are very happy."

"Nonsense. Children adapt. They will thrive at the girls' academy I have in mind. The school has an excellent reputation."

Livy couldn't argue against the advantages of a London school, but she wouldn't back down. "Fairview is our home. It is where we belong."

"Do be reasonable. The girls are in need of attention."

Livy could no longer keep her ire from showing. "How could you say such a thing? How could you accuse me of neglecting my own children?"

"I think the answer is obvious." She secured her statement with a heavy sigh.

Livy faced her without a thread of doubt. "Indeed, it is. You are an old woman who needs to find fault."

Mother Pratt glared at her. "Think what you like, my dear. I will not give up."

"Then you will be making a terrible mistake." Livy grasped her hands together.

Mother Pratt lowered her gaze. The fight seemed to have gone out of her for the moment, or was it only wishful thinking on Livy's part?

Livy was not without sympathy for her mother-in-law's circumstances. Living in this townhouse, even with Cousin Rosamund nearby and a full complement of servants, must be lonely.

Livy wasn't about to relent, however.

An idea sprung upon her. Why hadn't she thought of it sooner? What her mother-in-law needed was something Livy could give.

"You are welcome to stay with us at the farm for Christmas." Livy did so like a full house during the holiday.

The woman's face hardened. This was her true self shining through, the woman who would have her way. "You know perfectly well I don't travel in the winter."

"You could take the train down."

Her suggestion was met with a scowl.

"Do think about it. We would love to have you."

Livy believed her invitation to be top notch, but Mother Pratt would have to decide for herself what she wanted to do. Sometimes the idea of change took time to brew. As Livy had learned, acceptance was often a matter of priorities, not preferences.

Signaling the end of the conversation, Mother Pratt picked up her book.

Livy rose from the sofa and went to the window. The rain had started again. The girls would be disappointed to leave the zoo early.

"If you'll excuse me," Livy said, "I have some letters to write." Receiving no response, she left the room.

All that remained was the diagnosis.

James buttoned his shirt and pulled up his braces. He was glad the X-ray was over. The room had been cold, and dressed in only a cotton gown and carpet slippers, he had not been comfortable.

During the ordeal, he'd thought about his days at the gamekeeper's cottage. He'd thought about Livinia sitting next to him in the rickety cane chair talking about her childhood trip to London. He'd thought about her holding his hand the night of the storm when the night terrors put him in a terrible state. She'd stayed. She'd not found him weak or wanting. He'd remembered the softness of her lips when he kissed her.

The memories had kept him warm.

James moved down the hallway and came to a flight of stairs. The lift would be easier, but he didn't need a mechanical conveyance when he was perfectly capable of using the stairs.

Descending the smooth stone steps proved to be as much of a trial as climbing them had been. He feared losing his balance and pitching forward. He could not put his full weight on the offending leg, and relied on his strength in his good leg as well as clutching to the railing to reach the goal.

He heard footsteps behind him. A student nurse—a girl of no more than fifteen or sixteen—hurried down the steps.

"Can I be of assistance?" she asked. Her hair was covered with a scarf. Her uniform with the red cross was freshly laundered and starched.

He scowled. "I'm perfectly capable of managing for myself. Go help someone who is ill."

The gruffness had crept back in his voice. He had not wished to be unfriendly or ungrateful. No other conclusion could be drawn.

The last thing he wanted was to indulge in self-pity, and he was dangerously close to being there. Pity served no purpose, not even as an indulgence.

The youngster looked at him with a kindness he didn't deserve. She'd not been put off by his poor manners and foul disposition, thank goodness.

"Very well." She cast him an impish smile and continued down the stairs at a brisk pace.

He followed, albeit slowly.

The receptionist told James to wait in the doctor's office. The good doctor wasn't in, so he sat down in the straight back chair. The room smelled of sickness. A sour vapor hung in the air that hadn't been there when he'd come in for the consultation only a few hours earlier.

James tapped his foot on the bare floor. He had to

admit he was apprehensive about what the X-ray would show them, but he'd see for himself what the devil was causing all the trouble. The infection needed to be drained, perhaps, or another round of medication would be prescribed.

How much longer would it take this bloody wound to heal? His patience had reached its breaking point.

The doctor burst into the room, carrying a file and a photographic plate. The man swiveled into his chair and cleared his throat.

"I have your results, Major." He spoke cheerfully, but he hadn't made eye contact with James, which was worrying.

"As you can imagine, I'm anxious to hear what you have to say." James wanted badly to see the X-ray. Only discipline kept him from snatching the plate from the doctor's desk.

Dr. Wells pressed his lips into a thin line. So, it was bad news, James decided. He hadn't been fooled by the man's tally-ho enthusiasm as he made his entrance.

James braced himself.

"I am not happy with the X-ray." The doctor pushed the file aside and picked up the plate.

"What have you found?" James resigned himself to the worst news he could imagine.

"I'm afraid some of the bone in your knee has fragmented."

In the rush to provide care to so many, James realized, the doctor in the field hospital had removed only the shards of metal he'd found in the leg and had missed some bits of bone.

James sat forward. "A bone fragment is causing all the trouble?"

"More than one, I'm afraid." The doctor held the glass up to the light. He pointed to the offending bone chips. Remarkable how these X-ray machines worked, revealing the tiny pieces of bone wedged near the knee. No wonder he'd been in such pain.

James adjusted himself in the chair. Relieved the X-ray didn't reveal any more shrapnel, he knew, nonetheless, that he wasn't out of the woods yet. "Are the bone fragments the cause of the infection?"

The doctor shook his head. "Most likely."

"The country doctor thought there might be gangrene."

"We won't know for sure unless we look closer."

James frowned. Just as he'd feared. "An operation."

"Yes, a simple procedure, really." The doctor picked up his pencil. "I count two bone fragments here and here. I'd like to remove them. We'll clean out the initial wounds and cut out the dead tissue."

"Can't you just treat the infection?"

"My dear fellow, the infection is quite serious, and pills and powder don't seem to be the answer, as you have discovered."

Although James had hoped for a better result, he'd expected surgery would be recommended.

"What if I refuse an operation?"

"To do nothing is a risk." The doctor put the X-ray down and folded his hands on top of the file. "One I cannot recommend. Not when it's possible to remove the bone fragments and restore your leg."

James weighed his options. "Will I be able to walk again without a limp?"

"I cannot say for certain, of course, but that's the outcome we expect."

James couldn't continue the way he was. Something at long last would be done. He'd be invalided out of the Army if he didn't take care of this injury properly. He'd no desire to become a toothless dog of little use to anybody.

"I'm all for taking the bloody things out," James said. "How soon?"

"We'll schedule the operation straight away," the doctor said.

"No, I mean how long before I'm completely recovered? Before I can return to my regiment?"

The doctor frowned. "A fortnight. Maybe longer."

James gripped the sides of the chair, preparing to stand. "If an operation will put me to rights, then I say there's no time to lose."

The doctor affected a thin smile. "That's the spirit, Major. We'll admit you this very afternoon."

That was excellent news. James would ring up Livinia and tell her. Better yet, he would ask to see her. Such good news must be shared. How lucky he had Livinia to share it with.

"I will return after tea," he told the doctor. He almost jumped to his feet, but decided a more careful ascension would be prudent.

Dr. Wells wrote on a piece of paper and slipped the note into the file. "We will expect you then. I will schedule the operating theater for the first thing in the morning."

"Thank you," James said as he pumped the man's hand.

He could already feel his strength returning.

Chapter Twenty-Four

>>>«<<

Livy was delighted when James called. To hear his voice and in such good spirits sent her heart racing— as all happy surprises do.

"Would it be inconvenient for you to meet me later— this afternoon perhaps?" he asked. "We could walk in the park?"

There was hesitation in his voice. She guessed the reason. He did not want to disturb her or be the cause of further contention between her and Mother Pratt.

"I would love to meet you. A walk sounds lovely."

"Splendid."

"How did the examination go?"

"I have news on that front."

"Tell me."

"I will. When we meet."

"You are very wicked to keep me waiting."

He laughed. It did her spirit wonders to hear him in such a good mood.

They agreed to meet in St. James Park a few blocks from Buckingham Palace.

"Two o'clock?"

"I'll be there," she replied.

She hung the receiver on its hook. She was sure his news meant a full recovery must be imminent. How glad she was for him.

Livy hurried upstairs to her bedchamber, at sixes and sevens about what to wear. Her clothes were not stylish— they'd all economized because of the war. She did want to cut a fine figure. He was a proud man and she wanted him to be proud of her.

She settled on the green wool walking suit. He'd admired the color on her at Wyatt's birthday party and had told her so. It had pleased her tremendously that he'd noticed.

She put on her high button boots instead of the heeled shoes so popular with the young. She had her reasons. The walkways could be slippery and one had to be practical about such things.

She almost finished dressing when a sharp knock at her door startled her.

"Livinia?" Her mother-in-law called out, her voice shrill.

Livy must tell Mother Pratt about joining James this afternoon. Mother Pratt had expressed her disapproval in so many regrettable ways and Livy wished to minimize any conversation concerning the major.

An adult can pick her own friends.

"Livinia? Are you there?" Before Livy could get to the door, Mother Pratt opened it. She was in high color.

"What is the matter?"

Mother Pratt waved an envelope, looking distressed. "The post has just arrived. You've had a letter from Richmond. It must be Wyatt."

Livy's heart skipped a beat as Mother Pratt handed the letter to her. The address was indeed in her son's handwriting.

"Are you going to open it?" Mother Pratt asked peevishly.

"Of course." In her haste, Livy didn't trouble to find an opener but broke the seal with her fingernail. The long-awaited missive was only one sheet of paper.

She read silently. When she was done, she looked up. Mother Pratt's eyes bore into her.

"Wyatt has finished his training and has some leave coming to him," Livy said. "He will be here tomorrow."

"That was quick." Mother Pratt shook her head. "Never mind. You must telephone Elizabeth at once."

"Yes, she will want to come."

"I'm so pleased." Mother Pratt drew her handkerchief edged in black lace from her sleeve and dabbed at her eyes. "How fortunate we will all be together."

Livy couldn't agree more.

Her mother-in-law sat down on Livy's dressing stool. "I'd so hoped he would come to visit me. Will he be going to France in the near future?"

Livy handed Mother Pratt the letter. Her son hadn't mentioned how he was or when he would be sent overseas. All he said was that he had two days leave and would be coming to London to see them.

Fear gnawed on Livy that a few days leave meant Wyatt would soon be sent to the battlefield.

"We must have a dinner party," Mother Pratt said, after she'd finished reading. "We shall invite all our friends to greet my grandson and wish him well."

Selfishly, Livy wanted her son to herself for the short time they would have together, but she did not begrudge Mother Pratt her party. A gathering of family and friends would boost all of their spirits.

"Yes, that's exactly what we must do."

Mother Pratt clapped her hands together. "We will prepare a feast."

"I should think he would prefer something far simpler. The country is at war."

The old lady frowned. "I suppose you are right. We cannot appear too ostentatious."

"No, we cannot, but it will be a wonderful evening, I'm sure."

Mother Pratt rose from the stool. "We should not waste a minute. This will be frightfully short notice, but my friends will understand."

"You will pull it off, I have no doubt."

Livy fancied she saw a tiny smile lift her mother-in-law's lips as she exited the room. She wouldn't spoil the woman's cheerful disposition by telling her about the appointment with James.

She headed to the morning room where the telephone was kept. Thankfully, she'd no trouble making a connection.

"I never thought I'd be saying this, but I've missed Wyatt," Elizabeth said with enthusiasm. "I was just about to call you."

"Oh?"

"Mother, I have been accepted for nurses' training."

Livy's heart sank, but she would not say anything to dampen Elizabeth's excitement. "When will you go?"

"They want me to start next week."

Exactly what Livy feared. "Will you be able to come to London for your brother?"

"Yes, Mother. I will leave on this evening's train."

"Good. I will ask Grandmamma to send the motor around to pick you up. We will talk about your program when you arrive."

She rang off, reminded of how easily and quickly the telephone made communication possible.

Livy returned to her dressing room and put on the hat she'd borrowed from Elizabeth. The cloche style with an upturned brim made her look a bit younger, she fancied. Livy was anxious to hear what the Army doctors had found. Now she had her own news to tell.

Picking up her gloves, she went to the parlor. She was dismayed at how many invitations Mother Pratt had already completed. The party would be grander than she'd hoped.

"Elizabeth will be here on the evening train," she said.

"I will tell Holbrook. He will send the Daimler."

"Thank you."

The clock on the mantel rang the hour. Livy would be late and must hurry.

"Why are you wearing your hat?" Mother Pratt raised a brow.

"I am going out," Livy said.

"Aren't you going to help me?"

Livy hadn't expected her to ask. "I will leave the letter writing to you."

"Will you be back at a reasonable hour? The children will be returning shortly."

"I can't say."

"What could be so important?"

There was no avoiding the truth of the matter. Livy had nothing to hide. "I'm meeting Major Gunnison for a walk in the park."

Mother Pratt straightened and put her pen to the side. "Why, may I ask?"

"He's been to the doctor and has the report. I'm very keen to hear what he has found out."

"This is unpleasant news, Livinia. Why didn't you speak of this earlier?"

The answer was obvious. Livy had wished to avoid Mother Pratt's wrath.

"I don't tell you everything," Livy replied.

Her mother-in-law affected a frightful scowl. Years ago, Livy would've been intimidated and an apology would've been necessary.

These were extraordinary times, and the old rules didn't apply any longer.

"Very well." Mother Pratt spoke formally, clutching her handkerchief with bloodless fingers. As Livy exited, she knew she must say something or she'd be treated to a chilly reception during Wyatt's visit. Her son would be sensitive to any family disagreements. All must appear to be happy and in good cheer.

Livy turned around and faced the woman. "I didn't tell you because I know you don't approve of the major."

"I do not."

"You must admire his dedication to his profession."

Mother Pratt snorted. "You mean to tell me this...assignation is nothing more than bolstering the morale of our men in uniform?"

Her words were brutal and desperate.

"Our meeting is not an assignation, but yes, I would like to think I could be a comfort in some small way."

Mother Pratt harrumphed. "You wish me to believe this all is perfectly innocent."

Livy's blood began to boil. "Believe what you will. He asked to escort me through the park, and I intend let him."

"This streak of independence in you is not very attractive." Mother Pratt spat the words.

"I rather like it."

"A woman your age has no business gallivanting around the city like some...some...debutante." She flung her hands outward and knocked the stack of envelopes to the floor.

Livy's gaze dropped to the letters scattered on the

carpet. She could not look at a person who was so willing to be disagreeable.

On the brink of saying things she would most certainly regret, Livy took a calming breath. There was nothing to be gained by losing her temper—except perhaps seeing the woman's reaction.

"You have stated your objections to my friendship with the major most forcefully." Livy spoke with composure she didn't feel. "Nothing you say will change my mind."

With this, she opened the parlor door and departed. She didn't bother to shut it behind her.

Still shaking, Livy saw herself in the hall mirror. Creases at the corner of her eyes and around her mouth had become more prominent. Her hair showed a few more streaks of gray. She could not turn back the clock, but she had to admit she did feel a little like a debutante.

Was she being foolish? Perhaps. What did it matter? Was foolishness only reserved for the young?

The turmoil roiling inside her subsided. She drew her pair of kid gloves over her country-roughened hands. The soft leather slid on easily.

Holbrook was waiting at the door with her coat.

"I gather young Wyatt will be visiting," he said as he helped her with her coat.

She turned and smiled. "I'm very excited to see him."

"As we all are." He bowed his head.

"Thank you."

"He's a fine boy, Ma'am."

Livy grimaced. Wyatt was no longer a boy. What he was about to undertake was a man's work.

"You'll be surprised by how much he has grown."

"Indeed, Mrs. Pratt." He bowed again and opened the door.

She stepped outside. The chilly air nipped at her skin but the sky had cleared. She reveled in the fine afternoon, perfect for a walk in the park. St. James was a good distance and she hurried to the corner to catch the next trolley.

James arrived at the park early. He was familiar with these surroundings, having played here when he was a boy. His nanny had brought him to see the pelicans.

Very little had changed. The stand of chestnuts provided ammunition for their games. Places to hide were in abundance.

A newsboy on the corner shouted out the headlines. A new campaign in Europe was being planned. James paid a penny for a copy and told the lad to keep the change. The ginger-haired boy tipped his cap.

The iron benches provided a stinging cold seat in the autumn air. He made his way to one of those benches, intending to read as he waited for Livinia. The Battle at Loos had ended October 14. The Germans' line held despite the use of smoke and gas. Two British reserve units had sustained heavy casualties. Thousands had been lost. There were calls for the resignation of Commander Sir John French.

These were dire reports. What had gone so terribly wrong? He closed the newspaper. How frustrating not to be there, especially when the need was so great.

When he saw Livinia, he folded the paper in half and tucked it in his pocket. There would be no talk of war today.

A woman of forty years walks with an easy grace. There was none of the self-consciousness of youth nor the frailty of old age.

Livinia wore a practical walking suit in green, and her hair was dressed modestly, revealing her lovely neck—he wasn't such an old curmudgeon that he didn't notice such things. Her hat had been decorated with bits and bobs. Women managed to infuse their hats with the most mundane objects, giving the impression of whimsy. He approved of what he saw.

If he wanted a future with Livinia, he couldn't deny his feelings any longer. What would she think of him if she learned what kind of man he truly was?

She turned down another path. She'd been distracted by the myriad of rose bushes which hadn't yet been pruned back for winter. Most had gone to rose-hips, a riot of burnished orange and red.

"Livinia," he called out and struggled to his feet.

Her head came up and she turned. Her countenance changed in an instant when she recognized him. She'd been contemplative, he realized, and now her features were luminous.

Dare he believe he was the source of such happiness?

"There you are," she said, waving. He quickened his step. His leg hurt, but he intended to walk by her side.

As he approached, he was surprised by how his pulse beat double-time. By Jove, he was glad to see her. By the look on her face, the sentiment was returned in full.

She kissed him on the cheek. An expression of friendship, nothing more, and yet how he enjoyed being the recipient.

"Have you been waiting long?" She tilted her head in a flirtatious matter.

It was a curious remark. He'd been waiting for a great long while for someone to look at him with such affection.

He removed his hat and held it to his chest. "My dear Livinia, it is a lady's prerogative to be late, no matter the occasion."

"Is it?" She favored him with one of her smiles.

They stood facing each other, the only two people in the world.

Livy found James's behavior rather odd. He kept staring at her as if she'd appeared out of fairy dust. She thought she knew all his moods, but this one was new to her.

She threaded her hand around his arm. His muscle tensed briefly but to her infinite delight, he relaxed with the most engaging expression. Not a scowl in sight. Was she imagining things or did he seem happy?

"Shall we walk this way?" She tipped her head toward the path she'd been on.

"Indeed. The fall colors are especially beautiful down by the pond." He returned his hat to his head and pulled the brim down a fraction, shadowing his eyes.

This was not the precise placement of his hat that was his custom. The homburg, placed thus, looked rather jaunty, in her opinion.

She guessed at the reason. His visit to the doctor had gone better than he'd hoped.

They strolled down the path wet with leaves, his limp only slightly evident.

"I've had a letter from Wyatt." She couldn't keep her good news to herself any longer.

"Have you?"

"Just this morning."

"I expect his training will soon be completed."

"Indeed, he has finished and is due a few days leave before he goes to his next posting. He arrives in London tomorrow. How fortunate we are here so he won't have to travel all the way to Fairview."

"You must be very excited to see him."

"Oh, I can't possibly describe how much."

"You should prepare yourself," he said. "Your son will be wearing the uniform of his country."

"I have done, and I will be so proud." She squeezed his arm. "So many others have been called to duty. He must do his."

The war had reached them at Fairview, but she'd accepted Wyatt must do what his conscience demanded. She wanted to make sure James knew this.

James nodded. "I have no doubt you will do so with great courage and grace."

Livy had never thought of herself as courageous, certainly not like a soldier facing a ruthless enemy. James had been generous with his praise and she was grateful.

They strolled under a canopy of chestnuts. The morning's rain had not dulled their colorful display. Livy missed home. She missed seeing the meadows, now covered, most likely, with a dusting of snow. She missed the dogs' bellowing as they chased the cottontails across the fallow fields. She even missed the smell of bitter hops drying.

"We are planning a dinner party for Wyatt," she said. "Will you come? It's tomorrow evening. I know Wyatt will be happy to see you again."

His presence would be sure to cause tension, but Livy didn't care. The party would include Mother Pratt's friends. Livy could very well invite one of her own.

"I'm afraid I cannot."

Livy would not give up so easily. "Elizabeth is coming from Fairview. She has been accepted for nurses' training."

"An admirable pursuit."

"She will want to see you."

"I would like to see her." And yet he frowned. "Still I cannot come."

Livy was disappointed. She had stated her case and he

hadn't been persuaded. Nothing more needed to be said.

"You must tell me your news?" she asked amiably.

He patted her hand. He was a private man, but they had come together this fine day to share good fortune.

"They took an X-ray," he said.

"Is it the good news we'd hoped for?"

He smiled. "I cannot come to your party because the doctors are operating to remove pieces of bone tormenting my knee." He frowned briefly and let the emotion go. "The rather nasty infection I've developed isn't getting any better. An operation seems to be the only solution."

"An operation?." She was pleased there didn't seem to be any reluctance or doubt in him. He was so dead set against anything that would keep in the hospital.

"My ordeal will soon be over. I'm on the schedule for tomorrow morning."

"How very fortunate you came to London." She wanted to be positive for his sake, but she wondered why the rush to operate? Usually the patient's infection was brought under control first.

"I have you to thank," he said.

"Me?"

"If you hadn't kept after me, I might still be idling away at the gamekeeper's cottage."

"I don't deserve all of the credit."

"There's risk, to be sure," he continued, "but it will be minimal."

He did look rather certain. Of course, the surgeons were excellent.

"How long do you expect to be in recovery?"

"A few weeks, I'm told." He squared his shoulders. "I'm fit and in good health. It won't take any time at all for me to spring back to my normal self."

"You are eager to return to the front."

He could be most guarded with his feelings, but at this moment he had the most loving way of looking at her.

"Yes, Livinia."

"I know this sounds odd, but I'm comforted by your determination. It's as if you won't rest until the world is sorted out."

"I hadn't thought of it that way."

"You believe your duty is to your men, but don't forget the rest of us depend on you as well."

He raised her hand and kissed it.

She must, for his sake, accept his decision.

"Then I am very happy for you." She hoped happiness was reflected in her eyes and not foreboding. She wanted so badly for him to be well, of course, but when he was healed, he would return to the war.

They walked hand in hand, fingers intertwined. They could be strong for each other, would be for whatever the future might bring.

They came to a park bench.

"Let's sit a while," she said and took a seat. He sat beside her.

"May I come and visit you in the hospital?"

"I appreciate the offer, but I think not."

"A person must not be alone at such a critical time."

"I will have competent nurses and doctors to take care of me."

"I have no doubt, but they are not the same."

"Indeed, they are not."

His refusal hurt her. Why did he reject a simple act of kindness? The barriers she'd thought had come tumbling down were still proving insurmountable.

"I am disappointed," she said.

"You needn't be. I find recuperating to be a trial and a nuisance, and I don't wish to be a burden."

"Now you are talking nonsense." She withdrew her hand. She wasn't cross, only stupefied. How could he think those who cared about him would think a visit would be a burden?

"Have you called Gwendolyn?" she asked.

At the mention of his family, he scowled. "Gwendolyn has her own life to live."

"Your brother is in London. Surely he will want to see you?"

"My brother will not come."

"How can you be so sure?"

What in his past had caused a rift between him and his brother? What could be so terrible, he made no effort to mend his family ties?

"I must say I do not understand your attitude."

"You think me indifferent?"

"I don't. Not at all, but you pretend to be."

He shrugged. "It is the nature of my profession."

"I am not convinced you care so little."

He turned to her. His eyes were very dark. She'd not thought him capable of fear, and yet she was sure he was frightened. "You do not understand."

"Then help me to understand. What has caused you to be so estranged from your own brother?"

He rubbed his forehead. In frustration? In confusion? Perhaps she shouldn't have spoken so boldly, and yet she felt he needed some prodding.

"Do not leave a reconciliation until it is too late," she cautioned.

"Some wounds don't heal."

"They won't until you try. Why won't you end this feud with your brother?"

His shoulders sagged as if she'd placed a terrible weight there. She could spare him of all he was feeling by a change of subject. She would not.

"My dear, I made a grievous mistake when I was a young man. My family has never forgiven me."

"Perhaps you cannot forgive yourself?"

His face bunched up in a scowl. "It isn't that easy."

"How difficult could it be?" She pushed a little harder. He wasn't an articulate man, and left to his own devices would continue to remain silent about what troubled him. "What was so horrible that you keep yourself at such a distance from your family?"

He looked at her and then looked away. A minute passed and then two. She feared she'd gone too far.

"My brother's wife, Judith," he said finally.

Livy understood as clearly as if he'd spoken the exact

words. "You were in love with her."

"For many years, I'm ashamed to say."

"I'm sorry," she said. How inadequate she felt at this moment. She hadn't been prepared for this revelation.

He crossed his arms as a nanny and her charge—cooing in a pram—passed by them.

"My brother and I both courted Judith. She was a beauty and utterly charming, but in the end, insecure and frightened. She picked my brother because he stood to inherit. Robert could give her a comfortable home and the lifestyle she was accustomed to living."

"You resented him all these years."

"More than resentment. I blamed my brother for Judith's death."

His wounds went deeper, she realized, than the enemy's shrapnel.

"My dear man, you have lived with a terrible guilt for a very long time. You must set it aside."

"I have tried. There's something more, a secret my brother and I have shared for many years."

"More secrets?"

"What I have to tell you will come as a shock."

"I rather doubt it. There's not much that shocks me anymore."

"Gwendolyn is not my niece," he said. "She is my daughter."

Livy opened her mouth and then closed it. She mustn't yield to her own emotions. He needed to finish.

"Her mother and I were very young. When she fell

pregnant, she panicked and accepted my brother's offer of marriage. He could give her the security I could not."

"How very sad for you."

"I believe now it was for the best. Gwendolyn has thrived under my brother's care."

"Have you told her?"

He shook his head. "She is very dear to me. I wouldn't hurt her for the world."

Livy knew he couldn't. "You kept silent to protect her mother's reputation. Now you wish to protect your daughter."

"You see, I'm not the man you believed me to be."

"My opinion of you hasn't changed. I think what you have done is heroic."

"Hardly." He scoffed.

"You may not think so, but Gwendolyn will. You must tell her."

"Perhaps after the war is over." He looked at her. "In the event I don't return, I have a favor to ask?"

"Of course."

"Would you tell her?"

"Me?" She could not have imagined them speaking so frankly to each other only a few days ago.

"My wonderful, kind Livinia. You will know what to say."

She should say no, but he didn't have anyone else to ask.

"Very well, but I prefer you tell her yourself."

He sat back, looking relieved. The secret had been a

heavy burden to bear.

"How amazing you turned to Gwendolyn when you needed help," she said. "I know how difficult that must have been for you."

"I sought out a quiet place, and I knew she wouldn't refuse. To be honest, she's the only person in the family who talks to me."

She moved closer. "I am glad you have confided in me."

His eyes shone with goodwill. "I have enjoyed our talks as I have enjoyed your company."

"We shall continue to do so," Livy replied.

They would write each other letters. Each correspondence would be a sharing of their day, of ideas, and of their fears and their sorrows. This is what she could do for him. Would do for him.

"What is to become of us?"

"I cannot say," he answered. "The world is a dangerous place."

Livy rested her head on his shoulder. She'd not hesitated to do so believing the moment too precious to deny oneself the opportunity. He put his arm around her. They held each other, two people who'd found contentment and peace—if only for an afternoon.

Chapter Twenty-Five

>>>«««

J ames was assigned a bed by the head Sister, a woman whose gaze bore into him as if he was a naughty boy who'd just pulled a prank. He was reminded of the nanny who'd been employed to take care of him and his brother. The woman had been strict with her charges. She had never spared the rod where discipline was concerned.

"Here's a hospital gown and socks for your feet." She drew a curtain across a metal bar in one stroke to give him some privacy.

He stripped off his clothes as he'd been told to do and shrugged on the thin gown, tying the string at the neckline. The gown came to his swollen knee, exposing the inflamed surgical scar, several inches long and showing no improvement. The socks were too big.

When he was done changing, he sat on the bed and waited for the Sister to return. This time she carried a clipboard.

"This is just a formality, you understand. Do you have anyone you wish us to contact in case it is necessary?" She readied her pencil to write down a name.

"No," he said firmly. He wouldn't trouble Gwendolyn and her husband.

"There must be someone."

He realized what she was asking. Who would they call if the procedure was not successful? Who would take responsibility for his remains if the surgery resulted in his death?

"Mrs. Livinia Pratt," he said. "If the worst happens, she will know what to do."

The Sister scribbled the name, address and phone number James gave her. "What relation is she to you?"

"She's a friend, Sister."

The woman looked up from her writing. "Usually patients list a family member."

"My wishes are for Mrs. Pratt to be my proxy."

"Very well. I will contact her if the necessity arises." She tucked the clipboard under her arm. Her voice held a tone of efficiency. No doubt this was a question she asked often.

"Only if the worst happens." He was emphatic.

The nurse took a deep breath, no doubt ready to explain some hospital rule.

If she called Livinia, James knew what would come next. Livinia, believing he needed assistance, would be here in a shot. He couldn't ask her to come and hold his hand, even though that was exactly what he would like.

There was no reason to worry the dear lady who would be busy with preparations for her reunion with her son, and he didn't wish to interrupt the happy event.

He scowled, and the Sister clamped her mouth shut.

Without any more inquiries she left, having completed her unhappy task.

How did the nursing staff manage? To be surrounded by death and dying was not something a woman should have to endure. Except he'd learned women could be hard as steel if the occasion demanded.

James remained rooted to the spot. He was not about to lay down in bed this early in the evening. Nor could he roam the halls dressed as he was.

The room was cold and smelled of antiseptic. The chill seeped into his bones. Still, he considered himself fortunate. Compared to the deplorable conditions in the field hospitals, he was grateful to be having his surgery here.

Livinia had taught him to be thankful. He'd become a terrible ogre when it came to showing gratitude. It was not how he wished to be.

His confession yesterday in the park had been such a relief. Livinia had not found him wanting.

He considered himself a lucky man.

The soldier in the bed next to him moaned. James parted the curtain. The man's head was wrapped in gauze, his curly locks spilling over the bandage.

For the first time, James looked around him. There were eight beds in a room suitable for four. Every bed had a patient.

These were not the lads sent off to war with parades and brass bands. Not the boys waving proudly at pretty girls, their chests pushed out as they stepped smartly.

These were men, stooped in the shoulders and saddened by what they'd witnessed.

"Seems we both gave Fritz a run for his money," the young man said. He extended a hand. "Captain Joseph Stein."

"Major James Gunnison."

The boy saluted and made an effort to sit up, but James stopped him with a firm hand on his shoulder.

"Rest easy, Captain." He would not add to his burden by asking him to acknowledge rank.

"At what campaign were you injured?" Captain Stein asked.

"Loos."

"Suvia Bay for me." He gave a strangled laugh.

"Gallipoli. Bad business, that."

"The worst."

James thought it best not to ask more. The days of battles and campaigns were behind Captain Stein. There would be better days ahead in which to relive the agony and brutality, to talk of the loss. Right now, what this soldier needed most was to concentrate on his recovery.

In contrast, an injured leg seemed a minor inconvenience, and James was ashamed he'd made a fuss over a bit of shrapnel and bone.

"I must say I can't wait to leave this place," the young captain said, without a trace of a doubt.

"Have you been here long?"

"More days than I can count." His eyes glistened. "My family will be here soon to take me home."

James looked away. The captain was fortunate, indeed.

A young nurse came into the ward, carrying a tray. "Time for your medication, Captain Stein," she said cheerfully.

James sat back on his bed, and she closed the curtain between them.

He listened as she attended to the captain. He did not want to take the tablets, he told her. The medicine upset his stomach.

"It's for your own good," she replied, as stern as any matron.

She cajoled and scolded him until he relented.

The captain began to cough violently, presumably from drinking a glass of water.

"There, there," she said. "You're going to be all right."

Whether that was true or not was something she couldn't know, James would like to tell her. Why give hope that might be false?

The captain mumbled his appreciation and thanks. If he believed her, it was irrelevant, James realized. What counted was the will to go forward.

Hope was the catalyst.

Livinia had urged him to contact his brother, to forgive the past. Why was he being so stubborn? Why had he written a letter and not bothered to post it?

As the nurse passed his bed, James hailed her.

"Is there a telephone?" he asked too loudly.

She jumped and regarded him with eyes blinking. "Yes, sir, down the hall."

James grasped the back opening of the offensive gown and proceeded out of the ward. He was met in the corridor by the Sister. She narrowed her eyes.

"I must make a telephone call," he said. Apparently, she'd the ridiculous impression he needed her permission.

"Very good, Major. You'll find one down this hall on the left." She continued on her way.

The telephone machine was mounted on the wall, but no chair had been provided. The pain in his knee now radiated upward, reaching his groin. Standing was a chore. No matter. The conversation would be brief.

He told the operator the number. Two short rings were immediately answered.

"Gunnison residence. Maitland, the butler, speaking."

"Major James Gunnison here. By any chance is my brother available?"

"I will go and see, sir."

James waited, balancing on his good leg.

"Hello?"

The sound of his brother's voice made him apprehensive. He wasn't sure what to say.

"Robert, James here."

There was a moment when the only sound was the buzzing in the line. He feared they'd been disconnected.

Or had Robert hung up? Did his brother consider his call intrusive after all these years?

"Gwendolyn has told me you were in Kent with her

and Ronald," Robert replied stiffly.

"Good. I didn't know if she had."

"Something about an injury to your knee?"

"Yes." James paused to take a breath. "I'm in London now. I just wanted you to know I'm in the hospital, and the procedure to repair the wound has been scheduled for first thing tomorrow morning."

"Surgery? Nothing serious, is it?"

"The doctors are removing some bone chips," James replied. "There will be a week or two of convalescing, I'm afraid."

"That is to be expected, I should think."

"Yes, well, I just thought you should know."

"Of course."

"I'll ring off, then." An ache centered in James's chest. There was so much more to say.

"Jims?" It was the name his brother had called him when they were boys.

"Yes?"

"Are you allowed visitors?"

James had not thought he would ask. "Yes, although I'm afraid I will not be myself afterward."

"Quite."

James would like to kick himself. Why had he said such a thing?

"Perhaps when you are feeling better," his brother said, "when you're on the mend, you might come around for dinner?"

James smiled. "I would like to, very much."

"Then it's settled."

"I look forward to seeing you again. We have a great deal to catch up on."

"Take care of yourself."

"I will, Robbie. Good bye." As James hung up, he realized how much he had missed his brother.

His throat tightened and he'd difficulty swallowing. He wasn't about to fall apart in front of the nursing staff or these brave men looking to him to be strong. So he pulled himself together the best he could before proceeding down the hall and back to bed.

Chapter Twenty-Six

>》》《《《

W hen Livy descended the staircase the next morning, Mother Pratt's household was already a cyclone of activity.

Holbrook and his staff always set a fine table and Livy made it her first task to check on the dining room arrangements. Sixteen had been invited, along with the six of them, which put the count at twenty-two.

The dining room gave the impression of a banquet hall. Contrary to Livy's wishes, the party would be spectacular—just as they had been before the war.

Mother Pratt had ordered fresh flowers be put around. Their autumn colors added to the room's festive appearance.

Not that Wyatt would notice. Or maybe he would. Livy could never tell with her son. Would he appreciate the dining room splendid in gold and burnt orange chrysanthemums, with spikes of dark red gladiolas, and feathery grasses? Or would he be preoccupied with the war, as James always seemed to be?

She straightened a gladiola stalk. James would be preparing for his operation. How she rejoiced he was having the procedure at last. The pain he'd endured would become a distant memory, a trying time in his war years. His recovery would be a blessing, and yet she was uneasy about the speed in which the doctors had decided to proceed.

She dismissed her worries as unproductive. James knew what he was about, and he was in the care of the best doctors in London, probably in all of England. Still, she couldn't help but worry. So much could go wrong with anesthesia involved.

What of Gwendolyn and his past? The shock that he was a father had worn off. She was glad he'd confided in her. He'd carried the burden of guilt for far too long. One day soon, she hoped, his family would be reunited.

Satisfied all was perfection, and the way it had always been done, Livy joined her mother-in-law in the parlor. The children were occupied in their room. Elizabeth had not yet come down.

Mother Pratt stabbed at a needlepoint as the mantel clock ticked away. Livy had not told her mother-in-law about the operation. She would share the news with everyone when Wyatt arrived, the telling would be over and done with at one go.

"Thank you for having a breakfast tray sent up," Livy said.

"I hope everything was satisfactory."

"Indeed. I feel quite pampered."

Livy steeled herself from looking at the mantel clock.

How long did this kind of operation take? Was it a simple matter of taking out the fragments of bone? What about the infection? Would James be able to get up and around as soon as the anesthetic wore off?

"Have you spoken to Elizabeth?" Mother Pratt asked.

"Yes," Livy said. "Last night when she arrived."

"I trust she is well?"

"Very much so."

"Is she still thinking about the nursing corps?"

"She will tell you all about it."

The old woman's face puckered. "When do we expect Wyatt?"

"He didn't give a time. I hope soon."

Mother Pratt shook her head. "What does time mean to a boy his age?"

Livy heard the sadness in the woman's voice.

"Wyatt will join us in due course," Livy declared, which wasn't much comfort to either of them.

Since Wyatt's letter had arrived, Livy had detected a slight change in her mother-in-law's attitude. Her open hostility had been mitigated, but why and for how long?

Livy couldn't help but wonder and worry about what the day held in store for them all, and Mother Pratt kept her thoughts private and continued her needlepoint.

Livy hung up the telephone receiver, crestfallen. The nurse at the hospital had not shared any information about

James's condition. Such details were only give to family, she'd been told.

Resigned to being kept in the dark, she returned to the parlor where Mother Pratt and Elizabeth chatted. Her oldest daughter had dressed in Oriental silks. Her tea gown was a cornucopia of color.

They looked at her as she resumed her seat.

"What's troubling you, Mother?" Elizabeth had picked up on Livy's despondency.

She wouldn't withhold information any longer. "Major Gunnison was scheduled to have an operation on his knee this morning."

"So that's what all your fidgeting is about," Mother Pratt said.

"Have you learned the result?" Elizabeth asked.

Livy shook her head. "No one at the hospital will tell me anything, but he must be all right."

Her mother-in-law made sympathetic noises. "It must be very difficult on a person to go through such an ordeal."

Livy found Mother Pratt uncharacteristically sympathetic. She didn't trust the woman and wondered why the change of heart. Was it for Elizabeth's benefit?

"I'd like to go over to the hospital after Wyatt arrives and see how the major is coming along," Livy said.

"A very good idea," Mother Pratt said. "We all must do what we can to be supportive."

"Would you like me to join you, Mother?" Elizabeth asked.

"If you'd like."

Elizabeth nodded. "Wyatt will want to come as well."

"Perhaps another time?" Mother Pratt replied. "You all can't abandon me. I see so little of you as it is."

"Tomorrow would be better," Elizabeth agreed. "Too many visitors after an operation might overtire the major."

Fortunately, Elizabeth understood her grandmother better than Livy gave her credit for.

Livy smiled. "I will give you a full report when I return."

"Don't be long," Mother Pratt insisted. "I depend on you to help greet our guests."

"I will be here," Livy replied.

The doorbell rang. Mother Pratt's hand froze in mid-air. They exchanged glances. Livy heard the front door being opened and the sound of male voices. One of them belonged to Wyatt. Her poor heart was aflutter.

Her son had not told the time of his train's arrival into Paddington. He could be so forgetful about such things. If she'd known, they could've met him at the station. He had been, of course, able to hire a cab. A boy of nineteen was capable of finding his way around the city.

Now here he was, half past eleven and in time for luncheon.

The parlor doors opened. Wyatt strode into the room. Livy was stunned by the change in him. This wasn't the Wyatt she'd sent off to training. Her son wore the khaki service dress of an Army man. He removed his forage cap and tucked it under his arm and grinned in a boyish way. Some things would never change.

Livy leapt to her feet, unable to contain her excitement. She reached out with trembling hands.

"How good to see you." She wrapped her arms around his neck and hugged him fiercely.

Wyatt protested and pulled away. His face had gone all ruddy. Such demonstrations embarrassed him, Livy was well aware, but she couldn't help herself.

"He looks marvelous, doesn't he, Grandmamma?"

Her mother-in-law had watched from her perch. She'd kept her composure for propriety's sake. An emotional outburst was not her way.

"Indeed, you look very handsome," Mother Pratt answered.

Wyatt leaned over and gave the old woman a kiss on the cheek. "How good to see you both." Wyatt stood between them, shoulders back and head held high.

Elizabeth was the last to welcome him. She gave him a quick peck on the cheek. "Training seems to agree with you."

Wyatt laughed. "The food could be better."

"We'll soon put you to rights," Mother Pratt said.

"Thought you'd be on your way to nurses' training?" Wyatt asked his sister.

"I leave for my studies next week."

"Capital. The need for nurses is enormous, I'm told."

Livy fished a handkerchief from her sleeve and dabbed at the corner of her eyes.

Wyatt pulled down his tunic secured with a webbed belt. "I've been assigned to a Stokes Mortar team." He showed them the flaming grenade badge on his right arm.

Livy's heart sank an inch. Her son's job would be to diffuse unexploded ordnance. She was only too aware, remembering how James had been injured, of the danger.

"You must tell us everything," Mother Pratt said with a nod toward the sofa opposite her.

Wyatt sat. He was not yet beyond her influence.

Livy returned to her chair.

"As I said in my letter, my training is finished," Wyatt exclaimed.

The next question would be difficult to articulate.

"Do you know when you will be leaving for a posting?" Livy asked.

Before he could answer, the little girls arrived and did not hesitate to shower their brother with hugs. They both talked at once, asking every question imaginable.

"If only your father could be here." Mother Pratt's voice rose above the others.

Livy had the same regret.

"Major Gunnison is in London," Elizabeth said.

"Jolly good," Wyatt said. "He's recovered from his wounds?"

"He's in the hospital," Livy explained. "The surgeon removed bone fragments from his knee this morning. They seem to be the cause of his persistent infection."

Wyatt grimaced. "Bad luck, that."

"He expects a complete recovery," Livy replied.

"We all pray for the major's good health," Mother Pratt added.

It was a generous remark, Livy decided. She cast her mother-in-law a smile. Ever since Wyatt's letter had arrived, the prickliness between them had gone.

Had Mother Pratt changed her mind about having the girls live with her?

Livy wondered. Would the old woman give up that easily?

With his sisters on either side, Wyatt began to tell them of his time in Richmond.

Livy listened with interest. She couldn't imagine her son being subject to early wake-up calls or to the high standard of wearing a uniform with buttons polished to a brilliant shine. A necktie was a mystery to him, and he'd never known the first thing about laundry and soap powder.

She turned to her mother-in-law. "Now that Wyatt has arrived, I want to go to the hospital to see how the major is getting along."

"By all means." Mother Pratt frowned but briefly.

"The major will be in recovery by now," she explained to Wyatt. "He should wake up to a friendly face, don't you agree?"

"I will go with you," Wyatt said, standing.

"No, you will not." Mother Pratt's mouth twisted disagreeably. "You've only just arrived."

"We'll go tomorrow," Elizabeth said.

"I will take the major your good wishes," Livy said.

"You'll be home at a respectable time?" Mother Pratt asked again. Was it for emphasis or some other reason?

"Visiting hours are, I'm sure, limited," Livy said.

Mother Pratt turned an adoring gaze on Wyatt. "Perhaps you could accompany your grandmother on a walk in the park? The weather has been unusually agreeable."

"I will escort you wherever you like," Wyatt said, ever the diplomat. Wyatt had always been good about consenting to his grandmother's wishes. Unfortunately, she was never slow to express them.

Livy was proud of her son, of the man he'd become. He was generous and kind, and understood his duty.

How glad she was to have her family together. They would have a wonderful evening, she was sure.

She excused herself and found Holbrook waiting with her coat.

"Shall I have the motor brought around, Mrs. Pratt?"

"No, I'll take the trolley."

"Very good, Ma'am."

As she descended the steps into the front garden, Livy saw the drape in the bow window fall back into place.

No doubt her mother-in-law had been watching.

Livy shivered. What was the old lady up to?

Moving quickly, she caught the trolley at the stop on the corner. She climbed aboard, paid the driver, and found a seat. The trolley gained speed and they were soon hurtling down the busy city streets at a breakneck pace. Livy hung on to the brass railing for dear life.

Finally they arrived at the stop only a short walk to

the hospital. She descended the steps and hurried toward the large stone building. A patient—helped down the steps by nurses on either side of him—stared at her.

Livy said hello and tried to keep a cheerful appearance, but her heart broke to see his suffering.

A gentleman opened the heavy door and followed her inside. The place was a beehive of activity.

"May I help?" One of the nurses stopped when she saw Livy.

"I am looking for one of the patients," Livy said. "Major Gunnison."

"Sorry, but visitor's hours are over," she said.

"His operation was scheduled for this morning." Livy couldn't help but be disappointment. "Could you tell me how it went? My family and I are concerned."

"I'm afraid I cannot, but I will take a note to him if you'd like."

Livy didn't press. The girl must obey orders. "I suppose a note will have to do." She took the scrap of paper and a pencil the nurse handed to her and scribbled down her best wishes.

"Mrs. Pratt?"

Livy looked up from the note. "Yes?"

The woman approaching at a brisk pace wore an air of superiority. Livy stepped back so she wouldn't be bowled over.

"I rang the house and they said you were here. I'm Sister Evans." She dismissed the young nurse with a glance.

Fear knifed through Livy. She crumbled the note.

"The major has listed you as the person to contact if need be."

"Yes?" Livy braced herself for bad news.

"There's been a complication with Major Gunnison's operation."

"What kind of complication?"

The sister met her gaze. "I'm afraid the outcome of the major's surgery wasn't what we would've liked."

Frightened about what all this could mean, Livy grew impatient. "Tell me what has happened."

"Will you come with me?" Sister Evans beckoned her to follow.

"Yes, Sister, I will come at once."

Sister Evans showed her into a small reception room. "Won't you sit down, Mrs. Pratt."

Livy collapsed into a straight back chair.

"Dr. Wells will be in to see you as soon as he's finished with his rounds."

"Is he dead?"

"No, Mrs. Pratt."

Livy relaxed a fraction, having feared the worst.

"I must return to my duties," Sister Evans said. "Dr. Wells will explain everything." She departed, leaving the door open.

Livy waited in the reception room, staring at nothing in

particular. The light in the room faded. Hours must've passed. Why didn't somebody come and tell her what had happened? Had the surgeon forgotten about her?

Mother Pratt needed help with the preparations for tonight's dinner, but she couldn't go until she knew James would be all right.

She rose from her chair, tired of sitting, and looked out the window, to the rows of buildings across the street and the rooftops in the distance. Beyond them was her farm, and their peaceful, rural existence. She'd resented the war's intrusion, had tried to keep it from interfering with her family. She could no longer brush it aside and pretend it was far away. They were all connected to its demands and sacrifices.

She left the window and peered out into the hallway, hoping to catch one of the staff. To her surprise, Wyatt and Elizabeth rushed toward her.

"Mother, are you all right?" Wyatt hurried to her side and grasped her hand.

"We were so worried when you didn't come home," Elizabeth said.

She told them what she knew, which was precious little. They were adults, and there was no need to soften the truth.

"They probably found gangrene," Elizabeth said.

"Dr. Bainbridge thought they might," Livy replied.

"Will he recover?" Wyatt asked.

"Most likely, but it will take time." Elizabeth pulled a face. "I'm sorry. He was so keen to return to the front."

"At least the source of the pain has been dealt with," Livy said. "It will be only a matter of time to recuperate from the infection."

"Can we see him?" Wyatt asked.

"The Sister told me to wait here. I can't tell you how long it will be."

Elizabeth buttoned her coat. "We'd better go, we promised Grandmamma we wouldn't be long."

"I'll stay a while longer. I want to be here when he wakes up," Livy said. "I'll be home as soon as I can."

She gave Wyatt a hug. He didn't resist. Elizabeth embraced her. "Goodbye, Mother. Give the major our best."

As she watched them go, she realized how proud she was of both of them. She gave them high marks for compassion and caring, important qualities, especially in this time of loss.

James awoke, unsure where he was. For a moment, he thought he was at the gamekeeper's cottage.

The familiar odors of a hospital brought him back to the present. He tried to sit up, but his effort was for naught and he fell back against the thin pillow. His arms were like rubber. He'd never felt so weak.

He realized he wasn't alone. Livinia slept in a chair by his side. Her hair was in disarray, the pins having fallen out.

He drew in a breath, but even that took effort.

The Sister, attending to others in the ward, noticed he was awake.

"What is she doing here?" His voice sounded raspy. His throat hurt.

"She was here when you came out of surgery. The doctor took the liberty of informing her of the results."

Blast. She shouldn't be here. He didn't want her seeing him like this.

"What time is it?" He was annoyed that he'd lost track of the hour.

"It's nearly twelve o'clock, sir."

"Aren't visiting hours over by now?"

The woman drew back as if he'd spit on her clean floor. "Major, Mrs. Pratt has been here three days."

The information he'd been unconscious for that amount of time came like a blow.

"Three days?" he bellowed.

"That's correct, sir."

"Mrs. Pratt has been here all this time?"

"Oh yes, sir. Day and night."

James huffed. No wonder Livinia was exhausted.

"Now if you would try and conserve your strength." The Sister reached up to close the muslin curtain.

"Were there complications?" He'd no intention of relaxing until he knew precisely what had happened.

The Sister's gaze softened. "The doctor will be around to tell you in more detail, I'm sure."

"What did he find? Surely you can tell me that much?"

She bit her lower lip. "Gangrene had developed in the knee."

"I'm not sure I understand. I know what gangrene looks like. There were no signs of gangrene."

The nurse shook her head. "You were very close to septic shock."

"My word, I had no idea." He hadn't realized how very serious his condition had become. "Did the surgeon get the bone fragments out?"

"Yes, Major Gunnison, he did."

"Good. Excellent." He exhaled. "And the gangrene. Has it been dealt with?"

"I'll go fetch the doctor. He can better answer your questions." She hurried away.

Livinia slept soundly. He could easily reach her head and would like to stroke her hair. He'd not forgotten how soft it was. Mindful of where they were, he held back.

Despite his protests, he found comfort from her presence. He would be dishonest to claim otherwise. She'd watched and worried over him as skilled doctors performed admirably to mend his leg.

When she awoke, he would express his appreciation.

A nurse came into the room rattling a stack of bedpans. She set the top one at the foot of his bed.

He would like to avail himself of the pan but wouldn't as Livinia slumbered. Nor would he wake her.

The nurse seemed to understand his dilemma. She put her hand on Livinia's shoulder.

"Mrs. Pratt, the major is with us again."

Livinia raised her head and pushed the tendrils of hair off her face.

She looked up at the nurse and then turned to him. Her eyes were clouded with sleep but he'd not seen anyone so lovely.

She grasped his hand. Her soft, warm skin penetrated his defenses.

"You look remarkable," she said as she squeezed.

"I feel well, considering."

She smiled. "How glad I am to hear you say so."

"I understand the operation was a success." He looked up at the nurse. "How long before I can get out of this bed?"

The nurse exchanged glances with Livinia.

"He doesn't know?" Livinia asked her.

"Sister has sent for the doctor," the nurse replied.

"Know what?" he demanded. He hated when people around him talked cryptically.

Livinia withdrew her hand. The color had drained out of her.

"Speak up, woman."

She straightened her spine and her eyes flashed a warning. He had spoken too harshly. She was not a tongue-tied corporal who could be easily intimidated. He'd learned as much the very first time they'd met.

"Livinia," he modified the volume of his voice. "Please tell me what it is I don't know."

She glanced at the sheet covering him. He tore his gaze from her and looked. The sheet was tented over his bad knee.

"I'm afraid the doctor had to amputate," Livinia said. "The infection had become a great deal more dangerous than we had realized."

The horror of what had happened took some time to register. "The leg is gone?"

She nodded.

He jerked the sheet off of him. What he saw didn't look real.

"This wasn't supposed to happen," he shouted at everyone in the room.

Livinia stood and took a couple steps back, the chair moving with her.

"I'll go get a sedative," the nurse scurried away.

"What have they done? I gave no one permission to take my leg."

"James, the doctor saved your life." Livinia's voice wavered.

"Leave me," he said so severely it took his breath away. He struggled for air, and at last it came. "Leave me alone."

"Naturally you are upset," she said.

"Did you not hear me? I said leave me alone! I do not want to hear any excuses, and I don't need any more of your meddling." His shouting brought unwanted stares from the other men in the room. A nurse came running from the hallway.

James glared at her as well.

"Maybe it's best you go now, Mrs. Pratt," she said.

Livinia hesitated a moment, her face contorted. James shut his eyes, his anger consuming him.

"Goodbye, James," she said. And then she fled.

Chapter Twenty-Seven

>»>««<

Livy didn't return to the hospital. She wouldn't. James's outburst had been understandable—shock had put him in a frightful state. She'd come up against his bluster many a time and could forgive him.

That's not why she wouldn't go back.

If she hadn't required so much of him, if she hadn't invited him to Wyatt's birthday party or badgered him with her visits, perhaps he would've had time to rest. He'd spent the day helping with the hops harvest. Why had she let him?

It'd seemed so important at the time that he take part in the community around him. She'd wanted him to know people cared about him, and he didn't have to be alone.

In hindsight, she'd made a terrible mistake.

Sitting with Mother Pratt in her overheated parlor with the rain spitting against the windowpane, Livy struggled with remorse.

A strained silence existed between her and Mother Pratt ever since the morning when Livy had returned home from the hospital three days late.

Livy wasn't complaining. Silence was sometimes preferable to arguing.

Amazingly, no accusations had been made. There had been no harsh words or slanderous comments about Livy's character even though she had missed the dinner party and the rest of Wyatt's short leave.

Elizabeth had gone off to her nurses' training without a farewell from her mother. What kind of mother neglects her children in such an appalling way?

"What's troubling you?" Mother Pratt's fingers nimbly worked the needlepoint that never seemed to get completed.

"Nothing," she replied.

"Don't give me the run around, I can see you are miserable."

She attempted a smile, but it lacked any sincerity. "I worry about Wyatt and Elizabeth."

"Of course you do. As we all do."

"I'm surprised you don't fault me for not being here when they left."

Mother Pratt shook her head. "I admit my judgments of late have been severe."

Severe and unkind. Livy had to wonder where this conversation was going.

"Have you heard anything new about the major's condition?"

"No." Of course, Mother Pratt must wonder why Livy didn't return to the hospital.

Livy wasn't about to tell her.

"Such a pity for a man in his prime."

Pity was the last thing James needed, Livy thought. She wished she could share how much she'd come to love the man, but Livy didn't wish to discuss matters of the heart with her mother-in-law.

"We must pray for a satisfactory recovery," Mother Pratt said as she put the finishing stitch to a delicate primrose.

"Yes," Livy replied, unsure what a satisfactory recovery could mean. Mother Pratt put down her sewing. "Being a widow is a lonely business."

Livy's insides constricted. She was in no mood for a lecture.

"The world is changing in ways we can't even imagine," Mother Pratt continued.

"I suppose you are right."

Mother Pratt nodded. There was never any doubt.

"You think me a horrid old woman," she said.

Livy wouldn't be trapped into lying. "Sometimes you can be…possessive."

"I only want what's best for the girls."

"Really?" Livy exhaled. "I think you want what's best for yourself."

Her mother-in-law didn't even wince. Instead, she remained perfectly calm, with her back straight and her hands folded neatly in her lap. It was as if she'd expected what Livy would say.

"I've never told anyone," Mother Pratt said, "but after my husband died, I became acquainted with a gentleman—a man of outstanding character."

Had Livy heard correctly? This wasn't the woman she'd known for two decades, the woman whose dedication to her family had always been paramount.

"You're thinking my behavior scandalous, of course. I don't blame you. I've often thought it myself."

"I do not," Livy protested.

Mother Pratt continued as if she hadn't heard. "I shouldn't have encouraged him. A relationship, a second marriage was frowned upon in those days—especially to a man of a lesser station."

"What happened to your friend?" Livy asked with gentleness.

"He died several years later, I'm told. How different those last years would have been for both of us if society had been kinder."

A swell of sympathy overtook Livy with gale force. Her mother-in-law had followed the rules, had done what had been expected of her, but at a terrible cost.

Livy understood the source of her mother-in-law's unpleasantness and why her life had eroded to the point of bitterness.

"I'm very sorry for your loss." She rose and sat next to the woman who'd been such a source of conflict during her marriage and after Charles's death.

Her mother-in-law looked at her without the severity she was used to. "What I'm saying is don't deny yourself even a modicum of happiness if you possibly can."

Here was a rare moment of reconciliation. Although

the confession took Livy by surprise, she'd grasped the significance.

"You are correct to assume Major Gunnison and I had grown fond of each other, but that is over."

"Because of my objections?"

Livy shook her head. "Because he doesn't wish anyone to care for him or care about him, for that matter."

"It is his training." Mother Pratt said. "They teach these things in the military so the pain of loss isn't debilitating."

"More than just his military career holds him back." Livy had believed his past had released him. After their conversation on the park bench, he seemed happy. "He won't risk any attachments, I'm afraid."

"You must persuade him."

"I'm grateful to have your encouragement, but I've made my decision." The major had rejected her outright. It was his way of coping, of course, but Livy must respect his wishes.

Mother Pratt brushed a tear from her cheek. "Look at me, I'm such a foolish romantic."

"It's a side of you I find quite appealing."

She dabbed at fresh tears with her handkerchief. "I've misjudged you. You could've made life difficult for me."

"I know how important family is to you. We share that trait."

"I am most grateful, my dear Livinia," she said.

"That's why I brought the children to London. We must stick together, especially now."

"I want to be part of their lives."

"You will be. The children can come to London on their holidays. You are always welcome at Fairview."

Her mother-in-law nodded.

"It's time for us to go home," Livy said. "The girls have missed far too much school, and I have a farm to run."

Mother Pratt sighed. "As you wish. I hope my invitation to Fairview for Christmas is still open?"

"It is."

"Then I will accept."

Livy couldn't help but smile. How glad she was that they'd come to a ceasefire. Who knows? One day they might even like each other.

"You have a visitor, Major Gunnison." The ginger-haired nurse stood at the end of his bed.

"I don't wish to see anybody," he grumbled. No one seemed to listen anymore.

"She's most insistent."

"Send her away, I tell you. Can't a man's wishes be respected?"

She stood her ground. "I'm glad to see there's still some fight in you."

A fat lot she knew. He was well aware the hospital staff regarded him as a toothless cur. "Nothing to fear," he heard them say to each other. "His bark is much worse than his bite."

A second nurse entered the ward. He ground his teeth.

They buzzed around him, seeking to be helpful. Didn't they understand there was nothing to be done? All he wanted was to be left alone!

This nurse was dressed differently. She wore blue with a red cross on a white apron. A scarf covered her head and had been tied at the nape of her slender neck. On closer examination, he realized it was Elizabeth Pratt.

He struggled to sit up. He wasn't about to let her see him flat on his back. The impossibly cheerful nurse brought a second pillow from an empty bed.

Elizabeth took it from her. "I can manage."

She settled the second pillow behind his back.

His vision blurred and his head seemed to be spinning around. It took a few seconds for him to recover. He hadn't sat up for a while, as he'd not seen the point.

"There you are, that's much better." Elizabeth spoke as if she knew what he was experiencing. She drew up a chair and sat next to him. There was a maturity about her, a confidence he'd not noticed before.

"I didn't recognize you at first." His voice was hoarse, the sound grating.

"Not the kind of clothes I'm used to wearing." She touched the scarf. "I'm almost done with my training at the Red Cross Hospital in Netley."

"I'm very glad if that is your desire."

"Oh, it is. The work is hard, much harder than I could have ever imagined, but for the first time in my life I feel

I'm doing something important."

James met her gaze. She was young, capable, and willing to face the challenges ahead. The frivolity and carelessness of youth were gone. In time, she would come to appreciate what she'd lost.

He did not ask after Livinia. His monstrous behavior coming out of the anesthetic had been unforgivable.

"How have you been?" she asked.

"Passable."

"I'm told you make a poor patient."

James scowled. The Pratt women never did mince words.

Miss Elizabeth patted his hand. Such a display of affection jarred his composure, but he didn't pull away.

"There is nothing the staff can do and yet they persist on being helpful," James grumbled.

"Lying in this bed all day cannot be comfortable."

"I tire easily."

"Or wise. You risk pneumonia."

"You sound like the head nurse."

"Best you take your leave," Elizabeth said. "There are wonderful places to go for rehabilitation."

"What good would rehabilitation do me? For what purpose?"

"Only you can answer that."

He huffed. "Time to let the next generation take over. I've done all I can."

"You're going to pack it in?"

He met her gaze. "Who wants a man with one leg?"

"I don't know, but there must be something you can do."

Thankfully, she didn't try to soothe him with platitudes. Lord knows he'd heard enough in the past few weeks. None of them stuck. No one could grasped how useless he felt. He resented all of them for trying.

She gave his hand a gentle squeeze. "After I've completed my training, I will be assigned to a field hospital in Bayeux."

Much as he wished otherwise, he could not spare her the horrors of what she would see on the battlefields in France.

"We are told to keep a sunny disposition, to be cheerful at all times. I must confess, I'm not sure if I can."

He was her confidant again. She trusted her deepest feelings to his care.

"You will do splendidly." He knew she would face the challenges regardless of her fears because she no longer idealized them.

She smiled just like her mother often did. "Thank you for your confidence in me. I know how much you abhor weakness."

James turned away from her gaze. Had he been so superior, so arrogant?

He looked back at her. She regarded him with a worried expression.

"What is it you've not told me?" he said.

His observation brought a grimace. There was something wrong, he had not been mistaken. She was deeply unhappy.

Elizabeth looked down at their hands clasped together. "I have met a young man, a captain. He's a patient at Netley. The sisters warned us not to become involved with our wards. Who can predict such things?"

James nodded. He was not immune to these yearnings that belonged to the young.

"I'm not sure I can keep my emotions tucked away until my service is done," Elizabeth said.

She sought his advice. He could give her direction from his own experience.

"Detachment will keep you from despair," he said.

"When the war is over? How will I recover my humanity?"

Her frankness reminded him of his own concerns. "Where does it come from?"

Her reply came quickly. "From what I value, I suppose: family, friends, my community."

"Then that is where you must turn." It seemed to be so simple, and yet it was a lesson he'd not yet learned. He was nothing more than a curmudgeon who had driven his friends and family away.

She released him and stood. He didn't want her go. He had enjoyed her company.

"Is there anything you need me to do?" She raised a brow.

He shifted in his bed, aware she was reprimanding him.

"Perhaps you would convey my fondest wishes to

your mother?"

"I will," she said, "but you had better do so yourself."

He didn't even know how to start. He'd spoken out of anger to dear Livinia, and she had suffered from the ugliness of his words. How could he have been so unkind to someone so caring?

"How are your mother and the girls?" he asked.

"They are all fine."

"I expect they have returned to Fairview?"

"Mother and the girls returned to the farm several weeks ago."

This news came as no surprise. Fairview was where she belonged.

"And Wyatt?"

"He is somewhere in France. Mother has received one letter since he left. He's a notoriously poor writer."

James didn't give her any reassurances or make any promises. Elizabeth was too smart a girl to accept them.

"I must go," she said. "I will tell Mother you asked about her."

He felt the loss of her parting. Why it should be so, he couldn't fathom. She was not his daughter, and yet he would have been proud to call her his own.

Elizabeth replaced the chair from where she'd appropriated it. "Mother would like to see you, you know, although she won't admit it."

"I'm afraid I've been rather a grump. I am deeply sorry."

"I will convey your regrets to her as well." She kissed

his cheek. "Thank you, Major, for your help. There are so few people I can talk to who speak with such honesty."

It was a compliment he didn't deserve.

"When I come home," she said, "we will talk some more."

"Mother, I need to speak with you."

Elizabeth joined Livy in the parlor. She was dressed simply in a woolen skirt and jumper and looked very thin to Livy's practiced eye. Since her daughter had returned from nurses' training, Livy had seen more than a physical change in her. She was becoming a capable and confident woman.

Her girl would soon be posted to a field hospital in France but for this moment, Livy would have her all to herself.

With Wyatt so far away and Elizabeth soon to follow, Livy was beside herself with despair.

Elizabeth sat down on the sofa, her back straight and her hands folded neatly in her lap.

Livy had had a great deal of news of late, none of it good. She closed her book and steeled herself for what her daughter had to say.

"I've been to see Major Gunnison."

"Have you?" Livy fought to keep her composure. She did not want Elizabeth to guess how even the mention of his name made her emotional.

"He asked about you."

"Did he? I suppose that is to be expected. We were neighbors."

"You know his interest is more than that of a former neighbor."

Her daughter had stepped over a very fragile boundary.

"Elizabeth, what you are suggesting is none of your concern."

"I do believe you're blushing," Elizabeth said.

"I am not."

"Are you telling me you don't care for him?"

Livy didn't want to be coy but wasn't sure she could admit the truth. "That is private."

"I thought you'd want to know. He isn't recovering the way the doctors had hoped. He seems to have given up."

"How the major chooses to deal with the loss of his leg is not for me to interfere with."

"But Mother…"

"He made his feelings plain. He prefers solitude. What more can I do?"

"This is different," Elizabeth replied.

"Tell me how?"

To be honest, Livy couldn't. She'd never backed away from what was required of her. Why was this time so different?

"I have avoided the major for a very good reason. He asked me to stay away."

"Said in haste," Elizabeth replied. "And pain. There has to be a great deal of pain."

"My dear, I am not without sympathy, but the question of my involvement with the major has been settled."

"You know how meddlesome you can be." Elizabeth hadn't said it lightly. She played with the tassel on her skirt. "He needs to be useful. Who better than yourself to remind him of all he can do and the many things he might to look forward to if he'd only try?"

Now Livy did blush. Had Elizabeth known all along how important James had become to her? How she had dreamt that one day they would steward Fairview together? Did she guess how those dreams had been dashed by a surgeon's knife?

Livy could not fight this new enemy that was tearing them apart. She could not vanquish fear and unhappiness with words of encouragement this time.

"You must help him." Elizabeth's entreaties became sharper. "He will die if you do not intercede."

"Surely it is not as bad as you suggest."

"He spends his days, I was told, in bed."

"I cannot imagine him being that way."

"Precisely."

Livy sighed. To think James had fallen into a pit of darkness was inconceivable.

"I've always admired your courage, Mother. How you never back down from a challenge."

"Your admiration has been misplaced."

Elizabeth sighed. "Your feelings have been hurt."

Remarkable how much children see when you don't even think they are looking.

Livy was close to tears. "I feel responsible for what happened. Perhaps his leg could've been saved if only he had rested properly."

"You're wrong to blame yourself. No one knows what causes infections to become virulent."

"The major blames me."

"He doesn't, I assure you. In fact, he sends his sincerest apologizes for his behavior."

Livy looked at her daughter.

"How fortunate you have found love again," Elizabeth said.

It was true, Livy realized.

"Will you go see him?" Elizabeth needed an answer.

"What if I fail? What if all the care and cajoling can't save him?"

"Are you putting conditions on your love?"

That's exactly what Livy had done. How could she have been so blind?

"When did you become so wise?" Livy asked.

"I had a good teacher," Elizabeth replied.

Livy was taken aback by the girl's compliment.

"I will do what I can," Livy answered. She didn't mean to sound doubtful, but the major could be stubborn.

Chapter Twenty-Eight

⇿⇾⇽⇾⇽⇿

Nervous but determined, Livy arrived at the recovery wing of the hospital. Collapsing her umbrella, she searched for a familiar face and found none, not even Sister Evans.

"Excuse me," she said to a woman carrying an armload of clean bed linen. "I'm looking for Major Gunnison."

The stout nurse frowned. "His lordship is in the solar room."

Oh dear, Livy thought. Elizabeth had not exaggerated. James had gotten a reputation for being difficult.

"Could you direct me?" Livy asked.

The nurse nodded in the opposite direction. "Down the hall. The solar is the last door."

Livy thanked her and proceeded with heavy steps. She must prepare herself for what she was about to find.

Would seeing James again be more of a challenge than she was prepared for? Would they have sharp words as they had done when he awoke from the operation? She dreaded a scene.

Livy knew without question she must do her best to keep any expression from showing revulsion or pity. She must be cheerful at all times.

The hall was poorly lit. The air was stale. She passed several wards where the wounded were being attended to by doctors and nurses. Her heart broke to see so many. Some looked at her with haunted eyes. Others just stared into space. One lad cried out in pain and despair.

The solar was an addition. The flooring changed to a mustard-colored tile. The door was made of steel. She opened without knocking.

The overcast day left the room encased in gloom. Trees, barren of their leaves, bent low in the wind. Branches rubbed against the glass, a frightful sound.

Thankfully, James was the only occupant, sitting in a wheelchair, his back to her. His hair was dramatically long, reaching to his collar.

She hesitated in the doorway. This was such a breach of his privacy, and yet her love compelled her to intervene in his seclusion. He did not have to face the future—whatever it may bring—alone.

She took a step forward. His head came up and he saw her reflection in the glass. He grasped the wheels of his chair and spun around.

He'd not been shaved, giving him the appearance of a ruthless vagabond or worse. She suppressed a smile. She liked this roguish appearance. He was the hero of a penny dreadful, looking thus. Such a hero had caused her pulse to race many a time as it did now.

He was dressed in cream-colored pajamas and a pale mauve robe. One of his pajama legs was folded and pinned at his thigh.

The missing leg was there, or more accurately not there. One couldn't help but notice and feel sorry.

A single foot was clad in a black carpet slipper. It bothered her, this lack of symmetry, one leg whole and the other gone.

People would stare—it was something he would have to get used to. They might even be so bold to ask questions. He would learn how to answer their inquiries. There could be no avoiding them.

"I'm sorry to have disturbed you," she said and then regretted the choice of words. This wasn't the way she'd wanted the conversation to start—with an apology.

"What are you doing here?" he answered with a growl, the warning of a wounded animal.

"I thought you could use some company." There was hesitation in her step. How easy it would be to withdraw with more words of apology and leave him to his solitude.

"I'm not very good company these days."

Her heart swelled with tenderness for all that he was suffering. For his future plans cut short. Even for his isolation in this most sterile of places.

"Nonetheless, I am happy to see you," she said with faltering courage.

He inclined his head. "Shouldn't you be in Fairview attending your farm?"

She took the chance and closed the distance, the uncertainty between them. She stood an arm's length away, and he looked up at her at last.

The ghostly pallor of his face alarmed her. There were dark circles under his eyes. His skin was colorless, a man who'd not been outside in some time. He'd aged years in only a few weeks, the lines in his face and around his mouth deep.

"I will go home shortly. The Advent season is about to start."

"And the girls, are they with you?"

"They are with my housekeeper. They couldn't afford to miss any more school."

"Indeed. School is of the utmost importance in this day and age." He shifted in the chair. "Your mother-in-law has conceded?"

"Yes."

"Good."

His interest in her children she interpreted as a slender thread of hope and she wasn't about to let go. "I'm told you had a surprise visit from Elizabeth."

"I was glad to see her."

"You are her hero."

He frowned. "Don't call me that."

"And why not? What you did for Elizabeth at Wyatt's birthday party saved her reputation."

His expression softened, giving Livy more encouragement, but there was still pain in his eyes. "She's a fine girl. You've done a wonderful job raising her."

"Thank you. I appreciate you saying so."

He nodded, his brows drawn together. "Won't you sit down? I can't abide anyone hovering over me."

She dropped into the nearest chair. Relief was too mild a word to express how she felt that he hadn't demanded she leave.

"I assume this is more than a social visit," he said.

Seeing him this way, Livy realized how thoughtless she would be to pretend that all was well.

"I hated the way we last parted—with anger and acrimony. Friends must always find a way to make amends."

Color flooded his face.

Her own high color was palpable. She wished she could make the hurt vanish. She could not. Nor would she show false cheerfulness. He grieved. He had every right. He must do so before he could go any further.

"I will never resign myself to being a cripple," he said wearily.

"I wouldn't expect you to." She gazed into his eyes.

She'd wondered what she would see. In their depths, she recognized the strength that had brought him into manhood and had served him well in his profession as the leader of men.

A spark ignited in her core. She let the flames spread.

"Now that you've seen I'm upright and recovering as well as could be expected, you can report to your family. Your duty will have been done."

"They will all be happy to learn you are recovering."

He grasped the wheels of his chair and pushed himself

up to the glass. Obviously, he expected her to leave.

She would not leave now. Nor would she let him cut her off or put distance between them. At least, not after an accounting.

What he chose to do after she'd stated her case, she must respect. To do otherwise would belittle his wishes as if they held no importance.

"Much as you try to rebuff me," she said earnestly, "I will not leave you until we've spoken honestly. My will is as strong as yours. You'll not find a more stubborn resolve."

He huffed.

"I can help you with your recovery." She'd not known before this moment what she could do. She would be his nurse, his companion, his mentor. He'd not grown up in the loving arms of a mother or the praise of a doting father. His examples of love and affection had been cold and forbidding. When he'd fallen in love, he'd been rejected as inadequate.

Livy would give him her love unfettered. She would help shoulder his burdens and be his helpmate if he would only let her.

He shook his head. "You don't know what you'd be taking on."

"I'm quite sure that I do."

His scowl was reflected in the glass.

She held her hands together tightly. They would not betray her anxiety. "Tell me, when does your rehabilitation start?"

"There's talk of me being transferred to Queen Mary's Hospital in Roehampton. They specialize in my kind of wound."

"That's excellent news."

He shrugged. "The doctors are not optimistic that I will walk again."

"Fie. And you believe them? You never have before."

He twisted his mouth, unable or unwilling to smile. "Your prodding will not work this time, Livinia. I know when I'm defeated."

"Are you? I'm beginning to wonder if you'd prefer to wallow in self-pity."

He jerked, as if shocked by an electric wire. "You couldn't be more wrong."

"Are you so sure?" She'd no intention of backing down. "Enlighten me as to how I'm mistaken."

Rankling him had brought back his vigor. She'd believed once provoking him to anger would be doing a disservice to his health and well-being, but she'd underestimated its effectiveness. Stirring his emotions had put him in a quandary he must deal with once and for all.

She waited for him to speak. The silence between them only aggravated her poor nerves. It was not an easy task telling a man his shortcomings. No doubt the doctors and nurses had imparted the same message to him. He'd spurned their admonitions with a lack of cooperation.

Livy was aware of her own breathing, the steadiness that belied the apprehension gathering inside her.

What was he thinking? Had she made a mistake?

James clenched his jaw in a way that could be described as pugnacious. He grasped the wheels of his chair, making ready, she guessed, to retreat.

She blocked his exit. "You haven't given me your answer."

Livy hated talking to him thus. He was not a child. Still, she battled with unseen demons and she intended to win. She would use whatever means necessary, whatever tools were at her disposal.

His looked up at her. "Can't you just leave me alone?"

"Is that what you *really* want?"

He glared, but she didn't move away. "You are the most obstinate woman I've ever met."

"Coming from you, I'll consider that a compliment."

He lowered his gaze. The dark clouds seemed to pass.

Livy was encouraged by this change however slight. "What is it to be, Major, self-pity or something better, something more worthy?"

James tensed and then shook his head. "I've been a fool."

She reached out her hands, and he seized them. Tears burned her eyes. She made no effort to wipe them away, her hands being most agreeably occupied.

The warmth of his hands was a reminder of life. He'd lived through a horrible ordeal. He had been spared when others had not. They could not waste another minute.

Her heart filled to overflowing with happiness.

He released her. "I've missed you, Livinia."

"You don't know how pleased I am to hear you say so. I have missed you." She rose from the chair and stood next to him. "We don't need to put on a brave face with each other."

"No, we do not." His eyes moistened.

She leaned over and kissed him. His stubble scratched her face, but she reveled in the sensation. He returned her kiss, the first one tentative, the next one committed and uncompromising.

When he stopped, she stroked his cheek. "We will help each other, you know."

"Are you sure, my dear Livinia?" His eyes clouded with doubt. "I'm not an easy man to live with."

"So I've found out."

He met her gaze with a smirk.

"I am more secure in my love for you than ever," she said. "I would like us to be together for as long as we both shall live."

His smile was crooked. "Is that a proposal?"

Livy bit her lower lip. "I know it's not what our generation does."

"A man likes to be in charge."

"Do you consider me forward?"

"I expect we both will have to learn how to cope with these new ways."

"So are you willing to give it a go?"

"I cannot refuse you."

"Indeed, you can't," she replied.

She sighed with the most profound contentment,

wrapped her arms around his neck, and gave him a massive hug. She knew at this moment whatever the future would bring, they would face it, all of it, together.

Epilogue

〉〉〉《《《

Gwendolyn Asher, looking lovely in a pink chiffon gown adorned with an abundance of lace, raised her glass. She wore her mother's opera length pearls, their luster radiant in the flickering candlelight.

"Here's to my two fathers and my new mother," she said.

Ronald looked amused.

Livy was proud of the way the girl had handled the revelation of her family's long buried secret. She never said, but Livy wondered if she'd suspected Major Gunnison was her father. Looking at the two of them sitting across the table from each other, Livy could see a strong family resemblance.

"I am so pleased that we are together—a family at last," Gwendolyn continued. Her cheeks had turned a lovely shade of pink to match her gown.

"Here, here," Robert Gunnison said. "We have Livinia to thank."

They all turned to Livy, who felt the heat of the room. She'd believed the good years were behind her, but she'd been wrong.

Her gaze shifted to her husband. He looked so handsome in his perfectly cut evening jacket and starched shirt.

They shared a love and that made the future bright with possibilities.

"Aren't you going to say something?" Gwendolyn seemed eager that she do so.

Livy choked back tears. "How very happy I am for the part I played."

"I'll drink to that," James said.

They clinked their glasses, all smiles and *bonhomie*. No one can predict what the future will bring, Livy mused, but what did it matter as long as were together?

www.ingramcontent.com/pod-product-compliance
Lightning Source LLC
Chambersburg PA
CBHW030018180626
46810CB00001B/95